TWO QUESTIONS

Danielle Murray

TWO QUESTIONS

Cover design by Julie S Williamson

Quotes by Jennie Jerome Spencer Churchill, Lady Randolph Churchill kindly taken from her memoirs,
The Reminiscences of Lady Randolph Churchill, by Mrs. George Cornwallis-West, 1908.

ISBN-13: 978-1798873649
Imprint: Huarau Road

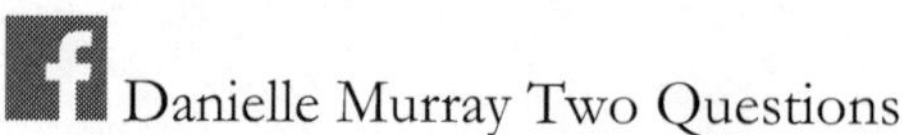

TWO
QUESTIONS

Cast of Characters

Meghan: Brooklyn Girl with no desire to leave home even though she does. Daughter to Lucie and Parker, sister to Ally. Granddaughter to Bubbe and Gramps (Fletcher) and Grand-maman in Montreal. USA to New Zealand.

Lucie: Meghan's mother. Married to Parker. Psychologist. Canada to USA.

Tish Louise/Patricia Louise Curtis Smith/Madame Smith: WW2 war bride married to Richard. England to USA.

Annie: WW2 war bride. Once married to Gramps/Fletcher. New Zealand to USA.

Bubbe: Meghan's Brooklyn grandmother. Married to Gramps/Fletcher.

Parker: Lucie's husband and Meghan's father. Son of Gramps/Fletcher and Bubbe. Commercial pilot.

Grand-maman: Lucie's mother and Meghan's French-Canadian grandmother who lives in Montreal. Related to Hermeline, Salome and also mother to Lucie's sisters Gilberte, Babette and Mariette who makes a mean sugar pie. And tourtière. Engaged to Doré before she married Lucie's father.

Gramps/Fletcher: Meghan's Brooklyn grandfather and Parker's father. Big time writer. Once married to Annie, Kiwi war bride.

Ally: Meghan's younger sister. Mother to Salem. Loves New England history.

Salem: Meghan's niece and Ally's daughter.

The Farmer/Blu/Harrison: He's the man! But he hardly gets a mention in *Two Questions* because the book is about the experience, not the relationship. May get airplay if there's a sequel.

Famous and/or Infamous Foreign Wives

Marie Antoinette: Last Queen of France. Beheaded in 1793, aged 37 years. Austria to France. Married to Louis XVI who was obsessed with padlocks. Child of Empress Maria Theresa who viewed all her daughters as sacrifices to politics and so married them off as she – not they – pleased. This did not always end well.

Tsarina Alexandra: Last Russian Empress. Executed aged 46 years old with her family in 1918. Germany to Russia. Married to Tsar Nicholas II (Nicky), son of Minnie who could have been a nicer mother-in-law. Granddaughter to Queen Victoria who also played the game of thrones with her children.

Consuelo Vanderbilt: American Dollar Princess. 9th Duchess of Marlborough. USA to UK. Returned to the US during WWII. She died in New York at age 87.

Jennie Jerome, Lady Randolph Churchill: American Dollar Princess. Mother to Sir Winston Churchill. USA to UK. Died aged 67 years old from complications following a fall down the stairs. Shoe lover who did not live to see her son become prime minister.

Wallis Simpson: Twice divorced American for whom King Edward VIII gave up the British throne in 1936. Became Duchess of Windsor on their marriage in 1937. USA to UK. Worth noting – Wallis all gets credit for coining the statement, "You can't be too rich or too thin."

And of course, Hepzibah. Because she was bad-ass…

Hepzibah Buell: Puritan ancestor to Meghan killed by French and Native American forces in the Deerfield Massacre in 1704. Twice fined for wearing silk.

Miscellaneous

Sisi and Franz Josef: Maine Coon Cats named after Elizabeth of Bavaria and Franz Josef I, Emperor of Austria. Elizabeth of Bavaria was not a happy camper.

Empress Maria Theresa: Bulldozer Austrian mother to Marie Antoinette. Great-great-grandmother to Franz Josef I just mentioned. Did not leave home for love.

Queen Victoria: Grandmother to Alix of Hesse/Tsarina Alexandra. Mother to Princess Alice and Princess Victoria (Vicky) who both married German noblemen. Also grandmother to Kaiser Wilhem. Did not leave home for love.

Grace Kelly/Princess Grace: American actress. Wife of Rainier III, Prince of Monaco. USA to Monaco.

Kathleen Kennedy Cavendish, Marchioness of Hartington: Member of American Kennedy family. USA to UK.

Princess Victoria/Vicky: Daughter to Queen Victoria, aunt to Alix of Hesse/Tsarina Alexandra, mother to Kaiser Wilhelm, German Emperor during WWI. UK to Germany. Didn't like it there.

Lucy Stone: Prominent 19th Century American suffragist. Did not believe women should give up surname after marriage as end result is legal annihilation of one's identify.

Jemima Goldsmith and Imran Khan: Former English/Pakistani International couple. After their divorce, Jemima returned to live in England.

Autumn Kelly and Peter Phillips: Canadian/UK international couple. Peter Phillips is grandson to Queen Elizabeth II. Autumn grew up in Montreal and lives in the UK.

Louisa and John Adams: Sixth President of the United Stares and his English born wife.

PART ONE

IN THE BEGINNING

Marie Antoinette

Monsieur, je vous demande excuse, je ne l'ai pas fait exprès.
Reine Marie Antoinette

You want to know what I have to say? What do you want me to say? What can I say? They have deprived me of my children, guillotined my husband and now they are to do the same to me. Of course, I am angry!

Do you think I wanted to be queen? Think again!

All I wanted to do was to live my own life with my family in my beloved Vienna. I did not ask to be here.

The French, they never accepted me.

Well, maybe they did at first. I was young. I was pretty. I was so terribly naïve. I was just a girl! But then they blamed me when there were no babies. How could this be my fault? My husband did not come to me for so many years and when he did, he did not know what to do! If my brother had not been sent by Mother to give him lessons in love-making, we would still be childless.

I was never good enough. I was always the foreigner, an outsider. Do you not think I knew they called me the Austrian whore? Or Austrian bitch? As if I could ever separate myself from where I was born! It was impossible.

Soon my head will be parted from my shoulders. It is with profound regret that I abandon my babies as I rejoin their father. But I shall die with courage. As I have lived. I shall not lose it at the moment when my sufferings are to end. And I shall pardon my enemies the evils they have done to me.

Non. I will show no fear. I will not shed a tear. I will not give them the satisfaction. I shall think of home.

Ich werde an Zuhause denken.

Maria Antonia
October 1793

1

I was born in Brooklyn, in the State of New York.
Jennie Jerome, Lady Randolph Churchill

Meghan's Method

Before my grandfather married my grandmother, he had another wife. Her name was Annie. He met her in 1944 when he was a US Marine stationed in New Zealand and he brought her back here to New York after the war. She deserted him a few years later. Apparently, she went back home. For good. Because she hated North America.

"She's dead now," my grandmother once told me.

"Supposedly."

I don't think Bubbe much liked living with Annie's maybe-ghost. My family never talked about her but she was always there. When I was a little girl, Bubbe told me that Gramps adored Annie. She said Annie was the love of his life. This, I have since realized, means my grandmother was not.

This is what I tell the man sitting next to me on the steps outside the central library when he informs me the small flag on his backpack is of New Zealand. And that my sister spent a year there and loved it but insists the shoes people wore were boring. I then return my focus to my aching feet and latest pair of heels which, at this moment, look far better on my body than they feel.

But the man with the New Zealand flag clearly wants me to talk, and so I talk. I tell him how when I was in high school, my dad and my sister and I used to spend Saturdays in the library researching American history and you can't say you've been to Manhattan if you haven't sat down to a chapter or two in the Rose Main Reading Room. I tell him that even though I've lived in New York all my life, I've only recently started spending summers in the city and the heat and stink aren't as bad as everyone lets on. I tell him about the mysterious missing Annie and how my sister couldn't find any trace of her in New Zealand, although to be fair, all she did was look her name up in an old phone book.

I talk because I can't walk and don't want to and even though I'm single and he's hot, he lives at the bottom of the world and I, ergo, am not interested in him and have no need to impress, endear, excite or arouse. I engage because I don't care where this is going. When I wonder how much more this man can take, I also tell him about my mother and Maine Coon cats and their mystery link to the last queen of France.

I laugh when he invites me to watch him play rugby with his 'mates' later on in the park. He doesn't laugh when I tell him my real name is Marie Antoinette. It's a game I created, a way of weeding out unkind people from my world. If you laugh, you're out. If you don't, you get to be my friend and call me Meg. I imagine Frank Zappa's kids also have this game. Or maybe they don't. Their dad was a total rock star. My mom is a psychologist. You would think she might have known better.

The man says he's a farmer in the North Island. He milks cows twice a day. I tell this farmer I'm a city girl and I have no intention of leaving the city but I will go to the park with him on one condition — that first he joins me in emergency shoe-shopping. It's another test. Can this man with the New Zealand flag on his backpack, who seems to want to know all about me, embrace my footwear fetish? Because my feet need immediate rescue and drugstore flip flops are not ever going to be an option. He agrees and we're off. We find me some cute pink summer slides. I watch him play his game. We have dinner. We share stories. Before I know it, maybe I am interested in this man who lives at the bottom of the world.

My biggest mistake is telling my mother. My mom's specialty is counseling couples where each partner comes from a different country and background. Either there are a lot out there or they have a shitload of problems because she's very busy. But Lucie is fine with that because she's obsessed with international couples and considers herself part of the club even though I'm not sure Canadian/American marriages count. I mean, really? The house she grew up in is less than four hundred miles away and she goes back so often, her cats probably know the way. Now Tish Louise, that I get. Tish Louise is a war bride from the Second World War. She came to America in the 1940s. On a ship. Before transatlantic flights and instant messaging were even a thing. Now that's an international marriage.

In any case, Lucie says fixing international couple-trouble is her superpower. She also says if she could change the world, her clients would come to her before they marry and not after. Because after the wedding it's usually too late. But her talents would probably be wasted anyway since Lucie says people in love and about to marry consider themselves indestructible and don't listen to reason.

Now that she knows about the farmer, it's all she talks about. Honestly, this is nothing. Sure, I love his wavy blond hair and seriously delicious soft accent which makes every word that leaves those lips sound like a poem. And true, nice guys with fabulous forearms are hard to find. But he has made it clear he's not here to stay and intends on going back to work the family farm forever and that's totally fine. Because living in close proximity to a herd of cows, no matter how beautiful this guy's blue eyes, is absolutely not part of my life plan.

If he wants to go back to New Zealand and be in the home he loves, I get that. Because New York is my home and I will not leave it. My family is here, my friends are here and my job is here. This is where I want to be. This is where I am meant to be.

That's the thing about being the child of a mental health care professional. You are self-aware. You have to be because no matter what you do, you are being analyzed. So you always have to be one step ahead, you have to over-think, question your motives, actions and reactions. You have to be prepared to challenge that one person who believes they know you better than you do. Because that one person may love you to the moon and back but you are still their special little twenty-four seven guinea pig.

That's why I am positive there's no way I'll ever leave New York. And I will never follow a man who will not follow me. I'm so not going to end up on a farm at the bottom of the world.

Patricia (Tish) Louise Curtis Smith

Two Questions. Of course, before those two questions, there are others. The ones posed as if in a terrible rush, as if I cannot possibly reply quickly enough.

Two Questions

When people realize how I came to be in America, first they want to know where we met and how. Am I really a World War Two GI bride? Was it love at first sight? How old was I? And Richard, how old was Richard? Was he in military uniform? What did he do in the war? Was he hurt? And how long did we wait to finally be together? Did my family object?

Once the excitement passes, the inquiry slows down. The people stop to think. And then I am asked the same two questions. Only now with hesitation. Suddenly my interrogators seem afraid of what I might tell them.

A Lucie Lunchtime Letter

Dear Meghan,

I know what you are thinking.

You are thinking you are so in love and this farmer from New Zealand is so wonderful that you will follow him to the end of the earth. If so, there are things you need to hear. And now, my darling daughter, is the time to tell you. Before it is too late and you are in too deep.

I know a thing or two about leaving one's homeland for a man. Having done this myself and having worked with many clients over the years who have also gone from one country to another, I believe I have a good idea of what it entails and I can tell you what difficulties you will face in your new life if you move away just for him. If you know about them in advance, you are better prepared.

Some of it you know already. You are the child of an international marriage and you have seen for yourself what this means. And you have heard me talk about my friend Madame Curtis-Smith and all my other war brides and your dollar princesses and poor evil foreign queens. But, ma puce, there is so much more you need to think about.

Oui. Evil foreign queens. Even Princess Grace was not particularly liked by the citizens of Monaco in the beginning. And she was a big movie star. Did not everybody love Grace Kelly? Apparemment non.

And as for Marie Antoinette and Tsarina Alexandra, both were detested by their adopted people and both were slaughtered by their adopted people. Things might have been different had they been local girls.

Ma puce, I will begin by saying this — relationships do not form in the here and now. Because, ma puce, there is always a past.

The past is your background. It is your culture, your belief systems, your values and your expectations. If you have the same past, relationships are a little less complicated.

Much of who we are is determined by where we are from. Just as I could never be separated from where I am from, you too will never be able to separate yourself from your background.

I suppose I have said enough for now. You have only just met this boy.

Lucie

2

Meghan's Method

As long as I can remember, my mother writes letters at lunch. Usually to her own mom and three sisters but also friends from home. Back in the day, it was by hand and stamped envelope into the solid deep blue USPS box at the corner of the street. Now, even with Grand-maman, she emails. When I moved out of the house, I was added to her correspondence list, which, given that I'm only five minutes away, makes little sense. But then again, so does texting someone in the next room. My guess is Lucie really needs to keep in touch. We all have our method. Mine is to imagine being interviewed by Oprah or Barbara Walters. Barbara Walters reminds me of my Bubbe. Not in the way she speaks so much but how she carries herself. The word 'dignified' comes to mind. Anyway, usually we're in a private room with big windows and exquisite French neoclassical chairs, but sometimes we're in front of a pretend audience (mostly female) or wearing headphones in a radio station. Location doesn't matter. What does matter is neither Barbara or Oprah can get enough of me as I ramble on about life, balance emotions and nourish my awareness. So I just keep talking. Out loud. Of course, I make sure I'm alone when I do my thing. Only the dog knows my little secret. As far as I know.

And just so you know, 'ma puce' is French. Translation: My flea. That is how my mother addresses my sister and me. And that is what her mom calls her. It's a term of endearment.

Having said that, my mother does not mince words nor perform pleasantries or other banalities of social life.

She gets right to the point. And unless you are on life support or in her office, she figures you're fine.

Tish Louise Talks

Do you have regrets?

Would you do it again?

Two simple questions with ever so complicated answers.

In return, I always have a question of my own.

Do you really want to hear the truth?

A Lucie Lunchtime Letter

Ma puce,

When I fell in love with your father, there was little information available as to how it would be living in a new country with a man I did not know. Bien sûr, I did not realize I did not know him. This knowledge only comes to you when you share a home. Mais cohabitation was not an option back then. At least, not in the United

States and the rest of Canada. But Québec was different. Québec is always different. Québécois were in transition. We had tired of religious suppression and wanted change. And my mother, who never liked having men, especially holy pious celibate men, tell her how to live her life, was all for it.

Mais oui, it was your Grand-maman who suggested I move in with your father before we married. My mother wanted me to be certain I was doing the right thing. But Parker told her it was not possible. Parker said that if we did this, his parents would never support our union. In their eyes, living together was a sin.

En tout cas, the first year of marriage is difficult for all couples. There are many adjustments to be made.

Parker and I got on well as we are both easy-going. My only problem was being away from home. I missed my mother and my sisters and everything in New York was strange to me. Language was also a concern. I could master English. The Brooklyn accent I could not.

I was lonely. You no doubt think Montreal and New York are not far apart, but in those days, it was a long way.

On occasion, I would read a story about a British war bride in the local paper. I found it frustrating that most articles concentrated only on the war and how the girl or woman fell in love with her soldier and provided little information on her present-day situation. Was she happy? Did she ever want to go back? Did she regret her decision to follow this man to his side of the world and forsake hers?

I met Madame Curtis-Smith at the park the year you were born. I noticed an accent when she was talking to her grandchildren and I asked her where she was from. She told me she had come to America as a GI bride and shared her story. We became instant friends even though your grandfather never liked her. He said it was because she used too many adverbs.

Actually, there still is not much information available. There are few books and little to be found on the internet. I do not know why as leaving home for love is now common. This is why I have been cataloguing experiences of women like myself. I have interviewed every foreign wife I could find, inside and outside the office. One day I will have enough material to put into a book.

Before I met Madame Curtis-Smith, I put out notices in the local papers and in *The New York Times* searching for war brides. Dozens came forward and were keen to share their stories. They too wanted the world to know the reality of their lives and not just the romance which had brought them here. Even though we all like to think so, not every war bride lived happily after. Of course, it was not all sad — many war brides were happy, and I needed to know this too.

How I wanted to talk to Fletcher before he died about his first wife that he brought back after the war. But your father said this was not a subject your grandfather wished to discuss. I suspect you know more about her than I do as you and your grandparents were close. As for me, I know nothing of her except her name. Annie. What a strange coincidence she should be a New Zealander like your farmer.

I used to spend a lot of time at the old May's department store on Fulton Street when I first arrived. Shopping releases dopamine into the brain in ways similar to sexual activity, and I needed the high. May's reminded me of the Woolworth's on rue Sainte Catherine in Montreal. Both are long gone. And McCrory's beside May's made the best Belgian waffles with ice cream. The minute you walked through the door you could smell them. Soon I ventured past downtown Brooklyn and across the bridge.

Making friends my own age was difficult. You, who like to say I have no social graces, should know that while your America likes to think of itself as this wonderful melting pot, its people are not very warm to those who do not speak the English language. Americans do not have the patience to listen and befriend and much of their exaggerated politesse is insincere. In contrast, Québécois are direct and we mean what we say. I found it hard to adapt to non-genuine exchanges, and so I learned to escape into the city where I could forget where I was. The New York Public Library midtown branch became my refuge. I was in awe of that impressive big reading room. The library served two purposes. It encouraged me to leave the house and it saved me from your father's mother. Hé seigneur! So many times, your Bubbe dropped in on me unannounced and uninvited. Think me cruel if you must, but if I could not have my mother in my life, I did not want a substitute. Certainly not one who visited every day. This was suffocating to me.

When I was young, I was fascinated with Marie Antoinette and it is at the NYPL that I reconnected with her. Many of her biographies were in French, and I read those first. And this is where I came across a small book display on Tsarina Alexandra, who was brutally murdered with her husband and children during the Russian Revolution. Her photos were on the wall and in every one of them she did not smile. I was haunted by her sad eyes. It is as if she knew all along how her story would end. Her real name was Alix, she was born in Hesse in Germany and she was a granddaughter of Queen Victoria. I pored over everything I could find on her. Poor girl, all alone and removed from all she had ever known and who missed her family desperately. I began to wonder if all those Marie Antoinette and Tsarina Alexandra biographers had missed a crucial component — a sense of being the outsider living day in and day out with an insider. Only one who has lived this truth will understand.

All this to say, I was not alone as a foreign wife. Even though I often felt it. I suppose since time began and humans started moving from A to B, men and women have followed their hearts from here to there. Mostly women though.

Lucie

3

Meghan's Method

'Hé seigneur!' is my favorite French-Canadian expression. I hear it a lot when my mom is on the phone to her sisters back home. I'm never quite sure which sister she's talking to because every call starts with the same standard greeting — 'Bonjour Madame' — and is followed by animated conversation and lots of hand motion. And this is weird — when speaking English, Lucie's voice has considerably less pitch variation and her feet are completely still. She told me once that lower body language is quite telling and that men move their feet when nervous but women do not. Then again, she has also mentioned that extroverts, practiced liars, arrogant people and alpha types are less prone to fidgety feet. I'm not sure what to make of it. All I know is the cats keep out of her way. They don't love her as much as she does them.

But they sure did have a thing for my grandfather. The man, probably due to his non-active approach, was a cat magnet. Whenever my dad was home in the afternoon, Fletcher would walk over for a cup of coffee and the minute he sat down, the cats made themselves comfortable on his lap. If they bothered him, he did not say. Gramps kept many thoughts to himself but not when it came to the overuse of adverbs.

"Verbs do not need props," Fletcher informed anyone within earshot when I asked him to review school papers before handing them in.

I now live in fear of lazy prose. I am no match for my famous grandfather.

And I knew it would not take long before hormones made their way into the conversation. Lucie's go-to on human behavior is Sigmund Freud and she sometimes fixates on sex because he did too. All because the man once said time spent with cats is never wasted.

But I also know a thing or two about Tsarina Alexandra and I am sure that girl left home for love — she moved to Russia to be with Tsar Nicholas II — but Marie Antoinette did not follow her heart. She wasn't in love with Louis XVI. It was a marriage of convenience arranged by the Empress Maria Theresa of Austria to form an alliance with France. And seeing as Marie Antoinette was only fourteen, her bulldozer mom was not going to listen to her anyway. Maria Theresa viewed her girls as sacrifices to politics and they would go where she wanted them to go.

By the way, I never think of Tish Louise as a war bride. Not really. And she calls it 'GI bride'. Don't ask me why.

Tish Louise — who Lucie still calls 'Madame Curtis-Smith' — is probably my mother's only friend in Brooklyn. She lives on Garfield Place so we both kind of hang out there because I love her too. Sure, she's British, and she married Richard during the war and came to the United States as soon as it was over. It's no big secret. But Tish Louise is so many other things that I just don't think about her as a war bride.

I have to tell you, growing up with a formidable mother is no walk in the park. Lucie is not as serene as she likes to think. You learn to wash your hands frequently and distinguish which pretty towels you can use today and which are for the far better people who may, but usually do not, come to visit later. Because, and I'm not kidding, Lucie has few real friends. At least not in Brooklyn. True, when I was growing up, my father Parker was excellent yang to all that yin. But my laid-back air force pilot turned airline pilot dad was away half of every month and my sister and I were left with the fallout. When it all got a bit crazy and I was too lazy to rock up to Bubbe's house or go to the shop, it was such a comfort to pop into Tish Louise's for a hot cup of tea. According to Tish Louise, there is not much in life that cannot be fixed with a decent cup of tea. Only she calls it a 'cuppa'.

Tish Louise is an odd sort in our neighborhood. She is tall and elegant and looks like, in her younger days, if there hadn't been a major war going on, she might have spent time fox hunting somewhere in the countryside in sexy riding crop pants and those cute little brown jackets. Or cruising along French country lanes in a zippy cool convertible with a scarf wrapped around her head like in the movies. I have always wanted to do that but I need better hair and ideally, a longer neck. Tish Louise has perfect posture and never hunches when she sits. And her dress is impeccable. I have never seen her in a pair of jeans and I'm sure she isn't slumming it in sweats on weekends behind closed doors either. Actually, she seems more suited to life on the Upper East Side than Brooklyn but she's not snobby about it. She never 'puts on airs' as she would say. Although for some reason, she never did have much time for my grandfather. She will deny it, of course, but whatever was going on between those two, the feeling was mutual.

Tish Louise loves squirrels and always keeps a full bowl of peanuts on her front window sill. She has the same name for all of them — Winston Churchill — but her favorite is a little white fellow. You don't see too many white squirrels in these parts. Squirrels in Brooklyn are gray. And this one isn't hyper like the rest of them. He'll sit on the ledge for hours and watch her yet he never comes inside. Of course, if Fletcher were alive today, he'd probably point out that's because the damn thing is sick and diseased because he may have had serious issue with adverbs but pleonasms — that's a fancy way of saying redundant words — can be both fun and functional. Anyway, my grandfather would be wrong, that damn thing looks just fine and obviously knows a good gig when he sees it. And while she usually listens to music by some English dude called Engelbert Humperdinck, I know she's mad for Gladys Knight's *Midnight Train to Georgia* because I've caught her at the kitchen sink singing as a Pip more than a few times. She confesses that it brings her back but I never ask her to where or when. My grandfather used to say music-evoked nostalgia is deeply personal so I don't think it's my business. But whatever it is, it makes her happy.

That is what I love about Tish Louise the most. She's always in a good mood. When I was growing up, Lucie was too distracted to be in a good mood. In New York anyway. Because in Canada she was a different person. In Canada, my mother chewed gum and let us eat Froot Loops for breakfast. In Canada, my mother was pleasant. She laughed and she didn't have rules, especially not about hand towels. Even her voice changed but then that may be because she was speaking in another language and I've noticed languages do that to you. In New York, my mother was your basic Empress Maria Theresa. Fierce. Overbearing. And yet vacant. Adults say kids don't notice these things but they do.

See, because even when Lucie was right there in front of you, she was never present. Was she thinking of Montreal or that stupid book stuck in her head? I don't know.

My sister and I were not the only ones to observe Lucie's dual personality. Parker saw it too. He said it was because when Lucie was back in her mother's home and away from responsibility, she mellowed out. But I reckon it was more than that. For one, Parker thinks my mother can do no wrong. He adores her. But back then Parker didn't spend as much time with her as my sister and I did. Not in New York and especially not in Canada. From the time I was little to just about my first year of university, I spent summers off the island of Montreal in the house my mom grew up in and where my French-Canadian grandmother still lives. As soon as school let out, my mom and the cats (Sisi and Franz Josef) would be waiting for Ally and me at the gate and off we'd go, five or six hours straight up the I-87. I swear it happened the minute we hit the border. My own personal Maria Theresa would kick off her shoes and mutate into some barefooted breezy flower child who preferred to be called by her given name instead of label. My relaxed Grand-maman, who never seemed to mind us and those massive Maine Coons setting up camp upstairs for two solid months clearly saw nothing unusual in my mother's altered state. Neither did my three aunts and so I came to realize this was the Lucie they had known all their lives. Carefree. My dad, who would commute all summer but still didn't see us as often as he would've liked, was also chill when we were in Canada. Parker loves Canada. But Parker kept his shoes on and didn't become an altogether different person. And I believe it was — and probably still is — easier for him not to think about the reasons why my mother did. Because if he dwells on it hard enough, he might have to admit to himself that in taking my mother away from her home, her family and her culture, he somehow transformed her.

Well, that's my take on it anyway. Luckily, my mother is not so batshit anymore. Getting licensed, setting up practice and finding a niche where she can help homesick people more miserable than herself has loosened her up. There's no point in talking to Lucie about it. Like all shrinks I know, she's bang on analyzing others and clueless about herself. But talking to Tish Louise, now that is easy. Though I suspect she sees my mother's side of things much more than she lets on. I remember this one time when I went over to bitch, Tish Louise politely told me to stop and suck it up, because maybe, just maybe, Lucie was worried about an upcoming paper or exam or worse, something was happening back home in Canada and maybe, just maybe, my mom was plain tired of missing out on all the stuff, big or small, important or not, going on with the family she loved and missed and who were so far away.

Tish Louise doesn't know about this farmer dude because she's in London visiting her sick sister. But unlike my mother, she won't go over the top about it. That is not her jam. Seriously. I've just met the guy and I've seen first-hand how leaving your life for love can change you. It's a disaster and I'm so not going there.

Still, maybe I should ask Tish Louise why she likes that Motown song so much. Does it help bring Richard back? Or perhaps it reminds her of her life in England before Richard came into it? Tish Louise and I had quite a few sessions about WWII when I was studying for my finals in eleventh-grade history. She sure knew an awful lot of fascinating details about the war. And I have to say this — Tish Louise was way more interesting than the teacher. What she did was make it real. I'm still in awe of what went into D-Day even though the invasion of Normandy came at huge personal cost to my mother's side of the family. Although, I suppose if it hadn't, neither my mom or my sister and I would be here today. That's one way of looking at it.

Anyway, maybe being a war bride, and all that it entails, is something Tish Louise would like to talk about. I should ask her.

By the way, I'm no expert on the workings of the unconscious mind — really, is there that much internal chat going on? — but I take issue with Freud sometimes.

How can sex be the motivation for all human behavior? My Brooklyn grandmother also had her doubts. When Parker was a boy, Bubbe got a job at a beauty parlor next to John's Bargain Store just to get out of the house. After a while, she got her cosmetology license (she paid six hundred dollars for a six-month course) and opened her own shop on Seventh Avenue. She said Gramps wasn't too thrilled about that but he learned to live with it and her being out all day allowed him to do his work in peace. Bubbe loved the salon. It was her happy place. But it's funny how we all see things differently. The way my mother remembers it, my Bubbe was forever on her doorstep like a sad puppy in the rain, begging to be let inside. But the Bubbe I grew up with wasn't a wet dog at all. I know because I used to drop by her shop a lot after school and that Bubbe was in her element, chit-chatting with clients as she chopped and styled. Bubbe kept the salon open seven days a week and didn't have time to stalk random in-laws. Like I said, Bubbe was dignified. Not desperate. And she was also perceptive enough to know when she was not wanted. Bubbe was people-smart.

"You don't listen all day to folks talk about themselves, and their kids and the family and who is talking to who and who isn't talking to who, without picking up a few clues into what makes humans tick," she told me one Saturday when I was helping out. Saturdays in Brooklyn are busy no matter where you go and beauty salons are no exception.

Of course, she never challenged my mother's qualifications but really, life experience has to count for something. She liked to think that talking to your hairdresser is another form of therapy, only much less expensive and you get to look better on the way out.

She also liked to think that shopping is what motivates people. Especially in certain parts of Brooklyn.

"Sex in this neighborhood happens only when stores are closed. Your mother and her Sigmund Freud would know this if they spied less on the white rats and more on the lovely ladies in the beauty parlors."

You could see the twinkle in her eye when she said this but I know she wasn't entirely joking. There's a time and place for everything and, like my Jewish grandmother, I'm big into shopping. Freud said a lot of things. He also said sometimes a cigar is just a cigar. I miss my Bubbe.

Tish Louise Talks

I was only young when the war started. As soon as I was old enough and received the call, I trained and worked as an auto mechanic and truck driver in the Auxiliary Territorial Service. Just like the Queen. Only she was our Princess Elizabeth at the time. Most unmarried able-bodied females were conscripted. We all did what we could.

I met Richard in 1943 when I was sixteen. He was not much older although he most certainly seemed it. He was twenty and a staff sergeant with the US Eighth Air Force. I was not looking to fall in love. And I was absolutely not looking to fall in love with an American.

The Americans differed from our boys. They were wonderfully confident and carefree and oh-so direct. My heavens, they would march up to us in the street and introduce themselves. Chat up the girls. It was ever so hard not to be charmed. And they all looked so smart and terribly handsome in their uniforms.

Remember, our men were fighting in Africa or the continent and on the seas and many had been lost at Dunkirk. At the same time, we were inundated with North American soldiers who were living in our towns, and frequenting our shops and restaurants and the dance halls. They were even coming into our homes. And not that it should have mattered but they had more food and were willing to share. I never truly went hungry but oh, how I longed for chocolate.

A Lucie Lunchtime Letter

Ma puce,

I used to think Louis XVI had a micro-penis and it was for this reason that he waited seven years before bedding his new wife. But it may have been the opposite. It was not just that Louis XVI's courtiers accompanied him to the bedroom and watched as he and the virgin Marie Antoinette reposed (ben coudon!) which stopped him from consummating the marriage but the fact he may have been too big for her too tiny vagina. The poor girl.

Poor Louis XVI. Freud would have found him bizarre. Actually, Freud was a friend of Stefan Zweig who wrote a fascinating book on Marie Antoinette in the 1930s. I am certain they discussed this most intriguing issue. Of course, they discussed it. One must remember that both Louis-Auguste and Marie Antoinette were youngsters when they married and Marie Antoinette looked more like child than woman and this was a concern to the sensitive dauphin. After all, he was a nice boy. As well as just a boy.

I doubt no two persons' sex life — or one man's penis — has been studied, analyzed and debated upon as much as that of the last king and queen of France. Even at the time, it was all anyone could talk about. It was a recurring subject in royal correspondence and diplomatic exchanges and a constant worry to Marie Antoinette's mother.

Marie Antoinette was a willing partner as she knew her part to play and did not wish to disappoint her terrifying mother. Louis-Auguste however, claimed intercourse hurt. And he preferred to toy with locks and keys in his workshop rather than bed his beautiful bride. Maria Theresa regularly wrote her daughter from Vienna with perhaps unwelcome how-to-inspire-passion hints. Doctors were brought in and suggested surgery but nothing worked. Finally, Maria Theresa dispatched her son Joseph (Marie Antoinette's brother) to sort things out. Within a year, the 'two complete blunderers' (in Joseph's words) were on their way to being parents.

Unfortunately, it was a girl. But Marie Antoinette was not disappointed. A boy would belong to the nation but a daughter she could keep to herself. Three years later she gave birth to a prince.

Monsieur Zweig suggests Louis-Auguste might have had a condition called phimosis. This is where the foreskin is too tight to be pulled back over the head of le pénis. Sex may be painful. Whatever the situation, it would appear Louis-Auguste was not keen on the act and his 'impotence' caused unrest. The joke was that the king, so fascinated with locksmithing, could not, in this particular instance, put the key in the hole. This was not the cause of the French Revolution but it did not help. The feeling was a ruler must have control over both his penis and his partner if he is to have control of his people.

Monsieur Zweig maintains that Marie Antoinette's excesses occurred in the first years of her marriage as a result of her increasing sexual frustration. This, I am certain, is a view he got from talking to and with Freud. I like to agree with Freud but I do believe if Monsieur Zweig had been talking to me instead, he would have surmised Marie Antoinette was not sexually frustrated but merely sublimating her rage. Why did it not occur to him she might be suffering from mal du pays? In my view, Marie Antoinette was both homesick and hiraethally frustrated. And after a while, once she adjusted to her new circumstance, she settled down into a strong, courageous, self-controlled woman. But the change came too late and her reputation was damaged beyond repair. When the revolution came, she was remembered only as 'a prodigy of dissipation' and she paid with her life.

You are correct in that Marie Antoinette was not a true foreign wife. She did not fall in love with a foreigner and follow him home. But she left Austria for marriage. And she hoped to fall in love with Louis-Auguste so I believe it counts.

And she was royalty. In those days, royalty did not marry for love. In those days, royalty married to form alliances and strengthen ties between two regions. It was agreed upon by the parents and the children went along. Maria Theresa depended on Marie Antoinette to secure the Austro-French alliance. This was not secure until a male heir was born. Which was why Maria Theresa worried for two-thousand nights.

Comme d'habitude, it was harder for the girls. Young princesses were expected to marry princes and those princes were often from faraway lands. So the girls grew up knowing, one day, it would be them who would leave home and never return. It was rarely the other way around. But I still think a fourteen-year-old girl, no matter what her station in life, yearns for romantic love.

Lucie

4

Meghan's Method

Ah yes, 'ben coudon'. 'Ben coudon' is Québécois speak for 'écoute donc'. It's a sort of 'really?' or 'for goodness sake' with a pinch of humour or frustration or both. And no, 'hiraethally' is not a word. Lucie made it up. She got it from 'hiraeth' which is Welsh. Tish Louise uses it now and then. More so lately now that I've asked her to tell me all about her life as a war bride. Tish Louise is not from Wales but her mother was. This explains why her pet name for me is 'Blodyn'. 'Blodyn' means flower so that's strange but not as strange as calling a loved one 'my flea' or 'blodyn tatws' which literally translates as 'potato flowers'.

The Welsh may be a bit weird but I do love the word hiraeth, which has no real English or French equivalent and describes a combination of homesickness, longing and nostalgia. In layers. Like yearning for a home you cannot return to or for something that is gone. Or a wish to be where your spirit lives. And I'm not sure what that last one means but naturally my mother has taken to it like a Burmese python doing just fine in the Florida Everglades. After it was dumped in the dark of night by an irresponsible snake owner who can no longer house the damn thing in its original ten-gallon terrarium because that damn thing grew bigtime, now weighs more than its soon-to-be former pet-parent does and feeds on rats as if it were popcorn. Lucie also likes to roll the R with her words. Hirrrraeth. Rrrreptile buyer's rrrrremorrrrse.

Fletcher said it was acceptable to borrow expressions from other languages because speech is not a constant and no one vocabulary ever has it all. Except maybe Yiddish. Not because he had any real command of Yiddish but Bubbe was a big fan and he often remarked that when she spoke it, she was never at a loss for words. If that sounds in any way derogatory, it is not. I believe Gramps found my grandmother to be quite adorable when she spoke Yiddish. I know I did. My grandfather prepared and packed lunch for my grandmother every day and walked it over to her in the salon no matter what the weather. He got her flowers twice a week and signed copies of all her favorite books. He never spent a night away from her. I don't understand why she ever thought she was second best.

Fletcher also said it was fine to invent words and if you were lucky, one might catch on. Like 'Neville'. Fletcher knew this kid in high school he apparently couldn't stand. He never would say why. All I know is my grandfather turned his name into a synonym for failure. If you've read his stuff, you probably remember the occasional reference. OK, maybe not. But it certainly stuck in my family. In this house, when you get things wrong, you Nevilled it. If you shrink a favorite sweater in the dryer, you Nevilled it. If you forget the most important item on the grocery list, you Nevilled it. And if you burn toast, you Nevilled that too.

Maybe that's why Tish Louise didn't gel with Gramps. She has a son called Neville. Named after her father. But that's not a good reason to actively avoid someone. I did ask her about it at the funeral but all she let on was that it was something that happened a long time ago, long before I was born even and sometimes it's best to let sleeping dogs lie. Which is also a polite way of saying it's not my business.

And I have let sleeping dogs lie. I will not inquire again. But I will keep her talking about the war bride thing. I only get snippets here and there, but I think she enjoys going over it. Even though she's probably gone over it in full detail a million times already with my mother. But

Tish Louise says I have different questions because we come to her from different perspectives.

If it ever gets out of her head, Lucie's book is about girls who fall in love with foreigners and follow them home. Personally, I'm not sure who cares about girls who fall in love with foreigners and follow them home but my mother figures quite a few people do and so her self-help manifesto masterpiece will provide a public service of some sort. When it's down on paper. I wonder if Gramps is the reason she keeps researching but doesn't yet write. Even after all this time, Fletcher Buell casts an intimidating shadow.

But my mother needs to lighten up and lay off. I've only just met the guy. And I know Bubbe would say he's a total mensch and I might agree. But I'm not that girl. I'm not going to follow him — or any man — home.

Tish Louise Talks

Of course, there was fornication. And lots of it. I doubt your high school teacher was allowed to tell you that World War Two was the biggest consensual sex spree in history. And that as much action took place off the battlefield as on.

Imagine this. All the local men are gone. Enter excitable impressionable soldiers in nice uniform with interesting ways and speech and on leave from the front line. Army boys with plentiful pocket money who have seen far too many horrors. Army boys taught to kill or be killed. Army boys raised with locker room mentality. And women and girls who, suddenly, because of the freedoms conscripted work affords them, want a bit more out of life and no longer feel the need to toe the line. Or women and girls, who, because the traditional breadwinner-men are gone, sell themselves to make ends meet. Naturally, the military hoped to put a stop to it and cautioned of venereal diseases. These warnings had little impact to young soldiers who might have their bodies blown to bits at any time.

A Lucie Lunchtime Letter

Ma puce,

I do not understand the Empress Maria Theresa of Austria. She treated her daughters like pawns in a game of chess. And yet she was able to stay home when she married. Francis came to her. And she was permitted to marry for love and adored her husband. But she did not extend the same courtesy to her children. She was ruthless.

Of course, the same might be said for Queen Victoria. She got her one true love and the other way around too. Prince Albert moved from Coburg to London. To be fair, her children had a say. They could refuse her attempts at match-making. Queen Victoria married four of her five daughters into German nobility. After Vicky and Alice went away, she insisted that the husbands of Beatrice and Helena stay in England. You know that Alice was Alix of Hesse's (Tsarina Alexandra) mother. Neither Alice or Vicky were happy in their new country. Both were lonely and unwelcomed. Her sons also paired up with foreigners and it was the wives who uprooted. Comme d'habitude.

Queen Victoria's European chessboard was quite a success. Victoria's descendants ruled not only Britain but for a time Greece, Norway, Prussia in the German Empire, Romania, Russia and Spain. But it was her DNA which introduced hemophilia into royal houses all over the continent. Alix married into the Romanov dynasty and became Tsarina Alexandra and transmitted the disease to her only son who was heir to the Russian throne. In those days, sufferers died young. There is still no cure. Hemophilia B has disappeared from the family but it could pop up again. I am curious to know if potential royal spouses are tested for the gene.

Oh, how I love to learn about the Tsarina Alexandra. A woman gone mad but intriguing all the same. But I digress. I suppose daughters have always been used as pawns. I think of the Virginia Jamestown Brides in the early 1600s when I say this. And a little later on, Les Filles du Roi in Québec too. These were both organized female migrations for the purpose of marriage, though whether the women involved qualify as foreign wives is debatable.

I have several reasons for thinking this way. For one, none of the women knew their future husbands before setting off from Europe to North America. Secondly, not all women left willingly so in some situations, it is more human trafficking than human migration. Finally, both husband and wife were of the same culture and background and so understood each other on a basic level. They may not have been on the same page but at least they were both reading the same book. Assuming they could read. Illiteracy rates were high back then. But they spoke the same language. That helps. Perhaps love only came into the equation with the war brides. If you look at it this way, then many of the nineteenth century dollar princesses also do not qualify.

Was not Madame Curtis-Smith brave? I could never cross an ocean for a man.

Lucie

5

Meghan's Method

My mother never stops. Mind you, we all have our quiet little passions, right?

Lucie used to be consumed with Marie Antoinette but my eponym has been dethroned by Tsarina Alexandra AKA Alix of Hesse. That's my sister's eponym. Or namesake. Whatever. Lucie maintains it's not because Marie Antoinette got boring (she did not), but because there's so much documentation available on Tsarina Alexandra now and new stuff pops up on the internet every day. So when she's not fixating on her work and international marriages and the sad suckers stuck in them, she's analyzing Tsarina Alexandra. That's just what she does. Lucie analyzes people twenty-four seven. She's also into half-marathons. She's the runner in Prospect Park pushing the funny cat stroller. But she only takes one at a time. Maine Coons are big.

Lucie tells me that a series of letters written by Alexandra to her mother has been found somewhere in Siberia. It's a one-way correspondence. Her mother never wrote back because her mother was long dead. And by the time she hooked up with Tsar Nicholas II, her father was also gone. As well as one hemophiliac brother. And her older sisters had all left home. And her other brother who was a grand duke was about to marry which was bad for him because men can also be used as pawns even when homosexual, bad for the wife-to-be because she was also a pawn and in love with another man and bad for Alexandra AKA Alix because she was required to move out of the palace she grew up in and had nowhere to live without being in the way. One would think palaces come big enough but according to both Lucie and my grandfather, two women running one household is never a good thing. I think it's the only point they ever agreed on, though how either one of them should know this without first-hand experience, I have no idea. Anyway, it's no wonder Alexandra never smiled. I probably know more about Lucie's evil foreign queens than I realize.

Parker's schtick is planes. Like Lucie, he turned his great love into his job so it worked out pretty well. He learned to fly before he could drive with money Bubbe gave him. It was their secret because Gramps disapproved. Gramps hated planes and stayed well away. To this day, my father cannot get over the irony of it all.

"He might have had better luck avoiding tall buildings," I heard Parker utter to himself in the weeks after my grandparents disappeared. When we all knew for sure neither of them was coming home.

After flying comes classical music and opera. I can't tell you how many hours I've spent in my room listening to the sounds of Mozart and Verdi wafting up from the basement. Those are his favorites along with Fidelio. My dad says Fidelio is Beethoven's only opera, and he agonized over it for years for a variety of reasons. According to my mom, Beethoven was a drama queen with a strong negativity bias, which is not a good thing. According to my dad, she thinks too much.

Parker's favorite tenor is a German called Fritz Wunderlich who met his end in mysterious circumstances in the 1960s. That he hit his head falling down the stairs is not the issue. It's how he came to fall. Was he tying his shoes and lost his footing? Was he stupid drunk and lost his footing? Or — and this is where it gets interesting — was he running away from a jealous husband while caught in a lovers' tryst on the second-floor bedroom of a hunting lodge and lost his footing? Parker says he doesn't care about that, he just likes to listen to him sing. But

Lucie says this goes to show you that we are all (A) motivated by sex; (B) have more than one story; and (C) hunting lodges are notorious for bad juju. Versailles was originally built as a hunting lodge so she might be onto something. Even if she is a killjoy.

Anyway, when I was growing up, Parker was the only dad I knew who listened to that kind of music. It's not something he picked up from the family home because his was a quiet house. Gramps needed to hear himself write. And did I mention Parker builds model airplanes from scratch in his spare time? He draws up the plans too. On the dining room table. Listening to his opera. He flies them in the summer in a corn field near Grand-maman's house in Canada. Being a commercial pilot is a good gig. You're away a lot but you also get a lot of downtime.

My sister is into Puritan history and all things 1692. I remember the day Gramps told her about his great-gran killed by Native Americans. It was Halloween and my sister was proudly showing off her Pocahontas costume to my grandparents before my mom and I took her out. Parker must have been on a layover because he wasn't there and it wasn't the sort of thing my dad liked to miss. Naturally, Lucie had to mention that Pocahontas was in an international marriage having married an Englishman before her untimely death in England at the age of twenty-one. From pneumonia. Or maybe it was smallpox. No one knows for sure. I think the year was 1617 and she met him — John Rolfe — in Jamestown which is actually in Virginia. Of course, Bubbe was being her usual attentive admiring grandmotherly self that day but you never knew with Gramps what you were going to get. Bubbe says this is what made him such a successful novelist. Because he could draw on any emotion at any time. My mother, who should know better, maintains it's easier to treat people with 'issues' than it is to live with them and secretly called my grandfather Grumps. In her defence, the man could be pretty grouchy. Unless my sister was around. Anyway, Gramps abruptly pipes up from his work desk in the corner and informs Ally about his grandmother from way back who was slaughtered in the Massachusetts Connecticut River Valley in 1704. I knew about the Deerfield Raid because it was covered in ninth grade history but my sister was still in elementary school and hadn't heard of it. According to Gramps, our ancestor Hepzibah Buell survived the attack but was left for dead on day five of the frigid three hundred-mile prisoners' march to Montreal.

"You see, the Indians and French Canadians were in on it together," says Gramps.

Gramps never did get on with my mother and he seemed to take great pleasure in pointing out that my mother's ancestors were likely responsible for killing his. But while Lucie appeared totally indifferent, if only because Gramps was so suddenly passionate in his story-telling, my sister was completely fascinated. She's been hooked on Puritan history ever since. Especially the part with the witches.

Tish Louise Talks

The American military strongly discouraged marriage with the British girls and Europeans. We were thought to be a distraction. Oh heavens, what utter rubbish! I would think we were just the opposite as we gave our hearts to young men far away from home. And in the time of war. It's hard to explain but love in a time of war is a most passionate thing. One never knows if one will be alive from one day to the next. Such uncertainty creates a sense of urgency. And of heightened emotions. Perhaps not among older married couples but we were young and had not yet lived a proper life. We wanted to live while we were still able to.

I'm not certain how many British women were married to foreign soldiers during the Second World War, but I do believe it was about one hundred thousand. Most came to America but at least fifty thousand went to Canada. And of course, to the Antipodes. There were Canadian war brides going to New Zealand, Australian war brides coming to England, Japanese war brides to the United States. All told, I have read a million women from fifty different countries left their home and families behind to be with their foreign soldier husbands after the war.

There were some, naturally, who viewed us as traitors. They said we should be with our own boys. I didn't give it any thought.

A Lucie Lunchtime Letter

Ma puce,

You might want to find out what his people eat. Food is much more important than we think. It is an issue when you live in a different country because it presents itself three times a day. Not only in terms of what is consumed but when and how. Are you expected to cook local delicacies? What if you cannot find your favorite food? What if the main staple is something which disgusts you? At what time is the main meal served? Could you eat your dinner on the floor every day for the rest of your life?

Lucie

6

Meghan's Method

I'm not worried about food. My mother isn't listening to me. I'm not going anywhere. I'm staying right here. This is my home. My whole life is here. My roots are here.

Like my sister, I fixate on the past and the people in it. I am big on graveyards. I can spend hours in Greenwood Cemetery here in Brooklyn. And back when my mother was getting her master's degree and needed peace around the house on weekends, Parker would take my sister and me out for long drives into the Connecticut River Valley where we would stop at old burial grounds and look for our forebears. There are an awful lot of dead Buells in the Connecticut River Valley. They're in Canada also, in a place called Brockville, which is west of Montreal. When my dad was visiting us in the summer, we'd drive out there sometimes because Parker said we are all related and it is nice to know where the family is hanging out. That's the thing about graveyards — they're full of possibilities. You have no clue who you're going to run into. An old ancestor perhaps, or someone linked somehow to an old ancestor. It's about connection. Tsar Nicholas II and Tsarina Alexandra have a nephew who's buried in the Brockville Cemetery. He's the son of Nicholas II's younger sister Olga and her second husband. The first was another male pawn with no interest in women and so the marriage wasn't consummated. And she repeatedly begged her brother to let it end. Tsar Nicholas II ignored her annulment requests for fifteen years until he was way in over his head in the middle of World War One and had bigger fish to fry. True, Olga didn't have to marry the guy but speculation is that she did it for the simple reason that option number two meant being sent away into a foreign marriage, and she didn't want that either. Olga was no slouch. She could see first-hand how xenophobic her country was towards outsiders like Tsarina Alexandra, so why would any other place be any different? And her whole life was in Russia and she really didn't want to leave. Until, of course, she had no choice but to run off later on in the game or risk execution like her brother, sister-in-law and their five children. As well as another brother. So Olga did go eventually — with a new husband and young family in tow. And the last Grand Duchess of Imperial Russia died living alone in a little apartment over a beauty salon in Canada where one son is now also dead and buried in Brockville surrounded by Buells. Lucie doesn't do graveyards but even she can appreciate that connection.

And yes, I have an interest in dollar princesses. But I'm hardly obsessed. It all started the day I walked past a building in Cobble Hill and read a plaque on its wall which indicated that this was the spot where Winston Churchill's mother was born.

'In this house in January 1850 was born Jennie Jerome, later Lady Randolph Churchill,' it said (and still does).

'She was the mother of the Rt. Hon. Winston Spencer Churchill. Prime Minister of Great Britain and Staunch Friend of the United States.'

'This plaque is erected as a memorial to Lady Churchill to evidence the esteem and affection in which her son is held by the people of this community.'

I was about nine or ten and didn't understand the odd link to Tish Louise's squirrels and was positive no one but my grandfather used the word 'staunch'. Now Tish Louise, it turns out, knew all about Winston Churchill and was keen to pass on her knowledge. Especially as she got a glimpse of the man himself when he dropped by the house sometime in the 1950s. The fact that Winston's mother had lived a few miles from my home had me enthralled. Who was this Jennie Jerome? What was she like? Surely the woman was more than just the mother of a staunch friend of the United States. And how did she come to be so far away from the house she was born in? And suddenly too, Brooklyn — the place I had grown up to believe was somehow inferior to Montreal although I don't think this was ever Lucie's intention — became more exciting. It was also a time in my life when Marie Antoinette was the last name on the planet I wanted as mine and because all the Jennies in school were perky with lean limbs and thick blonde wavy hair, I longed to be a Jennie too.

That Jennie J was actually christened a Jeanette and not a Jennifer and was dark-haired and brown-eyed like me made her all the more endearing. I figured she must have hated her 'ette' name as much as I did mine. By the way, it's not easy changing your name midway through your childhood when all the kids know you as one thing and aren't too keen to change to another. Thank God for the summer between elementary and middle school which allows for a bit of re-invention. I also thank God for stupid kids who think Meg is the English translation for Marie Antoinette. Parker, who was reading *The Thorn Birds* at the time, suggested Meghan — the name of the main character — because Jennie was too much of a stretch and Moon Unit was already taken.

If you've read *The Thorn Birds*, you might remember that even though the story takes place in Australia, Meggie was born in New Zealand. As my mother would say, 'Quelle coincidence.'

Now Lucie will tell you that Jennie Jerome was a foreign wife but as a pre-teen, I didn't care much. I'm not sure I do now either because to know Jennie J is to know she didn't see herself in this way. This was not her story. Her story was that of a woman ahead of her time. Jennie J was strong, independent, brave and fierce. She had attitude. People called her 'The Panther' because of her dark features (among other attributes), rumored to have been passed down from an Iroquois ancestor. It's nothing that can be proven but Jennie J's mother certainly believed in it.

"My dears, there's something you should know. It may not be chic but it is rather interesting…" is the manner in which Mrs. Jerome informed her three daughters. Like me, I'll bet Jennie J thought it fabulous news. We should all be so lucky to have Haudenosaunee blood running through our veins.

Jennie J met Lord Randolph Churchill at a party on the Isle of Wight off the south coast of England. Their son Winston was born seven months after their marriage and judging by his healthy size, he was not premature. Jennie J was married to Winston's dad for some twenty years but is said to have had as many as two hundred lovers in her life. Including Queen Victoria's son Prince Albert/King Edward VII. According to Lucie, 'sexual misconduct' is a common method of sublimating rage but seriously, if Jenny J was fuming, no one noticed. My view is Jennie just wanted to have fun. Of course, Prince Albert/King Edward VII AKA Bertie had lots of fun too (plenty of sexual misconduct and a hunting lodge on hand) but Jennie J was one of his favorites. After Randolph's sad demise (from syphilis, so it seems), she had two more husbands. Both were much younger than she and one younger than Winston even. And rumor has it, she had a snake tattoo on her wrist. Not chic but rather interesting.

Like my dad's favorite tenor, Jennie J also died following a fall down the stairs. She tripped on a new pair of high heels. Nothing suspicious. No toyboys involved. Her shoes were Italian. Most of the mystery which surrounds this woman was in life, not in death.

I doubt Freud would know what to make of her. Sigmund, too, enjoyed certain excess and when forced into self-denial, complained of the 'horrible misery of abstinence'. So what if Jennie J had as many lovers as she did shoes? He found life without cigars unbearable. If you have too much of anything, does that mean you are angry? Bubbe said women are allowed to obsess over shoes because aside from nightmare New York winters, they're the only constant in life.

"Everything around us is changing. Every day my body is different," my grandmother would say. "But shoe size, shoe size stays the same." She sounds kvetchy when I replay her words but she was far from it. My Bubbe was a hoot.

I used to visit Jennie J's grave when I worked at Blenheim Palace. Hers is a rather modest affair compared to where her parents are parked up at the Jerome family mausoleum at Green-Wood. But she's right next to Winston and her first husband Lord Randolph. I don't know where husbands number two and number three ended up.

I loved those summers in Woodstock. It's good for cycling and even after long days on the job, I never tired of it. Tish Louise suggested I might like to work there and she was right. I was in awe of the place. Jennie J was equally mesmerized. But she hated Blenheim Palace too. Not so much the building but the people in it and their way of life which was so completely different from hers. And Consuelo, who arrived twenty years after Jennie J, felt the same. Consuelo Vanderbilt is no doubt the most famous dollar princess. She married Jennie J's nephew (cousin to Winston) so she's there as well, in the cozy family plot. We had a lot of good times, after the tourists were gone for the day, just the three of us.

Tish Louise Talks

I've always been Tish Louise. I was born Patricia Louise Curtis. I fell in love with Richard but not his name. One's name is rather personal and Smith did not suit. I did go along with it after we married, for a few years at least, until my new American friend Jane convinced me to return to my maiden name. Over time, mainly to please the children, I've come to use both.

You would've liked Jane. We bonded over plants but she was also a writer. Just like you. She started her own magazine, in fact. She was much older than I but very forward thinking. I believe she knew your grandfather.

A Lucie Lunchtime Letter

Ma puce,

I missed croissants when I first came to Brooklyn. Marie Antoinette felt the same on her arrival in France where croissants were not available. It was not long before she had her pastry chef on the job and now we all think croissants are a French creation when, en réalité, they are from Austria.

Lucie

7

The amount of scribbling which goes on in a country-house, and in which Englishwomen in particular indulge, is always a source of astonishment and amusement to our Continental neighbours.
Jennie Jerome, Lady Randolph Churchill

Meghan's Method

Were we still speaking of food? Or writing, I should say. Lucie's lunchtime emails just keep coming.

Oh well, at least now I know why the French call croissants 'Viennoiseries'. I'm not sure what's on the menu in New Zealand but surely bagels are on offer. Some people can't start the day without a cup of coffee. I just need my morning toasted bagel and butter and I'm good.

Not that it matters because I just sold an article to that not so little magazine started up by Jane and I'm so not going anywhere anytime soon. I wish my grandfather could see me now.

The last Queen of France gets credit for another popular eighteenth-century product launch. According to legend, Maine Coon cats are descendants of six Turkish angoras Marie Antoinette smuggled to Maine as she plotted her escape from Europe. Rumor also has it that a ship captain by the name of Clough, who was in France during the Revolution, had a house waiting for her in Maine where she planned to set up shop when it was all said and done. But in her final days, an imprisoned Marie Antoinette would not abandon her two children who were jailed in different locations. Ergo, she failed to get away in time.

'Ergo' is one of my dad's favorite words. He swears Gramps said it all the time but if he did, I can't remember. In any case, Gramps often said memory was unreliable and the reason why we developed written language is because humans can't be trusted with the truth for longer than it takes for us to jot it down. He also said that if we tell the same lie over and over, eventually we'll come to believe in it. When I asked Fletcher once if he spoke from experience, I swear I made him cry. I can still see that single tear in my head, rolling down his cheek, as we walked over the Brooklyn Bridge on a bright, sunny Sunday morning. 'Severe clear' is what my dad calls those searing super crystal blue skies you see in New York like on the day of the attacks. But maybe I remember it wrong. Maybe my grandfather had watery eyes because he was in need of a pair of sunglasses. He never did wear sunglasses. Anyway, I am pretty sure Lucie took us to see Marie Antoinette's wannabe sanctuary in Edgecomb when we were little. You'd think it might be a museum of some sort, but no. It's a private home. Which, so it is claimed, Marie Antoinette now haunts. I highly doubt that because it's common knowledge ghosts can't travel over water.

Also questionable, and another bone of contention between my mother and grandfather, is how her white kitties morphed into the sizeable multi-colored modern-day Maine Coons. Cross breeding is not uncommon — killer bees, ligers and tigons, grizzly polar bears called pizzlies — but most hybrid offspring are sterile so it stops right there. This, according to Gramps, is as nature intended. And why close species often possess isolating mechanisms which prevent their getting it on in the first place. Gramps had no clue how Maine Coons came to be in New England but he was firm (AKA staunch) in his belief that my mother was way off base in hers. For as long as I can remember, Lucie maintains that Marie Antoinette's eighteenth-century rescue-cats hooked up with the local native bobcat and here we are, enter the magnificent majestic Maine Coon cat.

"Coons are an example of successful international relationships in the animal kingdom," she argued with my grandfather.

"Rubbish fantasy," he would reply, shaking his head in that sad way people save for no-hopers.

Now 'rubbish' was definitely one of Fletcher's favorite words. I used to think he picked it up from Tish Louise but my New Zealand farmer uses it and now I am beginning to wonder — did my grandfather's war bride wife Annie say it too?

Rubbish fantasy or not, this explains my mother's infatuation with Maine Coon cats. I must check to see if they've made their way to New Zealand. I'm just curious. That's all.

Now, most folk have never heard of the dollar princesses. Not even here in New York where a lot of it went down. Jennie J was one of the first. That girl fell hard for Lord Randolph Churchill. If not from day one, then at least on day three when she consented to marry him.

Most of the dollar princesses came about twenty years later. Like Consuelo, who married Randolph's nephew, a one Charles Spencer-Churchill, ninth Duke of Marlborough. The year was 1895. When I started at Blenheim, I knew all about Jennie J and how she made her mark at Blenheim by giving birth to Winston in a little chamber near the main foyer. I had, however, not heard of Consuelo Vanderbilt, and when I came across that portrait of her and her family in the Red Drawing Room, I was mesmerized. I gobbled up her autobiography even though, according to my grandfather, rich and famous people don't write their own memoirs and get others to do it for them and then take all the credit. Which is all kinds of wrong. Having said that, Consuelo deserves a hall pass because that poor girl was not only forced to marry a self-important man-snob she didn't love but was then made to live alone away from her tribe in another country. All this so her mother Alva could have the social status she felt she deserved. It was a miserable marriage.

To be fair, I think most of them were. Which makes them all the more fascinating. As is how it all came to be. Back in the late nineteenth century, consecutive years of excessive rainfall meant substantial agricultural losses for rich English landowners and their tenant farmers. Country estates were broke and castles were crumbling and yet it was unthinkable for a man of noble lineage to go out and work for a living.

Meanwhile, on this side of the Atlantic, the Civil War had come and gone and America was experiencing massive industrialization and huge economic growth. Fortunes were being made but, as is always the case, so too was a distinction between old money and new. For certain parvenu, like Alva, vast riches were not enough if it didn't get you invited into the right parties. And poor Alva really wanted to go to the right parties.

Just who came up with the idea of swapping capital for title is not known (my bets are on Alva) but immediately after Consuelo cried her way down the aisle, it became a thing. A good three hundred or so wealthy girls with no place in high society went on to marry into the British aristocracy, ergo securing spots in the smart set.

'Cash for class' arrangements were being made all over New York City and beyond. Guide books were put out to help facilitate the trade. It was practically an industry. And how much loot was involved, you ask? Consuelo's dowry in the day was two and a half million dollars. The arrogant man-snob scored big time and Consuelo walked out of the church a duchess but this was no win-win. Because Consuelo was born the epitome of class. She was intelligent, well-mannered, elegant and strikingly beautiful. I had a lovely conversation with her great-granddaughter once when I was at Blenheim and she was kind to me even though I turned into the village idiot in her presence. Lady H could often be found in the house working as an interior decorator. She resembles Consuelo and is also very tall.

A quarter of the British aristocracy married dollar princesses in those days and it was their capital used to restore those grand but shabby old homes. I hate to think what might have happened to Blenheim Palace without Consuelo's contribution. It's a massive place. I needed more than one summer there to work my way through it.

Anyway, at first, the Americans were cool with these women going over and mingling with royalty. But over time, people in the United States became resentful, seeing millions of hard-earned American dollars being spent elsewhere.

Without a doubt, the best hater has got to be Franklin H Work. Mr. Work was a billionaire New York banker whose daughter Frances ran off with the son of some baron in 1880. Frank was pissed and found the transatlantic marriage trade so infuriating that he stated that if he could do anything about it, he would make international marriages a hanging offence.

The funny thing is, Frank Work may have got the biggest prize of them all. Frances Work was the late Princess Diana's great-grandmother. So Frank Work's great-great-great-grandson is Prince William, future King of England. I wonder what the old man would say now.

Tish Louise Talks

Of course, you know that Frank Work is buried in Green-Wood Cemetery. In her trips to Manhattan after the divorce, I often wondered if Princess Diana might pop over for a private visit with her American forebears. But perhaps Frank's strong views were a turn-off and she stayed away.

Thankfully, my parents didn't object to the idea of international marriage. Not in the least. Heavens no, if the King of England could abdicate his crown to marry a twice-divorced American, how could they challenge me?

It was at this same time also that the American socialite Kathleen Kennedy married the Marquess of Hartington. She was the daughter of the former American Ambassador Joseph Kennedy and sister of John Fitzgerald who went on to be the United States President. Sadly, her new husband was shot dead by sniper fire while serving in Belgium and this was one month after her older brother Joseph Junior was killed in action. I knew nothing of these tragedies at the time but, you see, it serves to illustrate our reality. We could not live for the future because we didn't know if we had a future. Poor Kathleen, she perished in a plane crash shortly after the war. She was not yet thirty.

A Lucie Lunchtime Letter

Ma puce,

From what I understand, Americans and English are dissimilar on many levels. Just because they share a common language does not mean they are the same. From the dollar princesses travelling East over the Atlantic in the late nineteenth century to war brides going West in the twentieth, it cannot have been easy either way.

On the surface, Canadians and Americans are not very different. We share a continent and the same basic values.

We have the same general ideas about family, raising children, raising how many children and how much time to spend with relatives and friends. We observe the same holidays, household traditions and rituals. And the same basic rules of etiquette and common courtesies. And we hold similar prejudices too. We also share equivalent standards of living, housing and home heating, and have the same infrastructure and forms of transportation. We have the same medical practices (I would not want to give birth in a yurt), we have the same ideas about women's rights and their roles in society and also, we have identical ideas on personal hygiene and habits and how we manage time.

I understand why people might think we share the same culture. We look alike. But on the inside, we are not the same. Canadians and Americans have a different mentality. It is hard to explain to an outsider. Even harder to explain to an insider into both.

When you are living with someone every day, all these things which make up our ways of being, they are important.

Ma puce, society is not as rigid as when I married your father. Your Bubbe and Gramps are gone. No one cares if you live with someone before you marry. Before you commit to this man, go to New Zealand and see how you feel about where he lives. You must find out how things are done in his country.

Madame Curtis-Smith says if you want to know a man, see how he treats his mother. You need to see for yourself and observe how

Harrison interacts with you and others on his home turf as this is where he likely feels most at ease and is truly himself.

Right now, you are only getting one half of the story. You need to see all of him.

Lucie

8

Meghan's Method

I'm so not going to chase some dude to the bottom of the world.
Hell no. Not now.
Especially not now.
My career is on fire!
Hear me roar.
But maybe following your heart isn't a disaster.
Tish Louise certainly doesn't think so.
My mom is still here.
Anyway, it doesn't matter.
New York proved too much for the man.
It's over.
He's leaving.
Tonight.
On that midnight plane to Auckland.
And that's OK.
Really.
Like I said, it was just a summer fling.

Tish Louise Talks

Blodyn, I can see you are heartbroken. If you truly believe the affair was nothing but a summer romance, so be it. But if you feel that it is more, then you must go visit this man's home and home country before you take this any further. Find out the whole picture because all of us, men and women, always forget to paint the whole picture.

See where he lives and how he lives. Meet his friends. Discover the skeletons in his closet, if any. Another reason why the American military was against our unions is because after a number of soldiers were wed to foreign girls in the First World War, it was discovered they were already married back home.

Check out his family and remember that we are all formed by the unit we are born into. How his family functions will impact on your relationship. Note how your man treats his mother as it indicates how you too will be treated. Check out his father. We all turn into our parents one day. If you find traits you can't bear, beware as they may be passed on to your children as well.

Go to New Zealand. Goodness, it's the twenty-first century — there are no more excuses not to. Do not let your feelings for this man suppress your critical thought.

A Lucie Lunchtime Letter

Ma puce,

Before I met Parker, I never expected to leave my country.

Bien sûr, you know the story of how I met your father just after I finished high school. But I will tell you again. It does not hurt to know how you came to be.

My grandmother Hermeline was born near Plattsburgh. In her time, many French-Canadian families moved from Québec to New York for jobs. When I was a little girl, Hermeline told me that while all her American-born brothers and sisters were in Montreal, she had a twin sister living in the United States that she had not seen in years. This intrigued me. As did the fact her mother, my great-grandmother Salome, was buried in New York, while my great-grandfather who had died long before her, was laid to rest in Canada. Why are they not together?

Her story stayed in my head and when I was old enough, I decided to find this place where Hermeline's mother Salome is all alone. It surprised me as to how easy it was to do. This was in the days before the internet when all we had was regular mail and telephones. I wrote a letter to the local Catholic church requesting information and they replied immediately with the name of the cemetery and even gave me a map with her exact location. Americans are very kind in this way. Shots might be fired in disagreement but they are always wanting to be of service to you first.

That summer, I convinced my sister Gilberte to come with me and so off we went. When we got there, next to my great-grandmother's grave, was Parker. He was placing a stone on Salome's marker.

Your father was in uniform. I thought he was a soldier but later I found out he was an air force pilot. He was so handsome and I did not understand why he was paying his respects unless he was an American cousin and peut-être related to my grandmother's long-lost twin. My English was limited but I managed to ask him why he was there. He said that no, he was not related. It was just that he loved cemeteries and visited whenever he could and always placed a fresh flower or stone on one of the old graves because he wanted no one to feel forgotten. By the time he had finished his story, I had fallen in love with this young man.

My sister, who watched it all unfold in front of her, says it was fate and we were meant to be together. I told myself it would be OK because he was born in New York State — just like my grandmother.

I gave your father my phone number in Montreal and he came to visit in his little emerald green convertible the next week. He could do this as it wasn't too far from the American Air Force Base in Plattsburgh where he was stationed. He drove to see me almost every weekend after.

My mother did not trust this tall, dark and English-speaking American boy from Brooklyn who said he was Protestant with a Russian Jewish mother. But she had to agree with my sister that Salome was behind it. So, when your father asked me to marry him and come to live with him in New York, your Grand-maman did not object because it was my destiny.

Neither could I.

Lucie

9

Meghan's Method

So this happened. I kind of got married. Don't ask me how. The last little while has been a bit of a blur. But we got it done. We are now officially Mr. and Mrs. Harrison Max. Well, sort of. Because in keeping with French-Canadian custom and my Lucy-Stoner. complete disregard for certain patriarchal traditions which oppress women, I have absolutely no intention of changing my surname. Not to mention that Meghan Max sounds too much Hollywood celebrity and not enough serious journalist. Oh, and Harrison prefers not to be a Harrison. Yes, all this time, my farmer's actually been feeling my pain. Not that he dislikes his name but he tells me everyone in New Zealand calls him Blu and it just suits him better.

Shit – I might have known that had I been to New Zealand. What else don't I know?

By the way, it's entirely possible to plan a wedding in less than six weeks. Not to mention find that perfect dress, have a girls' weekend getaway, hold a stoop sale to get rid of all your cluttering junk, sell your car and quit your job. Now Blu Max and Meghan Buell are going on honeymoon!

Tish Louise Talks

Well, Blodyn, this is rather sudden. I offer my heartfelt congratulations to you and your man.

Yes, Jane and Lucy Stone would approve. So many things in life change after marriage. Your name should not be one of them. Isn't it interesting that Québec provincial law actually forbids a woman from taking her husband's name after marriage? Your mother also tells me that since 1789, French citizens are required to use no name other than the one stated on their birth certificate. So, in France too, taking your husband's surname must be illegal.

The first year of wedlock is a challenge. Wedlock is a most interesting word, is it not?

Richard was sent to the front straight away after we married. I wrote to him every day and every day I waited for his response. You can indeed learn to know someone through an exchange of letters, sometimes much more than in face-to-face communication. There is an honesty to letter writing not always found in person. Richard has always been a quiet man. His pen was far more talkative than his voice. Much like your grandfather, I would imagine. Only in a different way. This mysterious missing Annie you mention now and then — did you ever stop to think perhaps her story is in one of his books?

A Lucie Lunchtime Letter

Bonjour Madame,

I hope your introduction to your new home will not be as traumatic as it was for your namesake. One biographer referred to it as her 'De-Austrification'. During the handover, or 'la remise', Marie Antoinette was made to strip naked. They took everything that was Austrian away from her — her clothes, her beloved attendants and even her dog.

Once she was in France, she could have only French clothes, French attendants and French dogs. She was also required to change her given name — Maria Antonia was now Marie Antoinette. This was before the 1789 birth name birth certificate law, bien sûr. Mais, but what an awful thing to do to a child who has just left her home behind. Though I believe in the end, she sent for the dog and got him back.

The new Marie Antoinette was fortunate that French was spoken at the Habsburg Court so she was familiar with the language. Before her departure, she trained with a dialect coach to get the accent right. This was her mother's idea. Maria Theresa was not one to disobey.

Alix of Hesse changed her name to Alexandra after her conversion to the Russian Orthodox Church. I do not get the impression it was an issue for her. Her big concern on arrival in Saint Petersburg was having to learn two new languages. Not just Russian and its different alphabet but French as well which was the language of the court. She was good at neither and preferred to speak English even though she grew up in Germany. Her British mother, who died when Tsarina Alexandra was six, obviously had much influence in her life.

Perhaps small name changes were not so important when you think of everything else these women had to contend with. Or maybe it was just how things happened in all royal houses and they thought nothing of it.

It is good you do not need to learn a new language in your adopted country. Not being able to understand or be understood is an isolating experience.

Ma puce, did you know that etiquette in the French court required Marie Antoinette and her husband Louis XVI to take meals in public? Versailles was open to all who were suitably attired. People would visit to witness the king and queen eat. Up to one thousand viewers could be admitted to the galleries which overlooked the dining salon.

This was absolutely not one of those peculiar royal habits Marie Antoinette might have thought nothing of as it was not practiced in the Habsburg Court. Empress Maria Theresa urged her daughter to accept French customs but Marie Antoinette barely touched her food on such occasions. Her audience construed this as a show of contempt and yet another reason to dislike her. Ben coudon, who wants to eat when hundreds of eyes are feasting on you as you do?

Lucie

10

How strange life in a big country-house seemed to me, who until then had been accustomed only to towns. The Duke and Duchess of Marlborough lived in a most dignified, and, indeed, somewhat formal style.
Jennie Jerome, Lady Randolph Churchill

Meghan's Method

Yup. Versailles was open to the well-dressed public and thousands of people might visit the palace on any day and view Marie Antoinette go about her life. In one of her first letters to Maria Theresa, she complained that she put on her rouge and washed her hands in front of the entire world. When she finally had a child eight years into the marriage, she was probably too horrified to write mom about the one-hundred-plus observers who waited and watched while she popped it out. Especially the part where the two chimney-sweepers climbed up on the furniture for a better look.

I have decided that, as a reluctant star in an eighteenth-century version of a modern-day reality show, Marie Antoinette would likely prefer cameras to crowds. Versailles was ill equipped to handle such traffic and toilets were few which meant people — and their pets — pissed and pooped in corners and behind curtains. Marie Antoinette's home in Vienna was private, quiet and clean. Versailles was a loud free-for-all stink-hole in dire need of detox.

The poor girl. Her new home is a disaster zone. She's homesick. Her mother doesn't approve of her new make-up regime and she's married to a man more interested in padlocks than propagation. Whatever the penis problem, Marie Antoinette had only one job to do — provide an heir — and she is stuck with a guy who cannot, or will not, get it up. When she eventually succeeds, men covered in soot witness her give birth.

Seriously, how can one's authentic self survive that shit? No wonder she ordered in four pairs of shoes a week.

My mother need not worry. I was not de-Americanized on arrival. I was not stripped down at the border and I have not had to hand over my dog. I love it here. New Zealand is amazing.

Blu's family farm is a short drive from town. To be honest, it's more of a village, because there aren't many people here and few services and only two stores. Blu warned me that it was small but I had no idea how small. The world's nationalities clearly perceive this one word differently. My sister doesn't believe me when I swear to her the place was not on Google Earth before I left. Because it is now, under a cloud, and shit, she says, what was I thinking? Lucie apparently told her it would not have mattered anyway as I've become one of those people in love who consider themselves indestructible and don't listen to reason.

But my mother can take comfort in that my dopamine levels are fine. Luckily, Blu's house on the farm is well away from his parents because there's not much to do around here except make love. Still, Lucie worries that one mile between their house and our house is way too close for comfort and keeps asking how I feel about that. She professes that, after all these years, she has nightmares of Bubbe on the stoop begging to be let inside even though I inform her she's delusional and it never happened. Lucie doesn't want anything getting in the way of her having another grandchild. Preferably one that is not out of wedlock this time. I promise her we are working on it. Quietly.

Wedlock is an interesting word indeed. Makes marriage sound like a trap, doesn't it? But no. According to Gramps, it comes from the Old English word 'wedlāc' which basically means 'to pledge' and so it's quite a sweet expression. Only now it seems only used when talking about children born to unmarried parents. Not that I really care how my niece came in to this world. I just find it an interesting word.

So New Zealand is tiny. And very very far away. The flight goes on forever. The moon is closer to New York than New Zealand. At least that's how it feels from where I'm sitting right now because I can see the moon. I cannot see New York.

Lucie says that if you want, immigration is an opportunity to re-invent yourself. Lucky for Lucie, most Americans know little about Canada and even less about French Canada, which helps to explain why my mother long ago re-invented herself with a Parisian accent. That is because a French-French person speaking English sounds decidedly more sensuous than a Québec-French person speaking English.

If you don't believe me, look up Catherine Deneuve in the movie Hustle. Then compare the way she talks with Celine Dion on any random YouTube video and you'll see. My grandfather explained it in terms of schwa and flow. Gramps was tormented by iambic pentameter — rhythm of words, syllable timing and feet. It's all Greek to me but Gramps insisted it was his job to know. Mind you, my grandfather was a genius. He may not have been the life of the party, but he was still the guy you wanted on your team on quiz night. Lucie never cared about all that though. Her concern is that French folk speaking English come across as sexy and sophisticated and Québécois do not. Lucie knows how to market herself.

Actually, there's only so much you can do. That is, because depending on where you're from, people have a pre-conceived notion about you, your personality and your abilities. Already, I can see that most minds are made up about me. I am often asked if I am craving hamburgers. Why is it everyone assumes all Americans live on burgers? And haven't New Zealanders noticed that burgers are pretty common here too?

And, of course, most countries have an ethnic hierarchy in terms of acceptable and unacceptable (or maybe not so welcome) immigrants. Americans pass muster these days unlike in the eighteenth century when certain parts of the world believed us inferior and monstrous. Not our fault really, but a direct result of the North American climate. Apparently, humidity is not so good for the brain or the body. Gramps told me that too. Like I said, Gramps knew stuff.

Anyway, my mother would also be quick to point out that if you're smart, you make sure you do your big reveal before your plane hits the ground and not after because once you've arrived, you've kind of missed that boat, haven't you?

My bad…

The good thing is, I've met few people here so far. That's because Blu is super-busy on his farm, and I'm afraid to drive on the other/wrong/left side of the road. I don't get out much. Which gives me time to figure out what I want to re-invent. I'm like in the summer between elementary and middle school. I'll keep my current moniker as is but I'm definitely contemplating a snake tattoo on my wrist.

Tish Louise Talks

Love is like a garden.

Those are the very words my mother said to me the day before I set sail for America.

"Both require constant care and nourishment," she said. "Your partner needs never-ending attention. If you forget to water the garden, it may wither away. If you forget to weed or prune, it may be overtaken. If you forget to protect against harmful outside influences, it may become diseased. The only real difference is that a garden can be tended to by one person alone. In love, both partners must be equally committed to making it work. And grow."

I never forgot her words. Or the tears we both shed the next morning as I got on the boat. It was nine years before I saw my mother and father again.

And oh, how we humans are a curious lot. If our garden fails to thrive, we do not pass judgement or criticize the garden. We accept that we are most likely to blame for its failure and work to fix the problem. We look to find what we missed. But not so in love. Humans expect love to be easy and come naturally. But in time, some begin to take it for granted and stop paying attention. And when things go wrong, it is easier to blame the other person than to look inside yourself.

Of course, luck and misfortune play a part. Weather may be catastrophic. Tragedy and circumstance can destroy the soul beyond repair. So I ask, if love fades along the way, for whatever reason, was it love? Does love have to last forever in order for it to be real? If she were still here, I might like to ask my mother her thoughts on the matter.

A Lucie Lunchtime Letter

Ma puce,

Ah, the calm before the storm.

International marriages are hard, but I think it is doubly difficult for the displaced spouse who is not in his or her home country. This displaced spouse has to deal with lifestyle changes and culture shock and often, at least at first, with very little support system. And the marriage partner, the one person to whom the displaced spouse looks to for support, may turn out to be far from it.

Now I know this from my own experience, but also from my clients, that being a displaced spouse or foreign wife is not the same as most immigrant experiences. Most immigrants migrate alone or as a couple or family, and in their new land, they tend to congregate near other fellow countrymen. This helps them ease into their new environment gradually. Or sometimes, as in large migrant clusters, they need not ease into their new environment at all and may keep to their old ways and language without consequence.

When you migrate as a foreign wife, you are immediately thrust into your new environment and your husband and his family will expect you to adjust quickly. They will think your love alone is enough to overcome this lifestyle change and will lose patience with you if you hang on to your old ways. Bien sûr, you also have someone to show you the ropes. But at the end of a long day, when you just want to go

home and hide in your shell, communicate in your own language, perhaps listen to your own traditional music, set the house temperature at the level you are used to, cook your own food in your own way and eat it at whatever time
you and your culture prefer, you cannot. There is no break from this new way of being. You are expected to adapt.

En fait, I say 'foreign wife' because in my experience, it is mainly women who follow men and not the reverse. I think women pay a higher price for love. Or they are more willing to.

Lucie

11

Meghan's Method

Yeah, so it's a bit different here. Shopping habits are seriously primitive. Cafés close mid-afternoon. And shoe soles are consistently black. Does no one here understand that color is critical?

But I like that tipping is not a thing. That's what the hairdresser who doesn't have strong hairspray tells me. Unfortunately, she can't tell me why she doesn't have strong hairspray. I'd give her some of mine but I'm running out and I can't find the extra-strength they have back home. And I sneeze a lot in New Zealand but that's beside the point. I need Marie Antoinette's powder because the natural soft rainwater collected from the roof and sitting in a big tank next to the house is wreaking havoc on my hair. My head is lifeless. I prefer the monstrous humidity-induced look I left behind.

You know Marie Antoinette's famous pouf? After its debut (her husband's coronation — 1775 was the year), her friends and followers strutted coiffures which stood up to six feet tall and with the help of said powder and wire framing, was stuffed with fruits and feathers and flowers and all sorts of decorations. Lucie didn't tell me this, Bubbe did. Bubbe was a ninja with hair. She gave me a pouf like Marie Antoinette on more than one Halloween and my style never failed to impress on dress-up day at school. Only Bubbe never did let me in on what was in the powder. My unsympathetic new husband assures me that if I can't figure it out before I come to the end of my spray supply, he has plenty of wire hanging around the barns, which he calls sheds, to fix me up. All hail Blu, the alpha male.

So there's no tipping at the sink and no tipping at the cash register on your way out. And no tipping in restaurants either. Tax is included in the price tag so when you eat out, what you see on the menu is what you pay. The new me, with untowering hair and who talks less and listens more (my re-invention so far), finds this liberating.

But the new me still doesn't have a snake tattoo or likes to drive on the left/other/wrong side of the road. When I have it all figured out, I must take a driver's license test. It's like being sixteen again. And not in a good way.

I haven't spotted a single squirrel since I arrived. Or chipmunk, toad, raccoon, skunk, beaver, bear, bobcat, dingo, wolf or whatever. No moose signs on the highway either. Not that I've seen a moose on the highway. Or ever. Just the highway signs. No Groundhog Day because no groundhogs. It's funny what you take for granted.

Tish Louise would not be happy. She always seems so settled in New York, but I wonder if that — or something else — could have been a deal breaker. She really loves her squirrels. What if she discovered they didn't exist in America when she got there? Just how much of your life are you willing to give up for one guy?

Because there is a difference. I get that now.

Most people migrate because that new country offers a better life. That's about putting yourself first. Some of us are happy exactly where we are and migrate solely to please another. That's about putting the other person first.

Sure, you have your love, but it doesn't feel completely win-win.

On the plus side, there are no snakes in New Zealand. Which means I don't have to worry about seven-foot Burmese pythons crawling up my toilet. You hear stories about that happening in the New York papers and it doesn't matter what floor you are on. Just when I'm finally having a good night sleep because it has been a while since the last report, it happens again. So I can stop it with the bathroom garlic spray (because if it wards off vampires…) and placing heavy objects on the lid before I go to bed. Maybe a Jennie J snake tattoo is not a good fit for me.

Tish Louise Talks

Oh heavens, yes, my parents were naturally very sad to see me go. But also, they encouraged me in my new life. We had a lovely life in England before the war and better than most during, I should say. But make no mistake, the war was an awful time. They felt I might have greater opportunities in America and things were so hard for all concerned in England in the 1940s. My parents had lived through two horrendous conflicts and wanted me away from it all in case it should happen again.

They seemed to forget that America was not immune, having had its own internal and very deadly battle, and that was not so long ago.

Richard returned home straight away after the war and I joined him a year later. I cried an ocean of tears on that ten-day crossing, having left my family behind and not knowing what I was in for. Where once I was so sure of Richard and my love for him, the moment I was on my own and alone on the boat, I began to have doubts. I was terribly frightened at what I might find on arrival. And with good reason.

A Lucie Lunchtime Letter

Ma puce,

You must not underestimate the impact your upbringing will have on your new life in this new country. As the old saying goes, you can take the girl out of the country but you cannot take the country out of the girl. In your case, I think you can also say you can take the girl out of the city but you cannot take the city out of the girl.

Everything about you — your thoughts and emotions, your behavior, beliefs and priorities — is shaped by where you were raised. It is your common sense. But you must never assume that what makes sense to you makes sense to your husband and his people. One cannot fully appreciate how so much of what we learn in life and what we take for granted comes from where we are from.

Your husband and you do not share a similar background. You have not grown up with the same set of rules. What makes complete sense to you and what you think is simple common sense may not make any sense at all to him.

Couples in my practice have many unusual concerns. Like the American wife who cannot wait until ten at night to eat dinner at the same time as her Spanish husband. It is a problem for her every day. Or the foreign-born husband who places his extended family before his own because back home it seems this is the norm. Franchement, I am surprised they are in therapy. And that their therapist (me) is a woman.

In his world, women are not equal and the man is always right. He will be a tough egg to crack. Some international couples have distinct notions of time management. She comes from a country where schedules are rigorously adhered to and he comes from a country where things are much more relaxed. He complains she is always in a hurry and she is annoyed he is always late and she cannot rely on him. Neither can his employer and he does not understand — cannot understand — why it is important here. I have a couple where the man cannot adapt to cold New York winters. He is South American. I do not know how to fix it for him especially as compared to the Montreal climate, I find New York weather quite agreeable.

Some international couples tick along just fine until they have children and then all their old and very distinct values come crashing in on them and they disagree. For some, it is as soon as the baby is born and how to raise a girl versus how to raise a boy. For others, it is an issue when the kids become teenagers and sexually mature.

Most of my clients manage to navigate around their problems but sometimes it is impossible to tell if the problem is the couple itself or their many differences. Some people just are not meant to be together.

En tout cas, you are not the first displaced person. Nor was I. You will survive.

Do not let yourself fall into a sliding-doors trap mentality and constantly analyze how your new life compares with your old.

You must avoid becoming a geographic schizophrenic, torn between two countries and never settling, wandering like a lost soul.

This is what I tell my clients.

Lucie

12

Meghan's Method

Is she fucking kidding me?

Is my mother seriously telling me I'm the one who must avoid becoming a geographic schizophrenic, torn between two countries and never settling, wandering like a lost soul!?

Because that just does not make sense. Lucie hates it when people confuse schizophrenia with Dissociative Identity Disorder. She'll be the first to correct/inform some poor sod on the G train yacking with his buddies that 'split mind' and the old 'split personality' AKA 'multiple personality' are absolutely not the same thing. I know — I was there. And Lucie spends far too much time thinking about my situation. I know now, no matter what I do, I'll always be one of her case studies. Just like Louis XVI and his peculiar padlock passion, she can't help herself. It's what motivates her. That, her sad sucker clients at work, Parker and the cats, running and of course, case study number two.

Case study number two is my sister Ally. Alix is named after the Alix of Hesse my mother goes on about. But Alix of Park Slope wishes to be known as Ally. Just as Marie Antoinette formerly of Park Slope and now of New Zealand prefers to be called Meghan.

FYI, Park Slope is our Brooklyn neighbourhood. And Alix of Park Slope has more wow than Alix of Brooklyn.

True — Ally may be the willowy most-beautiful-woman-in-the-room sister with the in-your-face stunning blue eyes to my average looks and shorter build — but I'm the smart one. Shrinks aren't supposed to label their children but they do. They just think they don't and forget action speaks louder than words. But I suppose we're no different to any other family. We all have stuff. Ally and I are best friends. She's my other half, my rock and the only person in the world who gets me even though I don't like her choice in men. We also have the same sized feet and share shoes. And we are both convinced my father is insanely perfect and my mother is just insane. We are excellent Freudian lab rats.

Today is Ally's birthday. I have never missed being there for my little sister on her special day.

I was four years old when my mother gave birth to Ally in the front living room. She never did make it upstairs in time. But that's OK because Lucie planned a home birth, which doesn't strike me as any different to a yurt birth. As with my own arrival, Grand-maman was in town to assist my mother. She also provided me with Matante Mariette's tourtière. Tourtière is a traditional Québécois fine ground pork pie with a bit of chopped onion and cloves in the mix and is one of my all-time favorite meals. Damn, I miss that these days and have to agree with Freud on this one — abstinence is a horrible misery.

To be frank, I don't know what I hoped for when the baby arrived, but it was not a blond, pale-skinned screaming creature with such soft blue eyes. Lucie and Parker with their olive complexions are similar in appearance and me and my brown eyes and brown hair looked like any one of their offspring would be expected to look. The whole lot of us are that way, on both sides of the family. But not Ally. Ally is your all-American blond, blue eyed, tall, skinny but toned cheerleader type. If I hadn't been there for the delivery, I would swear my sister was adopted.

Birthdays are a super big deal in our family. My mom goes all out as if she's compensating for too many hand-me-downs. Because she wasn't a fan of kids' parties (too transformative for the non-invited), she made up for it in other ways. Movie nights, ice cream at Serendipity's, dinner at Windows on the World, etc. When I was in my freshman year of university, she had a balloon-o-gram sent to me in class. Ally insists that is nowhere near as cool as the witches' brew soiree Lucie organized sometime in high school which, I have to admit, was pretty good until the snakes got away. That was the last occasion I camped out at my grandparents before the towers fell and it was only afterwards that I realized how precious a time it was. Bubbe spoiled me with her straight-out-of-the-oven challah bread and Gramps drove me to Sarah Lawrence every morning. By the end of the second week, he was not only auditing my classes but giving readings in the amphitheater too. When my boyfriend du jour asked if I minded being upstaged by an old man, I laughed. I'm immensely proud of my grandfather, so no, I didn't mind. Besides, it was not Fletcher's fault that he was somehow recognized by the dean. And he only agreed to perform because I insisted. The funny thing is, I don't think I've ever seen my grandfather so damn happy. I remember that, as I watched and listened, I wondered why he never gave author appearances. Bubbe blamed glossophobia for it but the brilliant raconteur on stage in front of me clearly had no fear of public speaking. I didn't miss a single show.

Unfortunate birth order also means Lucie is quite the anti-Grinch. The woman with middle child syndrome who claims she hates shopping still buys Yuletide gifts year-round. And even if we never spend the holidays in Brooklyn, Lucie puts up a real pine tree right after Thanksgiving and illuminates the house in fairy lights, inside and out. I used to think she went overboard with that just to annoy my Jewish grandmother but my mom says you have to have a heart two sizes too small not to get into 'Le Noël' in a cold winter climate. My father, who is half Christian even though Gramps didn't do God and didn't care either way, loves the season too. Gramps once claimed he stopped believing in the Gilbert Islands, said it had something to do with the war and that was that, end of story. But since I was little, Parker has donned a Santa hat at home the whole of December and he's the first to wrap presents and the first to bust out the seasonal foods and drink. Especially egg nog. Parker loves egg nog. My father has also told me more than once not to tell Bubbe but going out for Chinese food on Christmas Day is one custom he was more than happy to give up when he married my mom.

Anyway, back to Ally. Ally insists she doesn't care that I'm not there for her birthday because she's pissed at me for leaving. Because it might be normal for men to dump her but not her older sister. Ally says I've abandoned her and she has grieving to do. It doesn't matter that I haven't died. Loss is loss and there's a process. Denial. Anger. Bargaining. Depression. Acceptance. Right now, she's Kubler-Rossing at anger and I just need to wait it out. I told you shrink-parented kids are introspective.

Parker is taking Ally to Deerfield this weekend. Bonding with long-dead ancestors held prisoner and slaughtered in massacres usually helps to put things into perspective. And Ally has Salem now. My niece is only young but already she suits her name even though Lucie doesn't like it. She finds it too radical but I tell her she should be grateful Ally didn't stick her with something like Hepzibah. And she of all people has no right to be judgy about what parents call their kids.

Tish Louise Talks

I wouldn't have done well in the first years without the support of my lovely mother-in-law. Which does beg the question — is love enough? I have no answer for that.

My mother-in-law realized straight away I was from a well-to-do family. She knew because she was a British war bride herself from the Great War. Richard never once mentioned it. Not even that she was from Britain. It is most amusing the important things young fellows forget to tell you. Information about one's people and homeland are absolutely essential, are they not? But in talking to other GI brides, I believe our American soldier husbands assumed we knew all we needed to know about life in America from the pictures.

'GI' by the way, comes from 'General Issue'. It is what the Americans called their soldiers in World War Two. Tis much better than 'doughboy' which is what they were known as in the First World War.

Now, did I know Richard was of a lower class than myself? I did not. Although I'm certain my parents were aware. It's not something young lovers talk about, now is it? He said he lived in a big old house in Brooklyn and he didn't say how big or how old. My upbringing wouldn't allow me to ask him his social standing. In London, I would have picked up on his background straight away but with Americans, how was I to know? I couldn't tell from his accent and I assumed his poor table manners were an American peculiarity, not a class peculiarity. If there were other cues, I didn't recognize them. But I wasn't too troubled as I was young and had endured enough hardship during the war to appreciate my new life and that some things I might have once viewed as terribly important simply were not. Perhaps I was also in love with being in love and didn't always pay full attention and

Richard did, in fact, mention his British mother. Although I am quite certain this is something I would not have easily forgotten.

My mother-in-law was thrilled to see I had come with all my English recipes. Mum spent weeks writing them down for me so I would always 'have a taste of home' when lonely. Richard's mother loved to cook. We both did. We shared our recipes and often prepared meals together. She liked hearing my accent as it reminded her of England although her accent was West Country and I'm from London. Mind, once one has been away for a while, English accents all start to sound rather similar. And my mother-in-law didn't go back. Not once. She never saw her parents again. Her heart must have ached but she wasn't the sort to let on. She showed me the ways of this new country and understood when I didn't understand. Like me, she was an outsider and was able to see things through my eyes in ways my Richard could not.

My mother-in-law also shared with me the stories of her own adjustment to life in America. She reminded me how easy it was for us compared to the French in World War I. There were some English war brides in the Great War, a number of Irish also but most were French. And the French women were not treated well on arrival. The Americans didn't trust them. Americans were convinced their boys had been preyed upon. People were openly rude. They believed French girls were immoral and of questionable background and all thoroughly disreputable and infected with sexually transmitted diseases. In other words — just plain dirty! How awful it must have been for them.

A Lucie Lunchtime Letter

Ma puce,

Your sister will adapt. One has to get on with life. We cannot mope all day. What is the point in that?

Some scientists believe inner strength is determined by genes. That the presence or absence of a specific gene variant makes a person emotionally delicate or resilient.

But then, maybe not, who knows…

We are all presented with challenge in life and we decide how to deal with such challenges. One can choose to be fragile like an orchid and in need of constant attention in order to thrive or you can harden up like a dandelion and bloom just about anywhere. It is up to you.

Your father and I are no longer speaking. At least not in the English language. When Parker visited me in Montreal before we were married, he thought my speaking in French was romantic and beautiful and would urge me to talk just so he could listen. But when I arrived in New York as his wife, he said I was in America now and I was to speak English. He became agitated when I spoke to myself in French. I only spoke to you and your sister in my own language when he was away at work because he said he did not want me to teach you French, as it was not fair to him if the rest of us spoke French and he did not. Your Bubbe and Gramps agreed with him. Neither saw the value in bilingualism which is very narrow-minded and such an American way of thinking. And bizarre considering your grandfather's love of words and your Bubbe's command of Yiddish. My mother was especially annoyed with Parker in our first few summers in Canada when he made no attempt to speak our language. Finally, one year she told him it was dégueulasse that everyone in the house had to speak English just so one stupid ignorant man could understand what was being said. He changed a bit after that and tried harder. But he still does not really know French, does he? Well, now he is going to learn.

Tsar Nicholas II spoke to Tsarina Alexandra in English. All their correspondence was in English. Many love letters passed between those two. But Marie Antoinette was not allowed to write to her mother in her native German. She had to write to her in French. Ben coudon!

Bien sûr, the human brain is remarkable. Over the years, the two languages have become ingrained in my head and I think in both. And like many bilingual Montréalais, I am also prone to using French and English words in the same sentence. We call it Franglais. I am happy to be proficient in English but I just wish it had not been pushed onto me. Do not fret if you do not understand your husband's expressions or his accent at times. Your father and I have been together thirty years and I frequently mistake what he is saying. And you know from seeing me with my sisters that I am a different person in French than I am in English. In French, I have a sense of humour. In English, I lack spontaneity. I am serious and careful with my words. I am no fun. You lose a bit of yourself when not speaking in your native tongue.

Lucie

13

Meghan's Method

Sometimes I wonder if the Bubbe and Gramps my mother remembers and the Bubbe and Gramps I remember are the same people. The Fletcher Buell I knew would never diss bilingualism. Just as he would not disrespect any slang word as it slips into the mainstream lexicon.

I also wonder why my mother went into psychology. Weakness and frailty annoy her.

My mother is a dandelion who thrives anywhere. She says happiness is a choice you make. Mind over matter. Sink or swim.

Lucie was six years old when my grandfather dropped dead of a heart attack on the front porch leaving my grandmother to care all alone for her three girls and another on the way. From what I hear, Grand-maman spent an hour or so crying in the bathtub and then climbed out, dried herself off and marched back downstairs and got on with the business of living. She had mouths to feed and firewood which needed chopping. Winter was coming.

Grand-maman is also a dandelion. But then my grandmother has made no secret of the fact she wasn't in love with my grandfather. She was in love with my grandfather's younger brother. But he, along with thousands of other Canadian soldiers, died a lonely and horrific but valiant death in Normandy in the weeks following the D-Day landings. Grand-maman and Doré were engaged the morning he enlisted, and she waited for him to come home for the whole of the war. When Doré didn't come home, that's when she Kubler-Rossed. Several years later, and because of family pressure, she married my grandfather. Women had fewer choices in her day. She did what she was told.

Grand-maman believes you only get one true love in life and having done the marriage bit, she never saw the need to do it again. She likes her independence and not washing men's dirty underwear more. So my great-grandmother Hermeline moved in and looked after my mom and her sisters and my grandmother found herself a job. When times were hard, she sold off bits of the farm. But all four girls turned out fine, everyone is good and settled and except for my mother, they are close by. OK, maybe Babette is mildly unhinged but it happens. Anyway, now Grand-maman lives on the last remaining section in her cute old but renovated house. Real estate is iffy in Québec what with the political situation (will they or will they not separate from Canada?) but she has million-dollar lakefront views and doesn't worry about her financial future.

Actually, Grand-maman doesn't worry. At all. She says she used to. In fact, she worried non-stop from 1939 to 1944 and it didn't change a damn thing, so she's done with it. Life is for the living and it's best to live it well because as far as we know, you only get one crack at it. And if you find great love with a great guy, you go after it. She also says not to waste energy on a man who doesn't know when it's time to order in a pizza so I'm confused. What if he is both those things?

Now that her fireplace has been converted into a home entertainment centre, Grand-maman has time for other pursuits but gardening is not one of them. Green fingers have no place in my family. This explains why, when all our neighbors were quitting Brooklyn for cozy crime-free bedroom communities, we stayed put. One night over dinner, when I was ten or eleven years old and my new best friend Tina moved to Riverhead right after my old best friend moved to Ho-Ho-Kus, I begged my parents for a house in the burbs with a lawn. Neither was enthusiastic. Park Slope suits my dad because it's close to the airports and Lucie was near the university and lived for her morning jog into campus. It was over my second plate of Parker's homemade spaghetti Bolognese that I learned that while commuting is bad, it's nowhere near as bad as the concept of yard work. Since mention of dead demented queens and international marriage couldn't possibly help her cause, my mother called in the one-man cavalry.

"Freud found flowers restful because they have neither emotions or conflict," I remember her saying as she handed .over the Parmesan cheese and looked me straight in the eye.

"But Freud lived in an apartment and did not deal with their physical needs. Ben coudon! If he knew the effort they require, he would not consider flowers soothing."

Even at that age, I was aware the introduction of her favorite twenty-cigar-a-day smoker into any conversation is her manner of shutting it down.

So my immediate family does not ever till soil, dig, sow, prune, clip, weed or hoe. None of that non-restful shit. But we help out with Grand-maman so she can stay where she is. My aunts and cousins do most of the work but we — les cousins Américains — turn up as often as possible.

In winter, we shovel. In spring, we tidy up. In summer, we mow. In the fall, we rake. That is a two-day job over the Canadian Thanksgiving weekend in October. On the Saturday night, we get pizzas from the Viviry restaurant up the road. It's a family tradition. Of course, not centuries-old or anything like that. Pizza only arrived in North America in the early 1900s and was considered poor uneducated immigrant food and hardly treat-worthy until after WWII when troops stationed in Italy came home with a serious fondness for it and made it go gangbusters. So pizza, like Tish Louise, is a by-product of the last great war. On Sunday, Grand-maman cooks a turkey. On Monday, we drive back home.

Thanksgiving in Canada is more low-key but not much different from Bubbe's American Thanksgiving family dinner in Brooklyn a month later. Except Grand-maman makes a sugar pie and Bubbe made pumpkin pie which is so not Jewish. And Canadians officially celebrate on the tail end of a long weekend versus the start in the States which makes no sense because you can't work off your calories at the mall the next day. Bubbe always said shopping is the absolute best exercise. Bubbe and I were very good at fat-burning on Black Friday. Bubbe loved shoes too. That was our thing.

I'm telling you this, in a roundabout way, because now that summer is over (in May?), Blu has advised me that for the next month we'll be chopping wood to keep the fire going in winter. I recall him saying back in Brooklyn that most homes in New Zealand were without central heating. I thought that was because it was not cold enough to warrant it. He never once mentioned anything about having to clear out what amounts to a whole fucking forest just to stay warm.

Was it Tish Louise who told me that men forget to paint the whole picture? It must have been. Well, I'm thinking that may be OK when you both have spent your lives on the same page but it's not OK if, from day one, you've been reading different books.

The closest pizza place here is forty miles away and I'm pretty sure after my next few weeks lumber-jacking, I'll be required to cook up meals for dinner. Not because the closest pizza place is forty miles away but because I think I've picked a man who doesn't know when it's time to order in.

Maybe I have been spoiled but with Lucie either at school or work all day when I was growing up, we went out or delivered in a lot. Szechuan, Thai, Vietnamese, Indian, Middle Eastern, Greek, Italian, Mexican, Jamaican, Polish, Kosher, etc. Everything was within walking distance. The man I married in New York was keen to try anything but now that we're back on his turf, he wants a basic 'meat and three veges' spread on the table every night. What this means is red meat, chicken or fish plus potatoes of some sort and two kinds of boiled/steamed vegetables, one of which must be green. Now I know that Lucie wasn't exaggerating when she said food issues are huge in international marriages because already, I'm so bored. I don't mind a plate of vegetables but can't he mix it up just a little? And what's wrong with breakfast for dinner? We did that. My grandparents did that. Bubbe and Gramps regularly served up bacon and eggs at the end of the day which only work with New York bagels because Montreal bagels are sweeter and thinner and don't toast as well. And, of course, it wasn't real bacon but Bubbe's liquid smoke egg plant bacon which is the best. Blu even partook in it after he moved in with Ally and me. And not once did he complain about it. But now? Fuck no! So yeah, the horrible misery that is bagel withdrawal is just one of my woes.

But I love it here. I do. I do. My home is with Blu. He is my heart. You've got to follow your heart, right? Isn't that what Grand-maman says?

Anyway, it doesn't matter. I'd rather live in his world than live without him in mine. I would. But dare I mention, the coffee here is just crap.

Tish Louise Talks

Start as you mean to go on.

This, Blodyn, is my advice to you.

Start as you mean to go on.

No marriage is without conflict as two people learn to live with each other. Indeed, no marriage is without conflict full stop. Do not give up your rights within the marriage solely because you are alone and in unfamiliar territory and feel you don't possess the strength to fight for who you are and what you believe in. Take my word for it, I have seen it happen far too often. Marriage migration will change you. It may even break you. It is easy to fall into a routine you can't undo once your confidence and sense of self have returned. It may take years for you to feel completely whole again and when you do and revert back to your old way of being, your partner may be unwilling to accept you. So, start as you mean to go on. Know what it is you want out of your marriage and indeed life itself and even if it takes everything out of you, hold your ground.

A Lucie Lunchtime Letter

Ma puce,

Tsarina Alexandra was vegetarian, not many people know that. I doubt she would enjoy a basic 'meat and three veges' spread on the table every night also. I wonder what foods she craved from home. I know she missed English biscuits.

During the American Civil War, army doctors thought homesickness so serious that it could kill. And in their view, it did. 'Nostalgia' is listed as cause of death seventy-four times. At the time, it was a respectable medical condition and there was no shame in wanting to go back to your mama. Doctors claimed this was the only cure for it.

Ces jours-ci, I would be more inclined to describe this so-called nostalgia (which I can only assume leads to an inability to function) as situational depression or adjustment disorder. Symptoms are much the same. Melancholia, weeping, etc. But I am not sure if the problem has as much to do with being away from home (in which case, homesickness) as it does with the horror of being at war (in which case, despair). I find it hard to separate the two. Either way, without the drastic change in circumstance, there would be no depression.

You know, I agree with those très sympa Civil War doctors. The only cure for le mal du pays is to go home. So I go back as often as I can. You would think after thirty years I might have adjusted to my situation and in most ways, I believe I have. I no longer suffer culture shock. Culture shock only lasts so long because things eventually fall into place. But homesickness can go on forever.

I cried often when I arrived in New York, this I can tell you. I used to get a particular pain down my arm. It was in my left arm and my left arm only. I was not dreaming. It was physical. I have a client right now who tells me she feels it in her feet. She says it is a very distinct ache. Not like the soreness she gets from being on her feet all day or wearing shoes that do not fit. She says it is different. I believe her. How can I not?

Tsarina Alexandra complained continually of aches and pains and was constantly taking to her bed. Which is unfortunate because her husband Tsar Nicholas II was extremely physically active. He loved outdoor exercise. But his adored wife, with whom he shared a very healthy sex life, just liked to rest on her chaise longue in her Mauve Boudoir at the Alexander Palace and go on about her poor health. Except apparently when she was reunited with her siblings or back home in Germany in which case Alexandra was seen to run around like a schoolgirl. Suddenly she was well. Or cured.

I wonder what those Civil War doctors might have to say about that.

Lucie

14

Gardening, too, has become a craze.
Jennie Jerome, Lady Randolph Churchill

Meghan's Method

Women with practical footwear drop in regularly. Clearly day sex is not a thing in this country otherwise they would think twice before they knock and mosey on in without acknowledgement. Where I come from, this is how people get hurt. Like, with bullets.

I'm not sure if that is just the Kiwi way or Harrison Max's foreign bride is the new circus act in town and it will soon wear off but, seriously, who does that? I can't lock the front door because Blu doesn't take keys with him when he goes out and he doesn't like being locked out when he comes back. I have a friend in Vinegar Hill who has nine double cylinder deadlocks on her apartment door. Once the ghost of Louis XVI discovers how to cross over water and haunt her, he'll no doubt be living the dream. She doesn't believe me when I tell her we have only one lock and rarely use it. I don't believe it myself sometimes. Ally, who's emailing me all of a sudden, suggests I try hanging garlic on the porch to ward off the unwanted.

"Well, it works on snakes, the undead and vampires," she writes.

"So why not humans?"

"Actually, do we really know this to be true?", I want to reply but I say nothing because Ally always insists no self-respecting witch is ever without her garlic supply. Because while garlic is not nearly as effective as salt in warding off evil and negativity, it's still pretty good. When I message her that these visitors aren't bad, she replies we're all bad on some level. I can only assume a man is making her emo and again, I wish I was home and with my sister.

Unlike my mother, I can't leave to avoid intrusions because there's nowhere to go. No stores (open or shut), no library, no Starbucks. No nothing. And walks on deserted country roads hardly compare to city strolls. Too much green, no pavement, not enough window displays and people-watching. I haven't heard a police siren in weeks. I miss it.

The uninvited women are kind and I should be grateful they've come to see me but I'm not because all they do is talk weather and plants. Everybody in New York has plants (Tish Louise has lots) but no one actually talks about them. Who does that? When the lurkers ramble on, I find myself going back to research for an article I wrote on Wallis Simpson right after I was hired at the paper. Wallis was the reason King Edward VIII gave up the British throne in 1936.

The commoner (bad) and twice-divorced (more bad) American (shitstorm bad) didn't like gardening. But it was the way a friend put it which made me wonder if this too, was also unacceptable.

"Agriculture passed her by," said her so-called pal. Still, it was good to know my family weren't the only ones with an aversion to yard work.

Wallis Simpson isn't exactly an aspirational role model. I'm aware of this. A lot of things probably passed her by. Still, I silently scream. Am I in a simpler place in time? People are different here. Have I taken the midnight train to Zombieland? Will I fit in? Do I even want to?

Lucie and I disagree on Wallis. Lucie views Wallis as a foreign wife because she lived her life outside the country of her birth for a man.

But Wallis was already married and living in England when she met the future king at a hunting lodge covered in ivy. That right there should have served as a red flag. Vines cause energy stagnation. The balance with nature was probably all off. But the status-seeking, I-will-never-be-poor-again Wallis was likely not too worried about environmental harmony when she hooked up with the-then Prince of Wales. 'Prince of Wales' is what the British call the heir apparent to the monarch so there have been more than a few over the past centuries. Such as Bertie, Tsarina Alexandra's uncle and special friend of Jennie J. And the current title-holder Charles, the one who married the beautiful Diana even though he was really in love with Camilla, great-granddaughter of Alice Keppel, one of Bertie's other special mistresses. Anyway, Wallis' husband (number two) at the time was American like her and so there was probably not too much culture-clashing behind closed doors. And while husband number three (by now an abdicated King) was British, she didn't leave home to be with him. Neither can she be considered a late-to-the-party dollar princess because while she did receive a title in marriage (Duchess of Windsor), she had no fortune to give. As a child, she and her widowed mother lived on the charity of others. Hence the Scarlett O'Hara 'As God is my witness, I will never be poor again' mentality. Although *Gone with the Wind*'s fictional Scarlett (not a foreign wife by the way) actually used the word hungry and not poor. But an empty stomach was likely of little concern to the weight-obsessed, extreme-dieter that was the you-can-never-be-too-rich-or-too-thin Wallis Simpson.

FYI, Wallis was born Bessie Wallis and she also underwent a re-invention at a young age. The minute she realized she shared her name with farm animals, she put an end to the Bessie bit and insisted she be known only as Wallis. Trust me, that kind of change takes pluck. So no matter what you think of Wallis Simpson — seductress, social climber, royal groupie or reluctant royal, vulgar, vapid, misunderstood or cow — this is a woman with more than one story. Her uppity in-laws didn't accept her and her adopted country rejected her. People she confided in critiqued her agricultural persuasions.

Even Alice Keppel, who might wish to refrain from comment, got judgy on her. So the story goes, Alice was lunching with friends at the London Ritz Hotel when King Edward VIII's abdication was announced in the dining room and the most celebrated courtesan of her time threw some major shade.

"Things were done better in my day," Alice, it is said, remarked. For all to hear.

Maybe Wallis, too, thought she was living in Zombieland.

Tish Louise Talks

I changed countries but my daily life didn't change significantly. I went from one large city to another. I was only just starting out. Habits were not yet formed, ways not yet set. I didn't give up a career for which I had worked hard to achieve. I have always wondered if it is harder to leave one's home behind the older you become.

We moved into Richard's family home here in Brooklyn until we found a place of our own. His relations were extremely welcoming although I suspect some local girls were rather resentful towards me and other GI brides. Especially the young single women. We had stolen their men.

I fared better than many GI brides. My new home was not in the Tennessee Hills or on a dirt farm where the women work as hard as the men and cook and clean too. And I was not in a cold single-room shack with a potbelly stove and a bucket of coal deep in the woods. Some girls arrived to no running water, no electricity and an outhouse. I heard the stories.

A Lucie Lunchtime Letter

Ma puce,

It is strange that with so many people the world over coming and going, there is little research on homesickness. There is no Elisabeth Kubler-Ross, no recognized expert in the field, no ground-breaking academic work or definitive set of studies.

Neither is there any distinction between short-term homesickness as when kids go away for summer camp or the first year in a university dorm versus prolonged separation from home when you have been away for years and years.

Rien. Rien du tout. But then I think maybe the reason for this comes back to the reality that there is no cure for homesickness. Except going home. And time. Time does ease the pain. And when you migrate, you make a life. Despite how much you long for your old one, you build a new one too. And then you suffer a conflicted homesickness, torn between two places.

Elisabeth Kubler-Ross was a foreign wife. Switzerland to America. Her marriage failed but she stayed. She had children. She was passionate about her career and research into death. She made a life for herself here in the US but left behind her two triplet sisters. Multiples are deeply interconnected and should not be separated. Although when they are, it makes for fascinating research. Did she not miss her sisters enough to want to go back? Maybe. But once you have been away too long, it becomes difficult to find your place back home also. Returning means starting over yet again.

And by the way, all Brooklyn women talk about is shopping. And the weather. Anglos feel safe talking about the weather.

Lucie

15

Meghan's Method

I miss employment.

Sometimes it's not what you know but who you know. I like to think I got ahead in New York because I was good at what I do. Still, from the minute we are born, we all have a network. Your grandfather knows important people, your parents are friends with so and so at such and such, your best friend in high school has an uncle in publishing, etc. And then you go to university and you make a whole new network, kids who grow into respectable adults you'll know on and off throughout your career. People who can vouch for you. In my industry, who you know and what you know are both important.

But none of that matters now. My CV and good name mean nothing. Even my beloved alma mater means nothing. That I have a degree from a top university has no value because not only has no one here ever heard of it, when they do hear of it (when I tell them that's where Barbara Walters went), they think it's a high school. That Sarah Lawrence College is actually a university confuses Kiwis. And no one is feeling it for Barbara Walters either. New Zealand has its own fantastic heroes, doing extraordinary things. So there's that.

Of course, there's plenty of work to be had milking cows but I can't milk cows. I spent a lot of time, energy and money at school so I could wear pretty shoes to work in a temperature-controlled, well-lit, hygienic and orderly space with the right amount of buzz, cell-phone cover and Homo sapiens. I'm not a girly-girl and need not lie on a chaise longue in a purple room all day to be productive but neither am I the nature-loving outdoorsy type. I like to see outside when I work. I do not wish to be outside when I work.

My lack of job success reminds me of what Lucie says. Lucie says most foreign cab drivers in New York are PhDs and that exotic-looking quiet check-out lady at the deli on Seventh is probably a rocket scientist. I guess no one cares what they did in the old country.

If I want a job here, I might have to get me some local qualifications which mean something in these parts. I hadn't counted on going back to school. I know that's what my mother did but she was just out of high school and it made sense. I've been out of university for over five years and it doesn't make sense. The way I'm looking at it right now, it doesn't sound so much like re-invention but rather, starting over. I wonder if the exotic-looking quiet check-out lady at the market on Seventh feels the same.

At least I'm not alone in all of this. Blu's a good husband. He's not obsessed with padlocks. He's very attentive. Then again, maybe Blu's just trying to keep me happy so I don't buy four pairs of shoes a week. Mind you, given my current store-deprived situation, how is that even remotely possible?

Tish Louise Talks

Before Richard came into my life, the idea of leaving England never once crossed my mind. I had no reason to. England was my home.

I still wonder what I am doing in America at times.

I suspect it's not unusual to look back and question the small decisions one makes from day to day and the moments, both within and beyond our control, which alter our destiny. More so when one finds oneself on the other side of the world, away from all one has ever known. Away from mum and dad. And living a life one never even conceived of.

As my only sister is laid to rest, once again, I look back and ask myself how it all came to be.

What if I hadn't gone to the Red Cross club that night? Or if I hadn't missed the first train and not bumped into Richard on the steps outside? Would I have noticed him inside the hall? Would we have spoken?

If we hadn't spoken, and our paths never crossed at all, how would my life have unfolded? Would I have remained in England? Would I have married a local boy and lived near my beloved family? Would I have had children? Who might I have become? Would I have been happy?

Life doesn't always go to plan. You, dear Blodyn, should know this by now.

A Lucie Lunchtime Letter

Ma puce,

It is disappointing — or maddening — to find all that you have worked for in one country means nothing in another. This is an experience common to many immigrants. You are right, I have not experienced this. I earned my degrees in America. But remember, I acquired them in another language.

The rage stage in an international relationship can be extra complicated when one partner has given up everything for the other. Humans are good at playing the blame game and in typical cases of homesickness, you only have yourself to blame. Naturellement, this excludes war and refugee situations. But if you are away at camp or university or have left your hometown to better your life or lifestyle and become homesick, the only person responsible for your current misery is you.

Ah, but not so when you marry a foreigner and follow him home. When you follow your partner home and suffer emotionally as a result, it is easy to direct or project your rage onto your partner.

And why not? If it were not for this person, you would not be in this situation. And if the home partner is not supportive of the immigrant partner as he or she adapts to his or her new environment, rage and resentment are magnified. And even if the home partner is supportive, there can be anger simply because the foreign partner is coping with so many life-changes while the other, the home partner who is in your face night and day and living la-di-da, is not.

It is a situation fraught with danger and I don't dare tell you how bad it can become if the immigrant partner comes to realize the marriage is not good regardless of culture and country. Because now what do you do? Do you stay or go? What if you have children? Hé seigneur!

Lucie

16

When I first came to England and was taken for walks in the country, I had so many bitter experiences with long gowns and thin paper-like shoes, before realizing the advantage of short skirts and 'beetle-crushers'.
Jennie Jerome, Lady Randolph Churchill

Meghan's Method

Yes, the Kubler-Ross model is now applied to many forms of loss. Break-ups. Divorce. Unemployment. Changing house. Even desertion when your only sibling and best friend ditches you and parks up at the bottom of the world.

"Where shoes go to die," as Ally says. Often.

My beloved baby sister has gone off-piste again. Her anger towards me, which I thought was over, has transitioned into woeful bitterness. Bitterness is a destructive human sentiment. But I'm not worried because I know I'm not wholly to blame here. Ally's into bad-boy charm. There's a guy in all of this somehow and my family is used to the usual fallout. That too, follows a pattern before Lucie tires of acrimonious victimhood and whips her back into shape with talk of deeper self-love and better days ahead. Mind you, I do believe my sister might be less cranky with me and would have long ago completed Kubler-Rossing had I not settled into what she now refers to as 'a footwear wasteland'. Had I ended up in Barcelona or Rome where the shoes are delish, maybe then she could make sense of my move. And she's young. Far too young to be parted for life from her only sister. It's a big, sad thing. And I think multiples are not the only ones who are deeply interconnected and should not be separated. All siblings need each other.

Sometimes I wonder about those five stages. I read somewhere that Elisabeth Kubler-Ross was sick for years before she died and she herself was none too thrilled about the process. And when she did finally give up the ghost, Lucie showed me the obit in *The New York Times* which cast doubt as to how far along she got. To have 'appeared to accept' is not the same as to accept. But that's OK. I get it. I'm not exactly top of the class at Grief 101 either.

Like my father and Ally, I remain angry about Bubbe and Gramps. And I will never make it to acceptance. Compartmentalization is the way through. But not like in psychoanalysis where the goal is to separate conflicting emotions and beliefs from each other. Hell no! My emotions and beliefs are not conflicted. Not in the least. Whatever happened to my grandparents and everybody else on that day was just wrong. Sacred herb smudging, mantra reciting and bathing in baking soda will not now — or ever — clear my aura of psychic debris. Nor will talk therapy. There is nothing to discuss and nothing for me to learn from. It's easier to just push it out of my head. End of story.

That being said, while Ally is back at the anger stage, I'm Kubler-Rossing at depression. Probably because I milked cows this week. And New Zealand is not pancake-flat like Long Island. I hate the cycling here. I want to go home. Even with all the noise in Brooklyn and the long commute into the city and the fact I might come across a python in the loo. Because I'm not safe here anyway. The other day I heard about a lady who found a snake hidden away amongst the bananas at the supermarket. The fact that it didn't kill her is besides the point. I just want to go home.

And I miss my stuff. I shouldn't have been so quick to sell before I left. I should have shoved it all into a corner upstairs and sent for it gradually. Because now that I'm here, surrounded by all of my husband's things and none of mine, I feel like I've given up more of myself than I had to. As if I've been stripped bare at the border. Even though I did so voluntarily.

Thank God, the walls are not plastered with out of proportion images of dead ancestors. Consuelo Vanderbilt had to deal with that problem when she moved into Blenheim. The palace is full of painted pictures of her husband's family. Made to look more prominent by exaggerating the head to body ratio by just a wee bit so one does not forget how special they were. Many dollar princesses encountered the same scenario in their new English homes because rich people do revel in important looking family portraits. Perhaps this is a reason why Marie Antoinette built herself a private retreat on the grounds at Versailles — so she could get away from it all and furnish however and with whomever she wanted.

True, I actually enjoyed all the artwork at Blenheim. But I didn't live there having them constantly watch over me. Maybe it's only annoying when the dead ancestors are your in-laws.

Tish Louise Talks

Farewells are complicated when great distance is involved.

Like the song goes, every time we say goodbye, I die a little. Parting is all sorrow. No sweet. I now hate the word 'goodbye'. When the number of miles between loved ones is significant, the likelihood of not seeing one another again seems far greater than when one is just around the corner. Saying 'goodbye' only serves to rub it in. The

American 'see you' is somewhat more positive and suggests you may in fact reunite, and hopefully, sooner rather than later. And not as a result of an emergency 'come-home-quick' middle of the night call. Those, my dear Blodyn, are the worst.

My mother died quite unexpectedly on December 25th, 1971. I had been in America for twenty-five years and not once had I returned home for Christmas. I knew straight away it was an overseas call because of the specific beep on answer and then the crackle in the line. I could tell it was bad news as soon as my sister spoke. And as I sat down at the kitchen table and listened to my sister recount the details of my mother's sudden death, which had taken place just hours earlier as I slept, oblivious to it all in my bed on the other side of the ocean, I began to unravel.

Twenty-five years I have gone without being home with mum and dad for Christmas, I thought, and now it is too late. I lost the plot. I returned that week to London, quit my job, moved into my sister's spare bedroom and stayed until the end of summer.

Yes, I have been angry at times over the years. Angry at myself for not being there for both my parents at the end. Angry that I couldn't be there for my sister when her husband left her. Angry at the naïve young girl I once was who truly believed love could conquer all. I have also suffered depression. And yet I don't regret my years with Richard and the life we made.

I was fortunate to return home on occasion, and I've become friends with other GI brides with whom I could have a good whinge now and then. But I learned it best not to lean on these people. Just because we arrived from the same country and in the same circumstances doesn't mean we are meant to be friends. And there is a tendency to grumble. It's unhealthy. One must look to the future and not the past. I have many close American companions. I was an outsider but I never allowed myself to be left out. Nor did Richard. Richard ensured I was included in everything he did and was accepted by his mates and their wives. I was lucky in that language was never an issue.

A Lucie Lunchtime Letter

Ma puce,

Maybe I exaggerate at times. We know enough to know that there are four stages to the acculturation process.

Honeymoon, Rage, Adjustment and Acceptance. I refer to them as the four Hs - Honeymoon, Hostility, Humour and Home. It is easier this way to explain to my clients.

The honeymoon stage takes place immediately on arrival when everything is fresh and exciting and just walking down the street is an exotic adventure. It is magical. Really wonderful. But, like all calm before the storm, it comes to an end. I believe you know this by now. This is when reality sets in and you realize you have missed your sister's birthday and suddenly discover you really like central heating and squirrels and you are there forever and you do not want new and exciting. You just want a bagel. You want old and familiar and you would like to see your little niece grow up too.

With this realization comes hostility. Or rage. Everything in your new surrounding makes you mad… Cultural differences, language barriers if applicable, miscommunications, food that does not taste like the foods you are used to and the general fatigue of never quite knowing the situation and fitting in. Do you remember when Madame Curtis-Smith said that marriage-immigration could change — even break — a person? This is when it happens. Along with rage is hopelessness. When you feel hopeless, you lose confidence in the world and in yourself.

Rage is tricky to predict. In my work, I have met immigrant partners who adapt immediately and many who are mad for years.

According to my war brides, it can be for as many as ten years. Maybe even fifteen. Oui, minimum ten years. It is a long time.

For me, I don't think I was so much angry as absent. Or vacant. Ma puce, don't for a minute think I don't know how my emigration affected my personality when you were little. I know what you and your sister think. I wasn't always present, I know it. But many factors are at play. Character and coping skills, age of transition, family circumstance at home, how the two countries compare in terms of size, wealth, healthcare, infrastructure, education and employment opportunities, cost of living, availability of goods, entertainment opportunities, women's rights, personal freedoms, food, weather, crime rate, dangerous animal wildlife, et cetera. There is much to consider.

Or perhaps it was because young children are not particularly stimulating and it is hard not to let your mind drift. Have you considered that? Say what you will about Marie Antoinette and Tsarina Alexandra but both were devoted mothers, better than I could ever be.

But, hé seigneur, the list goes on and on and, oui, even animals can play a role. I have a couple at work who chose New York over Australia all because of snakes and spiders. The husband told me there are over one hundred species of venomous snakes in his wife's homeland and he was petrified inside and out. He never did come across a snake in the toilet bowl but the final straw was the funnel-web spider in his son's bed. Its bite will kill in fifteen minutes. She is mad because he reneged on his promise to live Down Under and feels she is stuck here. Ma puce, have you thought of what your deal breaker might be? What if you were passionate about one particular thing or sport which was impossible to do or partake in (or follow as a spectator) in your partner's country? So there is that too.

After rage comes humor (or understanding). It is the adjustment stage. Things fall into place, you establish a routine and no longer feel so isolated, you make new friends and become more familiar with the locals and their customs and are able to laugh at some of your mistakes. You find things to like and come to terms with your new way of life and your old way of life. You are assimilating.

The last stage is home. Or acceptance. You accept this is where you are and that you do not have to completely adore or understand your new culture in order to be at peace with it. And you accept that you may never feel like you belong in this new environment but you can be happy.

The problem with this four-stage process is it takes a long time to work through and it is not clear-cut. And just when you think you are settled in, rage may return. I have clients who claim to have been fine for a very long time and yet as they grow older and confront being away from ageing and dying parents, are now experiencing terrible frustration and resent having missed out on family for all these years. They are not so much mad at the adopted country but just plain mad.

Ma puce, many people remain stuck in stage two. I believe acculturation is far more complicated a process than Kubler-Ross and the five stages of grief. Bien sûr, the model was originally applied to persons facing death but is now used in all forms of loss. Break-ups. Divorce. Unemployment. Changing house. But I'm not certain how it works with nostalgia and hiraeth.

With grief, eventually there is acceptance. Not so with homesickness. I have yet to come across a client truly at home. But then this could be why they are seeking my help. People who are fully integrated into their new culture and are not homesick usually don't need therapy. Or at least my kind of therapy.

You are so far away and it will not be possible to come back regularly so you must try to adapt. Be mad but move on too. Do not let it take ten years. Acknowledge the differences between your old country and your new country and accept you cannot change them. Try to make Kiwi friends and not seek out too many Americans in New Zealand just because you all relate. Too much relating can be toxic. There is a tendency to complain and it is not healthy. You have to move forward and not pine for what is the past. Nobody likes an orchid! Do this as much for you as for your Harrison.

Lucie

17

How dark those days seemed. In vain I tried to console myself with the thought that happiness does not depend so much on circumstances as on one's inner self.
Jennie Jerome, Lady Randolph Churchill

Meghan's Method

You got to hand it to the guy for trying. I couldn't have followed Blu home if home was Australia. There's only so much you can ask of a person. Parker took us all to Sydney for Christmas in 2001 so I know. That was the only time I remember him not getting into the holiday season, but you can't really blame him. He thought if we got away from snow and cold weather, he might be able to forget. It worked, I think, for a little while. Because wherever you go, there you are. Australia's very nice but it's also super terrifying. Snakes are just the tip of the iceberg. There are crocodiles, sharks, cane toads, and spiders the size of dinner plates. Tish Louise says that squirrels were deliberately introduced into Melbourne in the 1880s but have since gone extinct. No surprises why. The shopping is lovely, but no. Just no.

And speaking of cold weather, I am fucking freezing.

One small wood burner doesn't keep this building warm in winter. Why did Blu not tell me how cold it would be inside this house and that not only does this house not have central heating but hey, it's not insulated? This is insane. Blenheim Palace had central heating in Consuelo's day. When Jennie J gave birth to Winston in that cute little room off the main foyer back in 1874, there is no mention of having to slip on a puffer jacket. Heck, ancient Romans worked out a hypocaust home heating system thousands of years ago, so how hard can it be?

And Blu is not the chill dude I married in New York. Neither is he particularly open to expression. Or emotion. I remember thinking when he asked me that first week to join him on a visit to the Brooklyn Botanic Garden, this meant he was a new age sensitive metro-sexual kind of guy. Blu knew the name of every restful flower at the BBG so I had to be right. Now I'm reminded of one of Lucie's favorite little life lessons. Lucie says people tell you who they are and we ignore it. We pay no mind because we want other people to be who we want them to be. When Blu told me he was into flowers I thought he was telling me he was in touch with his feelings and not afraid to talk about them. Now I realize he really loves flowers. That's what he was telling me.

Blu seems to be telling me quite a few things these days. I can't seem to buy or cook food the way he wants. I don't know where to get errands done in town. I don't know how to do half the stuff he thinks I should know how to do. I'm no good with farm animals. And I don't know how to chop firewood. Because every self-respecting Brooklyn girl surely must know how to move cows and use an axe.

The other day the bastard yelled at me for not removing black marks off the walls. I thought they were permanent stains when it turns out it's fly shit. Did you know fly shit was a thing? And did you know fly shit can be removed if you scrub like fuck for an hour? Well good for you because I sure as hell didn't.

The bastard gets mad because I don't understand his accent all the time (which I used to find so fine) when he's grown up listening to mine every time he turns on the television.

Here I am, on the other side of the world from my home and we live less than five miles from the old country hospital where Blu was born and where he's surrounded by the family and friends he's always known and I have no one and no support system. I'm completely out of my element.

I still haven't made any friends on my own. How exactly does one do that at my age? At my age, people have an established line-up of friends and aren't auditioning to take on more.

I can't talk to him because he thinks I should've settled in by now and the bastard's fed up with me because I haven't.

I used to be so bad-ass. But in this new environment I don't understand, with a man I realize I don't know, my confidence is dwindling every day. My former self would have advised Blu that if he was so consumed with the obliteration of years-old household fly shit, he could've fucking well done it himself before I got here. What is happening to me?

And my former bad-ass self would have told Blu exactly where to go when he said JJ couldn't come into the house. Blu says that dogs are dirty and belong outside. For three months, this man lived with me in Brooklyn and saw first-hand that JJ lived inside, ate inside, slept inside and even had a spot on my bed. And for three months this man joined me as I walked my dog in Prospect Park because my dog doesn't poop and piss in corners and behind curtains. And when Blu came back to New York, begging me to marry him and come live with him in New Zealand and I told him I wasn't going anywhere without my JJ, he was lying on the couch with the dog right on top of him.

"Bring her too," he said. As JJ was licking his face. Which, in dogs, not humans, releases feel-good endorphins and gives dogs, not humans, the warm and fuzzies. That's why dogs like to lick.

Not once did he point out that he wouldn't let her in the house and make her sleep in a cold dog kennel by the woodshed. She only just came out of quarantine, isn't that traumatic enough?

Is that lying? I must ask Lucie and Tish Louise about that. I think they would say it is.

And how does one forget to mention the fact that his ex-fiancé is not only the local vet but his best friend's twin sister and his whole family just loves her to death? I don't mind that she's smart and gorgeous and wears really nice shoes. What I do mind is that Mildred (not her real name) likes to let on that she knows my man better than I do. I'm sure she does but it's still impolite.

I'm angry. Kubler-Ross Stage two. Homesicking at Hostility. And I don't care if woeful bitterness is a destructive human sentiment. I'm tired of fighting alone for me and what's mine. I need to start as I mean to go on but I'd prefer to just sleep.

Lucie insists I need a bike ride but I'm not feeling it. Too many hills. I prefer my grandmother's go-to cure. Bubbe considered collapse from fatigue or frustration as a perfectly acceptable thing to do.

"Fletcher, stop over-thinking will you, have a zizz before you make yourself sick," she would often bark at my grandfather. 'Zizz' may be an uncommon word these days, but it should still win you thirty-one points at Scrabble.

Sometimes I think all I need is a nice long bath to make it better, but baths take too much water and since we live on a tank supply from the roof and depend on rain to fill it up, water is precious and you do not waste it in the tub. I am so not a shower person. Blu never saw me take a single shower in New York. He could've mentioned that too.

And – get this! He says we need pretty flowers around the house and a vegetable patch in the back and since I am not working, it is my responsibility to put in place. But we already have 'pretty flowers' around the house and a 'vegetable patch' in the back and so why do we need more? How did I not know all this man does in his spare time is till soil, dig, sow, prune, clip, weed and hoe? And now he expects me to do so as well. With a smile on my face. Has he lost his mind?

I'm aware I sound pathetic. So it's cold, put on a sweater. So JJ sleeps outside, some humans are homeless or cohabit with local fauna intent on killing them. Shudder to think, Blu could have been Australian, this is true. Thing is, I know my complaints are minor. Individually. One by one. But put them all together and it all gets a bit much. Every day I deal with adjustments while he carries on living life the way he always has. And he's the one who's pissy?

I agree with Ally. Shoes here are ugly. And no, I still haven't found a job. I'm living with a stranger and I don't know what I'm doing here anymore. I thought I was a dandelion but maybe I'm not. What I wouldn't do to hear Parker's music wafting up from the garden floor and right about now, I would love to be able to just walk over to my mother's house or pop by Tish Louise's for a talk.

Tish Louise Talks

You and Lucie are as alike as two peas in a pod. But horticulture is good for the soul, Blodyn. And your mother should know this. Gardening-based mental health interventions are on the rise. Perhaps Harrison also needs a 'method'. Do try not to be so bloody-minded.

Lying is the act of knowingly telling something that is false. To mislead is to not share or admit the whole truth which ultimately causes misconception. When one places one's trust in another to produce a full picture of the home they are going to, whether he or she lies, misleads or leads down the garden path, the end result is the same. Are men more guilty of withholding the truth? I don't have the answer to that question. But I do know that many aspects of womanhood are beyond the scope of the male imagination.

The problem lies in what one considers important on one's canvas. We all have particular ideas as to what to include in the picture: male versus female, young versus old, native versus foreigner, type A versus type B, extroverts versus introverts, lazy versus active, and whatnot. This is because we all paint and interpret differently.

I made friends on the crossing with whom I kept in touch with for a long time. There was a girl in my cabin who was married to a soldier from West Virginia. Beth was so terribly excited about her new life in America and would regularly show me a photo of her husband standing proud in front of her future home. And an impressive home it was. It was only later, while visiting Washington with Richard, that I recognized the large property as belonging to Mount Vernon. Beth came to stay with me a few years on. She and her young son were on the way to England, the trip paid for her by her parents.

Beth's man lied to her. He didn't have a big house on the water. Instead, he took her to live in poverty in the mountains. Why did he fail to provide the full story? I cannot say. Surely, he knew his porky pies would come back to haunt him.

Of course, there's misunderstanding brought on by differences in nationality or culture. It never occurred to her man that when he spoke of 'lean and tender nutty tasting limb bacon' back in England, she might not realize he was talking about squirrel, not pig. According to her husband, squirrel is the best meat in the West Virginia woods. The brain is a delicacy. Perhaps so, but Beth refused to skin a squirrel, bake a squirrel pot pie and dig in with biscuits and gravy. As would I, perish the thought.

I never heard from Beth again. I suspect neither did her husband.

A Lucie Lunchtime Letter

Ma puce,

Marie Antoinette's mother wrote to her every month and asked her if she was pregnant. For seven long years she nagged the poor girl. The Franco-Austrian alliance depended on it. Bubbe did the same with me too. Alliance or not. It is not something Grand-maman would do. Me neither. But I am glad you call as often as you do.

As you know, there is tremendous documentation available on Tsarina Alexandra and her husband Tsar Nicholas II. As well as exhaustive never-ending analysis of how it all went wrong. Correspondence has been kept, diaries put into print and it seems every family member, family friend and family servant has written a book. I thought I knew everything about Alexandra that I could possibly know. But maybe not!

I am so looking forward to the long-lost letters from daughter to dead mother to be made available.

In all my research, I have never found anything which shows Alexandra missed her mother. Her mother, Princess Alice, died when Alexandra was young. It was a huge loss and one she must certainly have felt the whole of her life. It makes sense that she might speak to her in some way. Apparently, the letters span a period of over twenty years and she carried them with her all her life. She kept them with her to the end. If the rumor is true — that these letters have been hiding in a cold Siberian cellar all this time — then it is an incredible discovery.

No, I did not rage. I chose to sublimate my fury into other things. I started running. But I know I hated many things in New York for many years. I thought the people ignorant, brash and rude. I also found them superficial. Just like your Harrison says you are. Invitations to dinner here do not always mean an invitation to dinner. Food was a problem although not a huge problem. I found a place which made good croissants. I prefer New York bagels too, by the way. But chocolate? Chocolate is much better in Canada! And how I longed to speak my own language. I learned English quickly because I heard it enough in Montreal so I probably knew more than I realized, but I missed the beauty of the French language. I still do! In this stage, one compares a lot and complains even more.

I am probably at Stage Three. I'm happy in Brooklyn and I have come to love it although I like to return to Canada often. I once had a patient tell me she was not homesick but 'people sick'. She said she did not miss her home so much as the people she had left behind. When she shared this sentiment, I knew she was describing me as well.

I know you find it amusing that I should give advice to people that I myself am unable to follow. Is it wrong to visit Montreal so regularly? Who knows? But why should I not if it is so easily accessible to me? Your father does not object to my time in Canada. It has not interfered with our family life or my career so I see no reason I should not go home when I want to.

I do wonder, bien sûr, if I have prolonged my adjustment or integrated less as a result. I may have few American friends but I have more friends than your father and he has been here all his life.

Lucie

P.S. Maria Theresa's letter-writing campaign to Marie Antoinette reminds me of Grand-maman's Catholic priest story. After three babies three years in a row, Grand-maman decided to take a year off. Babette was a difficult child, she was in need of a rest. Her local priest was not happy about it. So much so, he paid a visit one day to inquire as to why she was not pregnant as was her duty. She told him she was not a milking cow and she had no intention of calving every year and to mind his own business! Père André never bothered her again.

18

In England, as on the Continent, the American woman was looked upon as a strange and abnormal creature… Anything of an outlandish nature might be expected of her. If she talked, dressed, and conducted herself as any well-bred woman would, much astonishment was invariably evinced, and she was usually saluted with the tactful remark, "I should never have thought you were an American" – which was intended as a compliment. As a rule, people looked upon her as a disagree-able and even dangerous person, to be viewed with suspicion, if not avoided altogether.
Jennie Jerome, Lady Randolph Churchill

Meghan's Method

I get the impression Blu thinks he is superior to me because I am American. Because Americans are lazy, Americans are superficial, Americans are ignorant. And not only that but he behaves like an expert in all things American.

To be fair, I have seen this behavior before. Until we had our first real grown-up jobs and before my time at Blenheim, Ally and I spent almost every school vacation in Canada and worked there in the summers. We could've stayed in Brooklyn but my grandmother's house, which was once part of the farm, is in a gorgeous half rural off-island suburb of Montreal and has this holiday feel to it so it seemed right to summer where my mom grew up. Besides, we have tons of family there and only Bubbe and Gramps in New York. More important, the Maine Coon cats are happy in Hudson. Lucie likes her Coon cats in good spirits. Anyway, we may not have gone to school with the local kids in winter but in July and August we were part of the regular crowd at the yacht club where I took sailing lessons and Ally joined the swim team. In fact, that's where we both got jobs as lifeguards and I hooked up with my first boyfriend. And my second. People just forgot we were American. I forgot I was American. Mind you, I'm equal parts Canadian. But I still noticed that everybody has this idea that they know everything there is to know about the USA because they see it in the movies or on TV. But just because you know the words to every *Friends* episode and watch repeats to this day and still can't figure out why Monica and Rachel never lock their apartment door (no doubt a nightmare situation for Louis XVI), it doesn't make you an authority on my country and its culture. Heck, even I'm not an authority on my country and its culture.

My arrogant husband believes that Americans are one-dimensional and incapable of forming genuine relationships and belittles the fact that right now, in addition to my family, I'm really missing my friends because as far as the wanker (Ha! Another new word I just picked up!) is concerned, only New Zealanders are able to form long-term deep and meaningful associations. It's incredible to me that this man who lived in my home with me (and with whom I believe I have formed a genuine relationship) for only three months now assumes he knows the way I lived my shallow American life before he came into it. He uses the fact that I didn't spend much time with my friends while he was in New York to mean that we weren't as close and committed as he and his obviously better friends are here in New Zealand. No, I didn't spend much time with my friends while he was in New York but the reason for that is because I was spending all my time with him while he was in New York. My friends, being the close, committed friends they are, understood my situation and forgave me for my one-time neglect. Because that's what forever friends do. Frankly, I'm also struggling with the concept that American friendships are inferior to other friendships the world over. Because, no.

I'm sick of smug superiority over Americans. Especially in light of the fact quite a lot of people here seem pathetically fascinated with every aspect of the USA. Even Blu himself admits he was in New York because he always wanted to go there. I can't say I ever felt the same for New Zealand.

And please don't suggest it's because I'm American and probably didn't know what or where New Zealand is. Not all Americans are clueless.

I just don't get it. If Blu has such contempt for Americans, why the hell did he marry one?

Tish Louise Talks

With age comes reflection. One tends to look backwards rather than forwards. Memories of events from seventy years ago seem sharper than what happened yesterday. I will never get back the times I didn't spend with my parents and my sister and her family. And my grandparents and childhood friends. One's heart can make room for more people — for beautiful children and grandchildren — but it will not forget the ones who came before.

You are at the beginning of your journey while I am at the end. Know that you can have so much love in your new life and yet still suffer a tremendous sense of missing. Not just at weddings and funerals and births and deaths but for simple things like popping in for a cuppa or family dinners and small celebrations or just going to the pictures or a walk in the park.

Your people are not replaceable. And you are not replaceable to your people. My family back home also missed out, not knowing my children as they should.

Staying closer to home would indeed have been easier in many ways.

A Lucie Lunchtime Letter

Ma puce,

Ben coudon! That is because Americans are constantly harping on about it being the greatest country in the world. It is tiresome and uninformed.

Having said this however, please know I have tremendous respect and love for the United States. It is a unique and special place and I appreciate the many opportunities the country and its kind and generous people have afforded me. I am here as a guest and while you may not think me as such, I am grateful.

It's not easy being so far from everything that you love and Harrison is just up the road from his family. I know you are mad about the dog and yes, not mentioning your pitou would have to sleep outside could be construed as a lie. But remember, if this is all he knows about dogs, then to him it is common sense. If you view it from this perspective, you will see he did not intend to lie. He just did not think of it. Period. Your common sense and his common sense are two completely separate things. I am sure I have said this before (or maybe you did, I can no longer remember who said what) but you are not on the same page because you are not even reading the same book. End of story.

No, Harrison is not the man you married in New York. The man you married was on holiday in a different country. We are all more relaxed and willing to try different things when we are on holiday. When we go home, we go back to routine. The man you are married to now cannot fly off to Montreal for the weekend to sample Matante Mariette's tarte au sucre or Lafleur's poutine and go on Buell cemetery hunts in Connecticut because he has a job and responsibilities. These responsibilities now include you. It must be a terrible burden to be in charge of another's happiness. All married couples feel this stressor but, in his case, Harrison knows you have given up everything to be with him and if you are sad, you are sad because you moved away from your home to be with him.

You have put all your eggs into one basket and he is the basket. No one likes being the basket! You must remember this is a difficult time for your husband also. It is not only about you. This is a huge amount of pressure for a young man. Harrison's life could have been easier if he had married the girl next door who shared his ways and culture, cooked his foods because that is what her family ate too, was able to chop wood and move cows (?) and knew about fly shit on the wall and did not argue the fact that dogs are meant to sleep outdoors. Instead, he married a diva who dotes on shoes, will not touch the food provided by the farm, complains about the cold inside and thinks rugby and cricket are a bore.

Know also that his supposed contempt for your country could be a manifestation of his insecurities. Has it not occurred to you that Harrison fears your new home may not now or ever live up to the old? And that you might leave him at any time because of this?

Stop being an orchid. If your neighbors do not call before visiting, go along with it. Did you ever call Madame Curtis-Smith before dropping by? No, you did not. You marched on over there whenever you felt like it and as if she were at your beck and call. These visitors are trying to make you feel at home. So let them.

Be grateful you have been welcomed, that you are not a war bride before the age of easy air travel and internet and instant communication and no one blames you for stealing their men. Be grateful you are not a victim of prejudice. The French used Marie Antoinette's background against her and the Russians despised Tsarina Alexandra from day one because she was German. As a French-Canadian American, you do not have it so bad. Nobody hates you for what you are.

Do not be so hard on Harrison. It is not easy to have someone pin all their hopes and dreams on you. You wanted him and he wanted you. But he did not know loving you would come with such huge responsibility. This is neither your fault nor his. But the pressure is enormous.

I do not want you to make the same mistakes as I. You are stronger than me. You got this, as you Americans like to say. The only way I know how to help you is to pass on the knowledge I have gained. You will feel lost for some time to come. You will be sad and you will be mad. But please do not let this become your only story.

Lucie

19

Meghan's Method

Just go along with it, says my mother who can probably credit her entire university career and current profession to the fact she was trying to get away from my Bubbe.

And I am not a diva. Or an orchid. I am bad ass. I am a dandelion. But I would rather be lavender. According to Google, lavender is indestructible and grows just about anywhere. Lavender was Tsarina Alexandra's favorite color.

And seriously, what is it with the plant metaphors? She knows all frigging flowers look the same to me.

But I will not rage.

However, I am mad that I'm away from my family and I can't put into words how that makes me feel so sometimes I focus on the absence of squirrels in New Zealand even though I realize their deliberate introduction would be an environmental nightmare. Who would have thought anyone could miss squirrels? Besides Tish Louise. I also long for raccoons. Raccoons are super cute. I suppose raccoons can be a problem in Park Slope but only if you have a lot of green space and we don't so we don't worry about them. Not like we do with toilet bowl snakes. Every house has a bathroom.

I'm mad that walks are boring and bike rides are all up and down. My grandfather used to say that Manhattan was like that until about two hundred years ago when city commissioners made it flat to create the north-to-south and east-to-west grid of numbered avenues and cross streets I'm used to. When I was young, Gramps used to take me for walks in the city at dawn on Sunday mornings because it was the only time it was empty and 'ergo, at its most beautiful'. Hey, Parker is right, he did use that word! Anyway, for a while, I found the chillingly calm lack of people eerie and was on high alert waiting for the bad things about to happen or nasty military men in black who might appear from around the next corner but neither ever did and I learned to appreciate the simple joy of life in New York City. And isn't it a shame that black is a yin color? I don't remember exactly when we stopped our little weekend ritual but as my grandfather got older and more easily tired, Parker suggested we stay closer to home. For some strange reason, Gramps started taking me in the car to Narrows Coffee Shop in Bay Ridge which I thought was not that close to home and actually a heck of a long way to go for a cup of Joe until Parker told me that he too, used to go with Fletcher as a kid and it was their special place. Looking back, I'm forever grateful for that last Sunday morning because neither one of us was particularly up to it. He couldn't find his walking cane and I was exhausted from a night on the town after watching Venus beat Serena at the US Open. I can still hear my grandfather's words over the phone that morning.

"Life is a slippery slope and if you do not deliberately manage the journey and let it slide, you let it stop," he declared in his gruff but sweet voice.

Actually, he didn't just say that just the one time. He used to say it a lot, especially towards the end. Gramps hated getting old and feared frailty. He said if you gave into it, it was all over and he wasn't ready to die any time soon and abandon my Bubbe who had quite a few more years in her yet. So we went. I had my usual toasted buttered bagel and he had his regular order of real bacon and scrambled eggs, hash browns and I can't remember how many cups of black coffee. Forty hours later, bad things did happen and he — and she — were gone for good. Well, he got his wish — Bubbe was not left alone. So there's that.

In the months before he died, Gramps had pretty much given up going anywhere, but he had a breakfast meeting with his publishers that day and he was never one to pass up a complementary chauffeured limo service. Bubbe decided to go too because she thought his agent was a good looking nice single Jewish boy and she liked his sense of humor. When I met David Weisz-Levy at the funeral we finally got around to holding for them (no, we did not sit shiva), I remember thinking she was right. He was beautiful and funny too. But he was also very much taken and his girlfriend with inappropriate shoes made sure we all knew it. Still, Bubbe would have been so pleased to know that, because David Weisz-Levy couldn't get on the overcrowded express A train at the 59th Street Station that morning, he was alive.

Anyway, while my Gramps didn't exactly pass on his enthusiasm for walking, I did acquire his aversion to hills.

"Walking clears the mind and makes room for new ideas," he often said.

"But hills are just a pain in the ass."

As long as you stay below 96th Street in the city, you're good. The one time we went to see the Harlem Fire Watchtower in the East 120s, we took a cab. Although we did have to Hillary up what's left of Snake Hill, aptly named so it seems, because the rocks were once infested with not just reptiles but actual 'reptile tribes'. We didn't stay long, just in case they came back. 'Hillary' is as in Sir Edmund, Fletcher-speak for 'climb'. My grandfather and I share more than a passion for words and level terrain. He too, placed heavy objects on top of the toilet seat at night and now that I think about it, he wasn't a huge fan of bananas. I wish I knew what he thought of his time in New Zealand during the war. Why did I never ask him when I had the chance? Did he love it? Did he hate it because it's all so up and down? Seriously, flat is way better. Shoes love it. Bicycles love it. Drivers in manual cars who hate hill-starts love it.

And I'm mad that I can't get excited about graveyards here. It's taken me a while to figure out why but now I know it's because I don't have history in New Zealand. Back home, every marker I come across presents a possibility. Could this person be an ancestor? Could this person have known an ancestor? Now I have no link to the land or the people here and every time I step into a burial ground, it hits me. I have no connection.

Actually, it's not just in cemeteries. It's everywhere. Back home, a simple stroll down Battle Pass in Prospect Park or stopping by the Arch at Grand Army Plaza reminds me of my place in the grand scheme of things. Now I have no place.

I'm also more than nonplussed that Kiwis seem to harbor a huge distrust for chocolate and peanut butter combination desserts and reasonably priced rubbing alcohol is nowhere to be found. Or bagels. WTF? Not to mention Sahadi's hummus and strong hairspray.

And I'm not happy about Christmas in summer. I'm not happy that there's no egg nog in the supermarkets and cold ham is served for dinner instead of hot turkey. It's all kinds of wrong that people here have not heard of egg nog and they all insist it's too hot outside to cook a turkey. And no one, not a single person tried my tourtière at Christmas dinner. My beautifully cooked pie just sat there untouched on the buffet table. Even when I told Blu's family it was from Matante Mariette's special recipe and a Québécois classic, they ignored it.

But I will not let this beat me. I will find my center because I am lavender.

I will rejoice because Blu is a good man and he doesn't hate cats as some men do. Marie Antoinette's husband Louis XVI hated cats. So too did Fletcher. Or maybe that's just what he said because he sure got a big kick out of the bodega cat near Bubbe's old salon.

Coon cats seem smaller in New Zealand than in the US. They don't have bobcats here either. No matter, my two new kittens will do me just fine. I'm glad we have reclaimed the back porch and added another room to the house and put in an extra wall and included a utility room with a cat flap large enough for JJ to crawl through. I'm glad that when I wake up in the morning, my fur-babies are all sleeping together. And I'm glad Blu is buggin' out about it because it's only fair. La-di-da. I have started as I mean to go on.

I will rejoice because it's summer. Even though it's at the wrong time of the year. I will rejoice because we're going to add another wood burner before it gets cold again. Even though it means I'll probably have to chop wood for a whole two months and there's still no pizza place nearby. Grand-maman says I should google something called a firewood processor.

I will rejoice because Blu loves me and I love him.

I am bad-ass.

Mind over matter.

Sink or swim.

Recalculate.

Tish Louise Talks

When raising children, we all tend to think only so far ahead. We plan for the future in theory but not in practice. We expect our children to move out but forget that we also serve as examples and as such, it may seem completely natural for them to choose a life in another country. Yes, of course, lots of young people move overseas these days but I suspect children raised in multi-national homes have a greater world view and may be prone to it more than others. And if one is born with dual citizenship, it is also that much easier. Residence permits and visas aren't an issue.

I cannot begrudge our Neville for leaving us and making a life in England as I did this to my parents. As did your mother and now you. Understand that one day, your children may do the same. What comes around goes around.

A Lucie Lunchtime Text

Ma puce, the letters will be made public next week. I am so excited!

Lucie

20

Meghan's Method

My dad loves his job. Bubbe said from the time he was little, Parker wanted to fly planes. People are impressed by airline pilots. When I'm introduced to parents of new friends, the usual line is, 'This is Meg, her dad is a 747 captain'. Nobody cares that my mother is a psychologist. I guess there are lots of shrinks in New York. I figure there are probably a lot of flyboys too but piloting big planes clearly has more prestige, more pop. Being a journalist has a certain wow factor to it as well. Back home, people were always interested in what I might be up to. Or maybe it was that link to my grandfather, who knows? Because that, I realized on my first day in the crowded amphitheater, is not the well-kept secret we all once thought it was. My point, however, is that some jobs seem more glam than others. But I can tell you, dairy farming is not glamorous work. Ever.

Blu gets up hours before dawn to milk three hundred cows. He's back for breakfast. He wants it cooked. Right after his lunchtime nap, the man is back getting the herd in for another round. In between, there's fencing, fertilizing, paddock fixing, thistle grubbing, mating, calving, feeding calves, cutting horns, cutting hay, blah blah blah. It's dirty. Your hands get wet. And it never ends. Blu hasn't had a day off in six months. I didn't know all this when I married the guy. My mother is right. Or maybe it was Tish Louise who said it. I should have visited the home and country I intended to settle in before I settled in. How did I become one of those people in love who don't listen to reason?

Lucky for me I'm not required to partake because if I did, I would probs drop dead of nineteenth-century nostalgia. Civil war doctors would definitely be sending me home. I have never wanted to work alfresco. Nor have I pretended to. I've been completely honest about myself in this relationship from day one. You can't wear nice shoes in dirt and if that makes me a diva, so be it. What and who I surround myself with on the outside has changed. What and who I am on the inside will not. I cannot let that happen. I am bad-ass. I am lavender. I have started as I mean to go on.

I have to laugh at my mother who always tries to provide me with tools to help me frame and identify what I'm feeling. Lucie feels it's important to frame and identify feelings. Thanks to Lucie, I see I'm just raging, and rage is a normal reaction to my current situation. So while I poke fun at my mother, I'm also grateful for her info. I can't believe I'm saying this but what I would not give to hear one of her little life lessons in person right about now.

I can't be mad anymore because I'm pregnant. Which means I'm a prisoner here. Is it wrong that this — the fact that I'm now stuck here forever — is one of the first things to cross my mind when the test turns positive? Because I know Blu is never going to let this baby go.

But then it looks like he won't have to.

No doubt The Hague Convention on the Civil Aspects of International Child Abduction was put in place by people involved in international relationships who were not willing to meet their partners halfway. I say this because what it does is 'provide' for the return of a child 'wrongfully removed by a parent' from that child's 'country of habitual residence' to another country, presumably the country of the abducting parent. It's a bitch.

Oh, don't get me wrong — it truly is a wonderful thing. For Blu. But not for me and every other raging sad sucker foreign partner parent looking at a ten-year timeline (maybe fifteen) of hostility and despair in someone else's country of habitual residence. What it is, is inconvenient. What this baby means for me is now I really have to stay. I no longer have an out clause.

There's something to be said about going halfway. Sometimes I wonder what it would be like in a neutral in-between place, where neither one of us knows the culture and neither one of us has family and friends. Where we are both homesick. Instead of an all for one and nothing for the other situation. Lucie tells me a lot of international couples prefer it this way. That way they can both rage for ten years. Maybe even fifteen. Fair is fair.

The Hague Convention is newish. Had my mother wanted, she could have wrongfully removed Ally and I back to Canada without consequence. But with Easter holiday, Memorial Day weekend, summer break, Columbus Day, Thanksgiving, Christmas and visits at the drop of any hat in between, she always had a good thing going and she knew it. But even though Lucie can fly cheap on my dad's airline passes, she doesn't. She says if you consider the taxi to LaGuardia and the one hour and a bit ride and airport delays and immigration line-ups and luggage carousel waiting and whatever, you might as well drive. And this way she can take Sisi and Franz Josef and as many bags as she wants and has her own car while there. Once you get out of the city, it's plain sailing the whole way up anyway. And on the trip back, she can stop at the outlet malls in Lake George. She doesn't, of course, because her brain, unlike normal people, doesn't flood with dopamine in stores. But there's always hope that one day she will experience a shopping high and so not once have I ever gone past with her without begging her to stop and give it a go. Or at least wait for me — with the cats — in the parking lot for just a little bit.

Though she would like to think so, my mother and I aren't in identical situations. If a car, gas money and some muesli bars is all it takes to get to where you need to be, the situations are different. If she can walk home in a zombie apocalypse then no, we are not in the same boat.

Thing is, I don't want to leave my baby-daddy. I may hate this place — or hate being here, I'm not sure how to separate the two — but I love my man twice as much. Lucie gets me but Ally thinks I'm being a schmuck. Schmuck was Bubbe's go-to word for losers. Bubbe found Yiddish such a gratifying way to get her point across. Especially with my grandfather, for whom vocabulary was so important. I think she thought it gave her an edge. Anyway, when Ally was in New Zealand, just before I met and married Blu and got here myself, she loved every minute of it and so she doesn't understand why I don't just deal. I tell her there's a difference in how you experience things when you know you're somewhere for a good time, not a long time. A temporary stay cannot compare with one that is permanent. Your head is in a different place. No pun intended. Ally could return to her better footwear and bagels and her mama whenever she wanted. If I stick with the plan, I can't.

Well, of course, I can go back. But not for forever. Is that the take-away here? Regular compassionate release from my self-imposed life sentence? Did it take minimum ten years (maybe fifteen) for the war brides to stop raging because so many never got to go home now and then? But Lucie pilgrims all the time and she still hasn't settled. Although to be fair, I don't think my mother was ever angry. I don't remember rage. Only that her body may have been in Brooklyn but her head was not and she was always looking for an excuse to go to her mama. Still does. But then I have to ask myself this now — is that a bad thing? Would I not do the same now if I could? My sister and I still got love and attention. So did Parker. He still does. And is it any worse than living with your head in a book, online or glued to your cell phone? And does it all just depend on the person and the places involved and maybe not so much how far you are from home and how often you get a fix?

Am I being unfair to my mother because all she has to worry about when things go bad is good quality sneakers and the walking dead?

Tish Louise Talks

I thought I knew everything when I was young.

As I get older, the more I realize how little I understand the world around me. Life is not black and white. I used to believe true love only came once in a lifetime but years of observation have taught me otherwise.

Had Richard gone home to America after the war without me, would I have found love again? I think so.

Perhaps my mother, who remarked on the day I left England that cacti do not thrive in the rainforest, thought so too.

Things are different now. 'You made your bed and now you have to sleep in it' was a refrain many a GI bride — or wife — was told by her parents (and community) back in the day. Women today have more freedoms. If they want to leave, they leave. Women today do not marry the first man they fall in love with. Women today know it is possible to love more than one other.

And it is easier these days also. Easier to follow your heart to another country. Communication is instant and free. Heavens, why was there no Facebook in 1946? Facebook is brilliant. I have connected with all my sister's children and grandchildren in the UK and hear from each and every one on a regular basis. I'm quite the rock star simply for being a GI bride!

A Lucie Lunchtime Letter

Ma puce,

Maybe I already know everything there is to know and this anxious wait is fruitless.

Bien sûr, you also know much about Tsarina Alexandra. You know she was Queen Victoria's favorite granddaughter. You know her hemophiliac brother was killed in a fall and that her English mother, Princess Alice, died when she was only six. But I will tell you more.

Alexandra's marriage to Nicky — with whom she had been in love with since she first met him at the age of twelve — deeply worried Queen Victoria. Not because she did not approve of Nicky but because Queen Victoria believed Russia was far too unstable and a dangerous place to be. What happened in the end proved her fears were well-founded. Not that Nicky did not play a significant role. Tsar Nicholas II was a good husband and father but an incompetent ruler. Alexandra's sister Ella also paid a price. The Bolsheviks murdered her too.

If only things had been different from the start. If only Nicky's father had prepared him for his role as Emperor, he might have known what to do. But Alexander III died young and unexpectedly. And Nicky was left in the lurch.

Now maybe we will have a candid first-hand account of how it all went so horribly wrong for Alexandra and her young family. Because if you cannot be honest when speaking to your long-dead mother, what then?

Tsarina Alexandra also never expected such responsibility so soon. Unlike her mother-in-law Empress Maria, Alix/Alexandra was Empress as soon as she married. The former Princess Dagmar of Denmark had seventeen years of marriage and life in the background learning the ropes before she became Empress Maria. Tsarina Alexandra was Empress practically on arrival and barely knew the Russian language, let alone the different alphabet.

Empress Maria (known as Minnie) could have been a little more accepting of Tsarina Alexandra and helped her along but she was not and did not. Minnie was also a foreign wife and the daughter-in-law of yet another foreign wife. But Minnie's mother-in-law, a Hessian princess who herself had struggled with life in Russia and adjustment to Russian Court ways and learning the Russian language, accepted Minnie completely. This Hessian princess that was Minnie's mother-in-law helped Minnie adapt to her new home and welcomed her wholeheartedly into the family. She was a kind woman. I am not so certain the same can be said of Minnie.

Non, poor Tsarina Alexandra did not have it easy when she arrived in Russia. She was blissfully happy with Nicky but dreadfully homesick and she missed her family dearly. She struggled with the language and acceptance into the Russian court and aristocracy. Behind the scenes and within the family, Minnie conspired against her and Alix/Alexandra quickly learned that Minnie — as well as all of Nicky's relatives — could not be counted on. To make matters worse, Minnie was unwilling to give up her top dog spot in society and encouraged former subjects to carry on loving her at the expense of the shy Tsarina Alexandra. The Russians were already xenophobic and especially anti-German and for the sake of the country, it was up to Minnie to take the lead and set an example. More than anyone, Minnie could have encouraged the Russian population into embracing Tsarina Alexandra as their new Empress. Instead, she was ambivalent and others followed suit. Minnie also, as a woman, could have been more supportive as Alexandra continued to give birth to girl after girl instead of the one all-important boy and heir. Instead, she made her daughter-in-law feel like a failure. And others followed suit.

Tsarina Alexandra was never given a chance to shine. She was an outsider from the outset and she knew it. I know from research and my own experience also that this sense of not belonging is not something that goes away. Nor does it stay constant. For some, it lessens over time. For others, it does the opposite. Lots of emotions, not just rage, come back to bite you in the bum. And for many, it does affect the way you look at things, big and small. Yes, homesickness is a puzzle.

Did she regret her marriage to and move for Nicky? That is what I hope to learn from her letters. I just want to know. And would she do it again?

History views Tsarina Alexandra as a crazy woman and she often takes the blame for the Russian Revolution. Ben coudon! Minnie was a bad mother-in-law who could have had a tremendous positive impact on both her daughter-in-law and her son. And Nicky was a loving husband and father but a weak and terrible leader. If it takes a village to raise a child, it takes a village to bring down an empire.

Lucie

21

I quite forget what it is like to be with people who love me.
I do so long sometimes to have someone to whom I could go and talk.
Jennie Jerome, Lady Randolph Churchill
In a letter to her mother, 1881.

Meghan's Method

Does Tsarina Alexandra have regrets? I tend to think regret comes in many shades of gray.

If Tsarina Alexandra knew then what she might know now, would she do it again? That's an impossible question. And she was pretty batshit. Marie Antoinette, who was in a similar situation, was not batshit. Maybe it was because she had more shoes.

My Bubbe was a village. Every kid in the neighborhood knew that if they got into trouble or needed help, all they had to do was walk into Bubbe's hair salon and they'd be taken care of. Poor Bubbe. All my grandmother wanted in life was to love and be loved. And to laugh. That's why I think she was so happy in her shop. She came alive there, as if it were some sort of escape. But escape from what, I don't know. No one knows what goes on behind closed doors, that is true, but my grandfather did love her. I know he did. And we loved her too. All these years later, I still can't pin it down, but I've always felt something a little off about her. What was she not telling us? What secret was she hiding? At the time, I figured Bubbe was sad because both her parents died young and she had no relations in Brooklyn. I never did learn how or why because Lucie told me not to pry but that just struck me as weird considering Bubbe was married to a man who, like my dad, was into family history. Of course, I planned to ask my Bubbe about it one day but I left it too late. I really should have made it a point to find out — she and Gramps were both old and dropping dead out of the blue isn't out of the question past a certain age. But I didn't expect them to go the way they did. No one could have foreseen that.

And I never did understand why Bubbe, whose faith was so important to her, married the godless gentile that was my grandfather. Lucie says it's because we all go against our better judgement in the name of love (or lust) and just hope we don't live to regret it. I can't imagine it's too easy to see your heritage slip away. And I guess it can happen no matter where you are because poor Bubbe was fighting a losing battle in her very own home. You don't have to go across the world to see your heritage slip away, it can happen right in front of you. And it was all over the minute my father met my Shikse mother. In more ways than one, it would seem. Bubbe and Gramps and their quiet because-he-has-to-hear-himself-work house could not compete with Lucie's big fun-loving, loud, non-practicing-Catholic but still Catholic family. It didn't matter that they were across an international border. My wannabe rambunctious dad got sucked in. My French-Canadian Grand-maman's house is always full of light and life. And Bubbe's dimly lit brownstone a few blocks over? Well, not so much. I guess that's why she turned her shop into a welcoming colorful lively little sanctuary. Bubbe's hair salon was an extension of herself in a way her home never was.

And yet I wonder, if my dad was so happy in Canada with my mom's Canadian family, why make our home in New York and not Montreal? He could have flown with *Air Canada.* I must ask him sometime. Does he have misgivings about the choices he has made?

Looking back, Bubbe probably did live to regret her not-quite-what-she-might-have-hoped-for marriage with a man she thought was still in love with another woman. She was just out of high school when she married my Gramps, and he was too old for her. What on earth drew them together? Did she think she could mend his complicated sorrows? I never saw the man completely smile unless Ally was in the room and yet for some reason, he kept my sister at a distance. So many things I didn't know about them that I would have asked about had I realized I was running out of time. Parker is of no use to me. For some reason, my father is clueless about his parents. Lucie says that's because most of us rarely question the way we are raised. We just accept it for what it is because it's our common sense. And these days, Parker insists that whatever answers I need to find are in Fletcher's books and I just need to know where to look. Had they survived that day, I'm sure Gramps would have written about that too.

But what I do know now is how my grandfather came to marry his Kiwi bride. Shortly after Pearl Harbour, New Zealand became a base for American military operations. Thousands of soldiers were housed in camps in preparation for battle in the Pacific, and Kiwis who felt bad about that set up an office where young men were matched with families who regularly had them over for weekends. Relationships formed, especially for fifteen hundred Kiwi women who fell in love with the US soldiers and were married to them during or shortly after the war. My assumption is that Annie was one of these women.

New Zealand, even with hills, was the fun part. The Battle of Tarawa in November 1943 was not. What happened there was huge. Sixty-six navy destroyers alone, aircraft carriers, battleships, dozens of transport ships and ten thousand men plus. After seventy-six hours, the Americans lay claim to the atoll but hundreds and hundreds of soldiers were lying dead and double that were wounded. Taking Tarawa from the Japanese was meant to be quick and easy but nothing went as planned. Gramps never said a word about the war but this has to be it. This is where he lost his God. Tarawa is the Gilbert Islands.

I should've known this before but I didn't. But now that I'm a jobless journalist with no friends, I google a lot as I await the birth of my first child who will tie me to this land forever. Lucie might say I'm exacerbating my homesickness, but I couldn't survive here without the internet. That's how I know all about the intricacies of The Hague Convention and where I need to go with my kid if I do decide to go with my kid. Because I can't go home, that's for sure. If I did, those gruesome people involved in international relationships who were not willing to meet their partners halfway and who came up with The Hague Convention would only hunt me down and haul me off to jail. I can't let that happen. Jails also have bad juju and sorry, but orange will never be my new black.

That's also how I know that not all of Lucie's war brides were happy in their new overseas lives. My mother is right — there's still not a lot out there on what happened to the war brides when they settled into marriage in a strange new world. Even now as the war brides and their former soldier husbands dwindle in numbers, I've noticed the media prefers to focus on the romance of their union rather than the reality. But there's enough information available online to know that many of these war bride marriages were unsuccessful. And I have found one book in which the final conclusion is that over half regretted their decision to marry and move away. Thank goodness Tish Louise isn't one of them. The Tish Louise I know was very happy with Richard. The only thing Tish Louise regrets is his surname. She told me once that 'Smith' is a way too boring and common moniker. She's happy in the USA. I'm sure of it.

I also have books to keep me company. I quite like my grandfather's stuff even though it can be pretty heavy and he doesn't write about the Gilbert Islands anywhere. Or World War Two. And if he's writing about this Annie, I'll be damned if I can figure out who she is.

Lucie says when she first arrived in New York, the only literature in her own language she could find were at the public library's midtown branch which was great but still not enough. That explains the shitload of books in the trunk of the car on all our trips back from Montreal. I couldn't handle not having books in my own language. Or in an unfamiliar alphabet like the Russian Cyrillic script or Arabic or Chinese. You don't think of that when you're in a big rush to follow your foreigner home, do you? Or maybe like Lucie says, because you're so happy and in love, it's one of those things you just don't want to hear.

Tish Louise Talks

No, I never asked Richard's English mother if she would do it again. I was afraid of what I might find out.

Some people are able to cross the planet for another and never look back. I am not one of those people. I was close to my family and my roots go deep. In leaving England, I set myself up for a lifetime of little heartaches. Loving Richard came at great cost.

Do I regret this life I have lived? No, absolutely no.

Would I do it again? No.

A Lucie Lunchtime Letter

Ma puce,

It is indeed possible to have no regrets about your life choices and yet know that, if given the chance to do it all over again, you would not.

Ma puce, the book is on hold but in the meantime, your old magazine has published some of the letters. They shed a whole new light on Tsarina Alexandra and her life. She is not a lunatic. She is a girl, trying to make her way in a new country all alone except for the man she loves. She is a girl in a country which hates her. She is a girl who feels her mother's loss deeply. She knows only her mother can understand her sacrifice in marrying away from home, the loneliness that this entails and the pain and horror of raising a boy destined to die from a disease she passed on to him. No wonder she wrote to her mother — does it matter that she was dead?

Lucie

PS. Your father says you asked him why we live here and not there. I will tell you the real reason. We live in New York because your Bubbe only had one child — your father. My mother had three other daughters and would not be alone if I left. You do not take an only child away from his mother. It would have killed your Bubbe and slowly, over time, it would have killed your father also, knowing he had left her behind. Parker offered to live in Canada and I said no. This was not the right thing to do.

22

Meghan's Method

'It's complicated.'

That is the headline of the article. The letters are just a few, not really enough for a book and my mother is not happy about that because she believes Tsarina Alexandra owed her dead mother more than one or two letters a year. I don't think there is much to them, really. Except for the one written the day Tsar Nicholas II abdicated. I call it the 'When rage comes back to bite you in the bum letter'. My old mag has done a good job with their presentation and, frankly, if I were still at the office, I would have killed for the byline. So now I'm jealous. I miss my old job. Maybe I should let them know I'm around. You can write from anywhere, right?

You can. I email my parents every day. Rarely something happens in my life now without them knowing. In Brooklyn, I would call once or twice a week and often drop by on the way home from work. Sure, Lucie drives me nuts, but I don't know what I would do if I didn't have her in my life. I wonder if when she's gone, I'll continue to write to her before I go to bed. I find it therapeutic. Did Tsarina Alexandra feel the same?

Tish Louise Talks

They say everyone has a story. We do. But I think we are many stories. I am a GI bride, but I am other stories also. This is not how I define myself. I am strength, I am love, I am family. I am wife, mother, grandmother, daughter, sister, friend, lover, one-time auto mechanic, homemaker, avid reader, chocolate lover, royalist, 1960s civil rights activist, Lucy-Stoner, volunteer worker, cancer survivor. I am the girl who emigrated for a boy and followed him home. I am the young mother with five boys who bakes both American brownies and English scones for the bake sales who became an anti-Vietnam war protestor. I am the woman who wished her hair was thicker and her waist a little thinner. I am the old woman who desperately misses her dead husband. I am the old woman in a green coat who takes peanuts to Prospect Park every day to feed the squirrels and hopes to see a white one. I am many things. We all are.

But of course, I still feel a pang for England. I have lived in America most of my life but I am English. I will always be English.

Tsarina Alexandra Writes (To Her Long Dead Mother)

15 March, 1917

My Dearest Mama,

It is over. Nicky is no longer Emperor of Russia. He was made to abdicate today. I am not Empress. Not that I care. I never wanted to be Empress in the first place. I just wanted to be Nicky's wife and live a quiet life with the only man I have ever loved.

Perhaps now I will get my wish. Perhaps now Nicky and I and the children can leave this horrid place. I hate it here, Mama. I always have. Not until this moment have I said so. I would not dare acknowledge my true feelings. But here it is. I hate Russia. I shall hate it to my grave.

The Russians, they never accepted me. I was never good enough. The Russian Court made fun of me. The servants mocked me. Do they not think I knew they all called me the German bitch? Or German whore? As if I could ever separate myself from where I was from. It was impossible.

Of course, I have Nicky by my side but have I had the support of his family? Hah! From day one, his mother especially was too cruel. I was too shy, too harsh, tactless. Too foreign in my ways. Just the third daughter of an insignificant grand duke. Not once have I had her support. So many times, I could have used her support.

I cannot explain it, Mama, but that woman did her best to make it difficult for me. She encouraged public sentiment against me. It would have been so simple for Minnie to take my side in court and in public. I feel that if she did, others would have followed her lead. To this day, that she did not makes me so savage.

I quite thought Minnie would come around when the babies were born but no. Instead, she blamed me for the girls. As did Nicky's family and the Russian people also. And then Europe too, began to keep watch as it would seem the stability of the entire continent was affected by the condition of my reproductive system. How did I not go completely mad? And yet such beautiful creatures they are!

Ten years I put up with such continual condemnation until finally I gave birth to a wonderful wee boy. And our joy is shattered when we learn he is a bleeder! Which, of course, according to all of Russia and

Nicky's family (but not Nicky himself, thank goodness) is my fault. As if I wanted my child to be so sick!

Nobody here understands me, Mama. I just want my son to live. Even Alexei's doctors were baffled by Grigory Rasputin's ability to heal when they could not. Time and time again Rasputin saved Alexei. Had it not been for Rasputin's intervention, he would have died at the hunting lodge in Spala. And yet the bastards have murdered him. What will happen to my little boy now?

And now I suppose it is me who will shoulder the blame for the revolt! All I wanted to do was help my man. Why did Nicky's parents not prepare him for his role in life? We have all suffered in consequence as a result. Surely, I cannot be at fault for this also.

Mama, do not get me wrong — Nicky is my beloved, my treasure, the joy of my heart and what would life be without love? But as I grow older, I am able to look back on that naïve young girl who thought love was enough to conquer all and I have to wonder — was I crazy to think living away from my people would be fine? Because it was not fine.

But today there is hope. Everything is changed. Maybe now life will be different. Maybe now I can go home. Maybe now we can all go home! Oh Mama, wouldn't it be too wonderful!

Ever your loving daughter,

Alix

P.S. Why are women blamed for not birthing boys? Surely men have some part!

23

Meghan's Method

I get it now. I get it why Tish Louise loves that song so much. You know the one. *Midnight Train to Georgia.* So deep down, is Tish Louise a cactus in the rainforest? And omigod, was her mother into plant metaphors too!

And is that what it all comes down to? Erik Erikson's Psychosocial Development Stage Eight. Integrity versus despair? Looking back on your life and wondering whether you got it right or wrong? Regretting the choices you did or did not make?

And if you could go back and do it over again, would you do it all the same?

In all the conversations I've had with Tish Louise on the phone or in person since I met Blu, she claims she has no regrets, not a single one. And yet she wouldn't do it again. She would choose not to live in his world and would rather be in hers without him. Having read Consuelo Vanderbilt's memoir, it's the same thing. And I'm sure Marie Antoinette — in a 'if she knew then what she knows now' kind of way — would tell her ruthless bulldozer mom exactly where to go. But I do believe that Jennie J would do it again. The way she lived her life — to the full — has me thinking that it would not have taken very long for the lonely newlywed to grow into a woman whose happiness did not depend so much on circumstance as her own inner dandelion self. Recalculating is quite the superpower.

Tsarina Alexandra is a mystery. Even when things are looking grim, she firmly holds on to the notion that Nicky is her beloved, her treasure, the joy of her heart. But supposedly there are more letters to come. Letters written just before what happened in the basement.

What about my clearly conflicted mother? In spite of everything she writes, she doesn't actually say, does she?

I want to be happy in my new life here. I have to be happy. Don't let me be the girl with regrets. Or the girl who wouldn't do it all over again. Don't let that be my story.

PART TWO

TEN YEARS LATER
AND
ALSO
LONG
BEFORE

24

Annie's Diary Entry

May 25, 1946

Today I have been married to Fletcher for three years and I've been in America for almost three months. It is not what I expected. Perhaps I made an error in judgement and shouldn't have been in such haste to marry this American man who so intrigued me and was more exciting and interesting and polite than the boys I have known in New Zealand. And so perhaps I've made an error in judgement and I should've listened to Mum. Mum didn't care about his perfect white teeth and beautiful grammar. It was my belief that she didn't want me to marry Fletcher because she didn't want me to leave her and Poppa in Auckland and not because of any possibility we were not suited or I would not enjoy life in America so far away from my people.

The local minister has advised me to keep a journal, to put my thoughts in writing. I did not seek him out. He came to me last week. He said he could see how unhappy I was. I did not think myself so transparent. He was very nice and he listened to me carry on at great length. Fletcher was at work and so I was able to speak unburdened. It was a great relief. I was surprised as the minister back home was a frightful character and not at all one I would turn to for help. It is different here. He asked me if I had anyone to talk to and when I told him no, he said I should write to my mother. I told him I can't tell Mum of my new life here as I don't wish for her to worry and in truth, it would serve no purpose. He returned this morning with a book for me in which to write my thoughts. His kindness made me cry. Again.

I have cried a great deal in these recent months. When I am alone, I am unable to help myself. I know I should be happy that we are finally reunited after such a long time apart, and I should be especially happy on such a day, but I can't say that I am.

I have been so naïve. All the other Kiwi and Aussie girls on the Monterey seemed so full of joy and carefree. I was no different. Imagine it… We were all going to live in America! All the American GIs in Auckland were so charming. I know Mum loved Fletcher's 'Yes Ma'ams' and 'No Ma'ams' even if she said it made her feel terribly old and matronly. Poppa longed for his after-shave. I heard him tell his mates that Fletcher smelled sweeter than any Kiwi man ever could and wouldn't it be nice if he could supply such lotions in the chemist shop. Fletcher didn't say much of his country but he need not have as we've all seen enough at the pictures and in the magazines. But it really is not the same at all. Vergennes is as removed from Hollywood as is Auckland.

Crikey! We have no electric power! I believe I am still very much in shock and can't understand why Fletcher would not have brought this to my attention before I arrived. He had been in our home on several occasions, to be sure he would have noted we lived with electric power. And so I live with candles and kerosene. And no running water and plumbing. The toilet is outside. What with the acute housing shortage in this country (how is this possible in the land of plenty?), we have no home of our own. Fletcher says he has written the Federal Public Housing Authority but there are few available housing units at this time and a long queue. At present, we board with Fletcher's father and stepmother. Fletcher's stepmother is an unpleasant woman and appears to resent my very existence. If I'm to be truly honest, however, I must say she resents Fletcher's existence also. Fletcher's father is a quiet man who does what he is told. Fletcher is also extremely obedient. I believe women in America are quite pushy and certainly, this is the case with Fletcher's parents. Mum might be a little shocked.

Poppa's birthday is soon. How I wish I could be at home with my parents. I miss Mum's lamb roast and her Sunday pavlova. Thank heavens the twins are always such a barrel of laughs. I do miss my younger siblings and am so grateful they are a comfort to Mum and Poppa now that I am gone. Still, Poppa says after I left, Mum took to her bed for a month. I had not thought of how such things might be for Mum and Poppa once I had left. Now it seems I have quite a lot of time to think about life here and there. I reckon if I had a baby, I would be too busy to think. The girls on the ship with their littlies did seem rather occupied quite a lot.

Meghan's Method

I think about a lot of things when I'm stacking firewood.

I think about what I would be doing this very minute if I were living in New York and how my Grand-maman is doing because she may be a box of birds but she is old. I think about JJ buried under the lone tree in the paddock behind our house. I wonder if I'd gone home after my first miscarriage when I was ready to pack it all in, if I would have come back to my Blu. I wonder if I hadn't, would I have considered it a starter marriage and moved on completely, not ever contemplating my life right now had I stayed. Was Tish Louise right? Is it possible to have more than one true love in life? And then I think about Tish Louise and wonder if she keeps squirrels in heaven. I think about peanut butter chocolate ice cream, bubble baths and orange school buses and what to make for dinner. I think about the opening paragraph of my next article because when I'm not at my computer is usually when good first liners come to me. I think about how lucky I am I don't have to worry about snakes in the wood pile and why is it people keep giving me garden tools at Christmas when it's obvious — just look at my yard! — that agriculture has passed me by. Although I do have several palm trees now. Palm trees don't grow in Brooklyn but last summer I saw some in planters at the MetroTech Commons and that was nice. I marvel that my sister is finally in a committed relationship and wow, isn't David Weisz-Levy's little brother such a nice boy and wouldn't Bubbe be so happy except why is it that David W-L himself is still single after all these years? I worry about the price of milk solids and that my son who looks like me worries too much. And I wish I could just figure out how to back up the trailer closer to the barn which Blu calls a shed. I think about a lot of things because stacking firewood requires little brain power.

Today I thought about Tsarina Alexandra becausc last week Lucie had me join an Imperial Russia Facebook group, and I see from comments written that while everybody agrees the poor thing was totally unhinged, nobody gets why. Lucie's hoping that someday, somebody, anybody, somewhere, anywhere, will get her point of view and come to see Alexandra as merely misunderstood. But I don't see it happening anytime soon. If Alexandra's 'when rage comes back to bite you in the bum' letter published the world over didn't manage to sway public opinion, I don't see how Lucie's one-woman crusade can. Still, I'm on Team Lucie. Every story has backstory. We're in the Marie Antoinette group too btw. Just saying.

Tsarina Alexandra's experience puts my life into perspective. I appreciate that my mother isn't long-dead and even though she drives me crazy, she doesn't fail me. I'm lucky that I don't have nasty in-laws, that the people in this country don't hate me and call me whore and bitch and that I don't need to give birth to sons to prove my worth. Even though I have two already and that's more than enough because if I go for a girl that means I need a bigger car and I might end up with another set of twins and I certainly don't want that. People didn't think like that early last century, did they?

I imagine they also didn't consider added airfare costs per child for trips back home. Or that you can only fly so far into a pregnancy and then that's it, you're grounded. No, I imagine they didn't. They went by boat. How come no one denied boarding to women with-child back then? What are thirteen hours in the air compared to months at sea?

And you know what? I feel bad that Tsarina Alexandra was blamed for all those girls. And what's wrong with girls? Parker always says, "A son is a son until he takes a wife, a daughter is a daughter for all of your life" and even though my father now likes to add "unless of course she marries a New Zealander and buggers off to the bottom of the world", I like to think it's true. He also says 'bugger' a lot now too, having picked it up on one of many trips to the bottom of the world. I just wish Alexandra was aware that at the same time she was desperately trying to conceive a boy, a woman scientist in the USA was working on the chromosomal basis of gender determination. If Alexandra only knew what Nettie Stevens probably suspected but which was only fully proven later — that it's the father who's responsible for the sex of a baby — she would have realized that it was Nicky who was at fault in all of this and not her. I can imagine how satisfying it would be to look her mother-in-law and just about everyone else squarely in the face and point that out. But then I suppose Alexandra alone must still take full credit for her son's hemophilia. No wonder she was a bit off her rocker.

Speaking of rage, I'm over the sad sucker raging. I live my good life, raise my boys and love my man with all my heart. I go home every year even though the journey is long and I still think Mars (or was it the Moon?) is closer but it doesn't take me five days at sea to get home, and for this, I am grateful. I pity Marie Antoinette who never got to see her mother again, who never returned to Vienna, not even for a short visit even though she could easily make her way in a zombie apocalypse. Why did she not ever go back? I don't know the answer to that question.

What I do know is foreign wives today do have it easier. Tish Louise and the war brides and Jennie J and Consuelo and countless evil foreign queens and dollar princesses spent hours writing letters to loved ones back home and waiting for the mail drop and whatever package it might bring and I can't remember the last time I put pen to paper. But I do spend a lot of time with my laptop. I am lavender (which is still my version of dandelion) because of the people who invented airplanes and the internet and smartphones, and I like them more than the city commissioners who flattened Manhattan so I could wear heels to work. I am a lavender because Ally and I and Parker and I text and talk on the computer every day although I'm not a fan of video communication which requires hair and make-up and that's a sore spot with me because I have come to terms with my new life at the bottom of the world but my hair has not. Sometimes I think I miss my old hair more than anything. You expect to change a lot of things when you emigrate but you don't expect to change your look. But I am lavender because Lucie calls every morning if it's not too late here in New Zealand and that gives me strength. I visualize her rage-running through Prospect Park pushing her Coons and yelling into the mic. Now and then she spots a white squirrel and attempts a selfie because she reckons she only sees them when she's talking to me. She believes it is Tish Louise's way of saying hello to the both of us. I question the lame thinking for so logical a person but I'm the one who, when I do get homesick, dance to *Midnight Train to Georgia* like no one but Tish Louise is watching so really, who am I to talk? Because sometimes I do have to remind myself that I would rather live in his world than in mine without him. And sometimes I wonder if my life would be a lot simpler if I had fallen in love with a guy from Atlanta or maybe Savannah. Georgia is walkable with a good pair of colored-sole sneakers. It's all good. Except for the snakes. I hear Burmese pythons are slithering their way up from Florida.

Sisi and Franz Josef have passed on and made way for the replacement cats. I suggested the names Imran and Jemima, Autumn and Peter or Louisa and John Adams but Lucie went with Wallis and Ed because they roll off the tongue easier. And Lucie continues to maintain that Wallis Warfield is indeed a foreign wife to the abdicated King Edward VIII even though I'm not sure why. From what I've been reading these days, Wallis thought Edward VIII was a bore and hoped to prevent his abdication and only married him because she felt bloody awful that he did it all for her.

I wonder if giving up a throne is harder than giving up one's country? At least Wallis could still count on her family for support, but Edward VIII's family deserted him. His own mother — Queen Mary — turned her back on him. And when it was all said and done, they kicked the poor man out of England and told him not to come back. So he lost his country too. Hiraeth overload.

Wallis and Edward were more dog people than cat. FYI — Slipper, their cairn terrier, was poisoned by a snake in France and buried in a proper grave with a proper headstone. Near a hunting lodge no doubt. I figure that Austria is not a dream destination for herpetologists so while I carelessly stack my wood, I sometimes question if Marie Antoinette was pissed knowing that her move from Vienna to Versailles meant she had to be more careful how she walked in long grass. Because on average, one to two persons a year die from snake bites in France and antivenom back then was not even a thing. But nasty vibes and dangers are everywhere I suppose. Maybe letting JJ bring in the cows was not such a good idea but she sure did enjoy it. JJ and Blu were quite a pair. My puppy never once looked back. In more ways than one.

I had a heart to heart with Mildred (still not her real name) when JJ died. Your husband's prior long-time love is not exactly the person you want to run into at such a time but, well, she is the local vet. Or was. That was the day she told me she was moving to Australia because having the two of us nearby was killing her. It's sad to think your happiness brings pain to others and of course, it occurred to me her situation might be difficult. But leaving a country for lost love (versus found) seems extreme. Then again, so does pining for ten long years. What's with that? Mildred says living in a giant snake pit will be fine because she wants closure. I didn't tell her that my mother the shrink says there is no closure. Not really. Or ask her why she dumped Blu in the first place.

But I'm still here. Becoming my mother. Like Tish Louise said, we all turn into our parents one day. And for some, sooner than others. Just like Lucie, I'm fascinated by other women who have done what I have done and maybe I should write a book about it but not at this time. For one, I'm not ready to write about Tish Louise. Her death is too raw and just plain sad. I'm not good at endings but then the very need for a Kubler-Ross model proves not many of us are. And like my mother, I'm vaguely absent. My body is in New Zealand, but I have a New York state of mind. I don't know how to get around being vacant. I love my boys but young children aren't overly stimulating. And most of my work is in New York. And even if I didn't have my old job back and write from afar, New York is everywhere. On the television and in the movies, on the news and in song. Frank Sinatra and Billy Joel be damned. If I want to forget my home, I should come from somewhere less in your face.

When I do forget, people remind me. 'Where are you from?' is a question I hear constantly. My accent gives me away as soon as I open my mouth. And yet as a white immigrant in a predominantly white country, I blend in more than most. But when I do something weird or different, people say it's because I am American. My behavior is viewed as a function of my nationality, not my personality. People also treat me as a representative of my president and forever ask me how I feel about the current administration. Because I prefer not to engage because it's nobody's business, I tell them that Barack Obama lived next door for a short while when I was growing up and we knew him by his more American handle. Like myself, he underwent a re-invention on the name front. Actually, I suppose it was more of a restoration. Anyway, at the time, he had a girlfriend called Genevieve who talked funny and when I asked her why, she said it was because she was from Australia where the kangaroos lived. She never mentioned the snakes. But this means I did it too. It means I asked the same annoying question. Of course, we didn't know the former President that well, he kept to himself and wasn't into sitting on his stoop all that much, but even as a kid, I could tell he was something special. People seem satisfied when they ask for more information, and I tell them he had a grandmother called Toot — short for Tutu — and a thing for tuna fish sandwiches. The secret, he once told me in his typical wistful Obama way, was in 'finely chopped dill pickles'. That's how his grandfather in Hawaii — also known as Gramps — made them. He just smiled when I asked him why he was looking up towards the sky if his grandfather wasn't dead yet. I think I had a crush on him. It was kind of hard not to.

Lucie says she's never had to deal with similar interrogation in New York. Most people know little about Canadian politics let alone who's in charge. Unless some hotshot young thing comes along to spice things up, I doubt that will change.

But I too, am to blame. I search out *The New York Times* online first thing every day. I Facebook with old friends at the expense of making new ones nearby. I choose to lead a double life. I may not know the day of the week here, but I always know what time it is on the East Coast and when there's a Big Brown Bag sale on at Bloomingdales.

25

Annie's Diary Entry

July 21, 1946

A fortnight ago I attended my first Fourth of July celebration. There was a parade on the main street in Burlington which is a larger town nearby and so many people came out to watch. It was a gay happy day. I am not sure if this is a regular custom or merely an extravagance now that the war is over and most American soldiers have returned home. Every man, woman and child held an American flag. I've never experienced such patriotism. I ate my first hot dog which was utterly disgusting. At night, there was a huge display of fireworks which was quite beautiful.

All this is strange to me as many Americans I encounter without my asking or prompting identify themselves as Italian or Irish or Polish, or whatever their ethnicity, before they define themselves as American. I'm not entirely sure if they explain themselves to me this way because I am a foreigner or if they do this at all times with all others. But I think it's the latter as it does happen rather quite a lot. Fletcher's stepmother says she is Irish but Fletcher says she was born here and has never been to Ireland and her family has been in Boston for several generations. Since the potato famine. That's a century!

Until now I had thought of everyone in this country as just being American. There is animosity between all these groups. Fletcher's stepmother says the Jews are tight with money but she uses another word for it and the Polish whom she calls Polack are dirty. But I have heard others say the Irish are lazy and they drink too much and Italians are greasy. There are no coloured people here but further South they are treated poorly indeed and now I understand why the American GIs were unkind to the Māori in New Zealand. In a country which claims to be a melting pot of cultures, there are deep divisions.

At this moment, I am bathed in sweat. It's very very hot and the people here call it the 'dog days of summer' though no one can tell me why they call it such. When I asked Fletcher's stepmother, she huffed and replied, "Well, that's a stupid question! Because it's hot and humid day after day." Which does not answer my stupid question at all. I'm afraid I like this woman less and less. If only we had our own home and didn't have to live with this awful creature, I think perhaps I could be happy here. Electric power would also help.

I reckon I am not very good at writing. I have tried to put my thoughts down more regularly and while I think my thoughts all day, when it comes to putting them on paper it seems too hard to bear. It makes it all quite real that I am not going home for a long time, if ever. I've written to Mum every week since my arrival, and I tell her the good things. I told her about the parade and the swimming hole not far from town which provides such relief from this heat. There are quite nice streams about with big large rocks and such cold cold water. But I do miss the ocean. It's terrible not to be able to see it regularly. I had no idea how attached I was. It seems amusing as on the long voyage to San Francisco, I believed myself happy to never see it ever again. I know now I took the ocean for granted. Boston is by the sea but this is a long journey from Vergennes.

Fletcher has been working on a farm. Had I known he wished to milk cows, I would have insisted we stay in New Zealand. Uncle Jack and Uncle Bryn both have reasonable size dairy farms in the Kaipara and would have gladly given him work. I'm quite certain of this. Uncle Bryn milks forty cows per day. Now Fletcher puts in long hours and I see very little of him. I feel Fletcher's stepmother finds me underfoot and yet when I try to help with jobs around the house, she is cross. Well, she seems cross no matter what. She is cross all the time! I don't see this woman smile or laugh! As I have made few acquaintances in town, I'm alone with her in the house all day. I understand that there are jobs here for women but Fletcher will not have it even though I helped Poppa in the shop for many years and I suspect I could easily work at a chemist here. He says I must stay home and care for our children. As there are no children at present and it would appear none are on the way, the time passes slowly.

I saw a lady at the grocery the other day with curlers in her hair which I thought extraordinary. When I pointed her out to Fletcher's stepmother, she told me I was being rude. But one would never venture outside the home in Auckland with hair curlers. I've told Mum in one of my letters and I know she'll find this most amusing. Americans are much less formal than New Zealanders. I am quite certain I will have absolutely no need for the linen damask tray-cloths Mum lovingly packed into my trunk.

Mum's last letter informs me that now that Paula's beloved Stephen has returned from the war, they are to be married. How I wish I could be there for Paula. All these years we dreamed of such a day and now she's to wed without me by her side. I am lonely for my oldest and dearest friend. I wish her well in her new life. And yet in my dark moments, I feel almost envious. How easy it might have been just to fall in love with a nice Kiwi boy. I love Fletcher dearly but I feel torn.

Vergennes is a French name, named after a French count. I recognised a bit of French spoken in Burlington and Fletcher informed me there are French people here from Canada. I didn't know French was spoken in Canada. I thought it was an English-speaking country. Fletcher says they came here to work in the mills and factories after the American Civil War and stayed on. Fletcher's stepmother hates them because they stole the mill jobs from the Irish. Fletcher says they are Catholic and the 'Chinese of the Eastern states' and I'm not to talk to them. As I sit here on the outside looking in, I do find it most ironic that not only is Vergennes a French name but Vermont is English for 'Green Mountains'.

A Lucie Lunchtime Letter

Ma puce,

Actually, the color is not orange but national school bus glossy yellow. It was a tint specially formulated for North American school buses before the Second World War because it is noticed in one's peripheral vision faster than any other color. Fletcher was an emotional cripple, but he was also a wealth of knowledge and happy to share. I miss him too.

Grief is a funny thing. Your grandparents' passing was tragic in many ways. Just when you think you can put it behind you, an image will pop up on the news or some disoriented tourist will ask you for directions. Your father always says he does not know how to get there. Like some of us here, he refuses to visit the site and feels strangely contemptuous towards who do.

I realize I just said 'passing'. Now I know that I have been in New York too long. In Québec, people die. Les gens meurent. What is the point of using soft words to soften the blow? La mort est la mort. It is what it is. And yet now I use a gentle word when what happened was anything but.

I talked about World War One War brides in my class today because I think they were true pioneers in intercultural and international love. Like Madame Curtis-Smith's mother-in-law, who was an English war bride from World War One. And yet I am unable to find much information on these women. The United States does not even know their numbers.

The WWI war brides were not the first group of women involved in intercultural and international marriage (we must not forget the dollar princesses and all those evil foreign queens), but I believe they were the first to leave home for love.

For a long time, marriage was a business contract. As with Marie Antoinette and her sister-pawns in Maria Theresa's game of thrones, it was a way to form alliances and trade ties. Nobility arranged marriages in order to control the movement of wealth through inheritance. If you wanted romance, you took a lover on the side. It was no different for common folk with a bit of land but little money. Marriage was a way to grow your family and workforce. Because if you owned a farm plot, why not keep things simple and marry your beautiful young daughter off to the neighbor's creepy middle-aged son? This way at least now you could share tools…

Until recently, life for most people was difficult. Just meeting basic needs like food, water and shelter — those needs at the bottom of Abraham Maslow's hierarchy — was a struggle.

I am sure you know all you need to know about colonial New England from your sister and grandfather. The first North American Buell (father to the unfortunate Hepzibah) arrived with the Puritans in 1630. William settled in the Connecticut River Valley, married Mary and produced seven children and dozens of grandchildren. From the beginning, his community was a success because colonists came as families. Families breed more families. But in Virginia a few decades earlier and in French Canada a few decades later, colonists were mostly men and the settlement failed to prosper. Even worse (from the point of view of those in the mother country), the men were mixing with local girls. Loving relationships were formed. Pocahontas was not the only native American wife of an Englishman.

Clearly the Europeans found it acceptable to bring disease, steal land, rape, murder and enslave, but this, this would not do. Pas du tout. So a plan was put into place to coax women to the New World. Enter the Jamestown brides and Filles du Roi. And their dowries. Which for the English women included not one, but two pairs of shoes.

Now I know two pairs of shoes is not your idea of a deal breaker (or even mine) but in those days, if a girl did not have a man to fall back on, her future was bleak. The idea of a new life in a new land and those two pairs of shoes probably did not seem so bad. Intimate love was not the prime motivator. Survival — meeting basic physiological needs — was the prime motivator.

In 1620 and 1621, one hundred and sixty 'maids, young and uncorrupt' plus footwear arrived in Virginia. Marriage was the main goal but reportedly, no girl was forced to wed against her will. The scheme worked and the population soared.

Meanwhile in Québec, France was also barging in. Initially, it was just a base for the beaver fur trade inhabited by men and some nuns. But when their long-time rival and now New World neighbor (the Puritans), began to thrive in New England, France decided to step it up.

New France needed numbers, and the only way to grow the colony was to include women. A similar dowry was put in place by King Louis XIV and from 1663 to 1673, eight hundred females made the journey to North America to be married to men they had not yet met. As in

Jamestown, these women were allowed to choose their husbands. The programme was a success (even if they only got one pair of shoes) and the population more than doubled in a decade. Two-thirds of Québécois trace their ancestry to the Filles du Roi.

This is not to say all marriages back in the day were a matter of convenience. I like to think love has always played a part. Certainement, in recent times, as humans more easily came to meet their primary physiological and safety needs, people began to want more out of life and with that, they longed for intimacy and companionship in marriage. Except for Fletcher's Puritans of course, who found all fun sinful.

Time's up! I will tell you more of what I talked about in my class next time.

Lucie

P.S. Grand-maman is developing quite an obsession with a database of Filles du Roi recently made available online and now counts nineteen direct lines. Like I said, sixty-seven percent of us in Québec are descendants of the Filles du Roi.

26

Annie's Diary Entry

August 5, 1946

Today Fletcher asked me why I do not behave and talk like an American girl. I feel awful. Girls here are called Cindy Jo and Bobby Sue. Girls here say 'tomayta'. I have attempted to shave my legs like the girls I see. Girls here are silly creatures and poke fun at my accent even while they have little knowledge of the world outside America and are surprised that I speak English (if they understand me!) when I tell them I've come from New Zealand. Girls here have no idea where this is. Girls here say things they don't mean. 'Why don't we get together sometime for coffee' means nothing. It's what Fletcher calls a casual invitation and such invitations are not to be taken seriously. Why bother then? Why be so insincere? And dare I mention the coffee here is dreadful?

Meghan's Method

Was my grandfather an emotional cripple? I don't think so. I just think he had things going on in his head. And a bit of baggage.

Parker agrees with me.

"Lucie, not everyone wants to be — or needs to be — an open book," I have heard my dad say to my mom more than once.

As far as Lucie is concerned, full disclosure frees the soul. Her whole family is like that. I'm not sure how before-Lucie-Parker lived his life, but married-to-Lucie-Parker has no choice. Nor do his children. Talk it out or put up with the consequences. But my mother didn't scare my grandparents. Gramps and Bubbe kept certain thoughts and feelings to themselves. They were private people and it drove my mother nuts. But we're all entitled to our secrets, are we not?

Grand-maman believes we are, but deception rots the insides. She may have no time for worry, but she apparently still feels bad she never told my grandfather she loved his dead brother more. Even though she knows not all truths need to be shared and there was no good to be had from it and sometimes freeing your soul is just a veiled form of self-indulgence.

"Times were different back then," she tells me.

Grand-maman is working on her family history. Not only on the tree but the personal stories she's able to pass on. Now that she's on email, she sends me stuff all the time. Like me, she fixates on women. There's mention of Salome and Hermeline and Hermeline's lost twin sister Mina but little reference to men. She says it's because she spent more time with her female relations and simply knew them better. And maybe because the males were more likely to keep their thoughts and feelings to themselves. Ally is loving this new information as much as I. One thing both sides of my family have in common is that we prefer to look behind us, not forward.

Lucie also likes to keep me informed. Now that she's teaching courses on International Couples at Brooklyn College, she sends me everything that goes on in class. I doubt those students have ever seen such a passionate tutor. She's given up on the book and says it's up to me to write it and it makes more sense anyway as I have the training and DNA for it and she doesn't.

I swear that was her raison d'être when I was home this summer and she made sure I returned to Blu with copies of her beautifully catalogued notes and individual stories. I had to buy another suitcase and the airline gave me grief over my extra load until my mother informed the check-in agent that Wallis Simpson travelled on her honeymoon with over two hundred pieces and she was only going to Austria while I was on my way to near-Mars with a very important cargo load. Anyway, I'm not sure I'm up to her task even though I'm confident I can write almost as well as my famous but reclusive grandfather even though I probably suck at iambic pentameter and rhythm of words and syllable timing. I didn't agree to it but neither did I disagree. But since I got back to the farm and have more time what with the boys in school, Hepzibah Buell has me thinking I should.

Actually, I've noticed I rarely disagree with anyone when I go home. When limited time hangs over every encounter, you don't rock boats because you know that if you offend, you may have to leave before you work it out. Maybe that's OK with some families but before my big move, mine was never one to ignore an elephant in the room. Not with Lucie running the show. Things are a little different now, at least with me. The modus operandi has changed, and honesty has taken a hit. I don't want to piss my people off and have them die on me when I'm gone. I don't think you think that way when your people aren't so far away and I'm sure Lucie hasn't experienced this in quite the same way as I as she's closer to home than I. But I no longer take any goodbye for granted in case it's the last one of its kind.

Hepzibah's story is cemented into my brain because after my Gramps put it out there, Ally never let it go. She even worked in Deerfield as an intern one summer (the old village is now a museum), which was really annoying because she and Salem were not home when I was. Parker was so excited for her, which is weird because in a way, isn't going there the same thing as going to Ground Zero? Parker says no because those who mourned are now also gone, because far less selfies are taken and because its buildings still stand and offer historical value.

What can I say about Deerfield? That whole thing went down because, as usual, England and France were at war and as a result so too were their colonies on North American soil. If it wasn't King Philip's War or King William's War, it was Queen Anne's War. Poor Hepzibah could never get away from it. Neither could the indigenous population who were constantly being pulled into the fighting. Hepzibah was killed in 1704. But eleven years before her death, Hepzibah was widowed with eight children and living in Deerfield when a party of Canadian natives descended on several homes outside the village palisade. According to Ally, Hepzibah's fate on June 6, 1693 is a bit fuzzy. One report has it she was inside the wall tending to a sick child when she heard of the ambush and rushed home to find her three daughters scalped. Another says she was present and also tomahawked. Either way, she survived but seventeen-year-old Sarah did not. Several years later, Hepzibah remarried a widower whose wife and three children had also been killed by Indians while he and his other children were marched off to Montreal and held captive until a treaty between France and England (obviously not long-term) saw them returned to Deerfield. You would think Hepzibah and her new husband Daniel might have decided to leave Deerfield for a safe zone but no, they were still there on that cold winter night when Canadian attackers raided again. Well, at least Hepzibah was (Ally says there's no record of Daniel's whereabouts at the time). Daughter Mary, who survived her scalping in 1693, was killed as were fifty other villagers. Hepzibah, along with one hundred and eleven captives, was taken prisoner and sent on yet another march up north. She didn't make it. My great-gran several times over was slaughtered on the fifth day and her body left in the Williams River somewhere in Vermont.

Daniel, whom Ally cannot prove was not at a hunting lodge during the attack, quickly found himself a younger wife and lived another thirty years.

What keeps Ally interested is that before it all went so horribly wrong, Hepzibah was fined twice for wearing silk. In Puritan New England, pimping your style (like all forms of fun) was sinful. My sister is on a constant search for more information on our defiant fashionista foremother because Ally says this is proof that while Hepzibah's later life was tragic, her manner of death isn't her only story. According to Ally, Hepzibah was bad-ass.

A few months before my grandfather died, Parker took the four of us — he, me, Gramps and Ally — to Deerfield to visit the mass grave. It's a four-hour drive so it was a bit of a road trip, but Gramps hadn't been that way in years. For obvious reasons (her ancestors were to blame for Hepzibah's death and Gramps never let her forget it) my mother didn't go. Neither did Bubbe because, in her words, "When your husband works at home all day, you need your time alone in the house." Now that I'm married to a farmer who never leaves the farm, I get that. Anyway, my grandfather was sure Hepzibah had received a proper burial but when we got there, we learned there are no bodies in the mass grave which is actually just a mound put in place in the early twentieth century as a memorial. And while it is assumed that those killed in the Deerfield attack are in fact buried in the Old Burying Ground, Hepzibah isn't one of them. Did no one, not even her husband Daniel, go looking for her, or her body, on the march up to Canada? It seems not — Hepzibah's final whereabouts is a mystery. The Williams River is twenty-seven miles long and for some reason, Gramps went all panicky and said he refused to set foot in Vermont, and so we didn't go look even though Ally begged him to reconsider. We thought his unexplained aversion to the Green Mountain State particularly odd. We had gone that far, what was the harm in going another hour up the road? It still strikes me as strange, and one of the rare occasions my grandfather said no to my sister. Perhaps Gramps was on to something. Ally and I went looking this summer — a not so slight detour on the way up to Montreal — and managed to spot a covered bridge but no markers. Maybe Gramps just knew it was a waste of time.

If you forget Deerfield actually happened for real and pretend it's something you saw in a movie, it makes for a good story. Like my sister, but not as much as my sister, I wish I knew more about Hepzibah. It would be nice to have a proper account of her life. Was Hepzibah really bad-ass? Did she marry for love or merely to meet basic needs? Would she have preferred to live nearer to her parents instead of in the danger zone that was Deerfield? Did she consider the fifty-four miles between her old home and new an insurmountable distance? Did she believe in zombies and think Mars was closer too? And was the silk worth the fines?

Maybe that is a book for Ally to write because she has the DNA for it too. Even though she flat-out refuses to look into the brain-eating angle and says I'm being ridiculous. I tell her the Puritans believed in witches so why not the undead?

Frankly, I am not sure how I feel about my Puritan ancestors. They have a lot to answer for. They firmly believed they were entitled to Native American land and assumed that because the people here long before them had different ways, that they were inferior. They did not play well with others. I am sure the same can be said about the old folks further North.

Still, it's the lack of info on Hepzibah which makes me think maybe I should write my mother's book. As I grow older, I'm more curious about my female forebears. I love that Tsarina Alexandra's letters have been released. I'm glad that Queen Victoria's diaries and letters to her children have been saved. I feel the same about Marie Antoinette's correspondence with her mother Maria Theresa. And that Jennie J and Consuelo wrote books. And that Tish Louise let me video our conversations on Skype and in person and that my stuff, along with what my mother put down in notes, provides lots of information. These records give me a glimpse into how women who came before me lived day to day. I've had enough of the well-documented lives of my forefathers for now, I want to hear about my forgotten foremothers whom I can better relate to. Like Hermeline and Salome. Sure, Marie Antoinette and co were much removed from regular common folk but nonetheless, it's a peek. And maybe my thirst is not so new. I remember being fascinated with Fanny Kemble's pre-Civil War memoirs of her life on a Georgian plantation which I wrote about for a magazine years ago. It didn't even dawn on me then that this English-born actress turned American abolitionist was a foreign bride. Lucie hadn't heard of her so was quite interested in my research and now I know why. I also wish I'd pressed harder with Bubbe. Bubbe was particularly proud of her Jewish heritage and yet never spoke of her family. Hardly a mention of her mother or siblings if she had any. Or photos. Bubbe says everything was lost in the fire. Parker says he doesn't remember meeting a single relative but he does remember the fire. He was very young, he says, and it was in the attic. No one quite knows how it started but it was quickly contained and no one was hurt. Parker also reports he didn't question Bubbe's missing relatives because it was just the way it was. She was not the only Jew in Brooklyn without kinfolk after all. You would think Lucie would be all over it but nope, she will tell you straight up that less time with his relations meant more with hers and anyway, that elephant was in another room in another house. I asked Bubbe once when I was growing up (seriously, how could I not when one side of the family was so completely different from the other?), but no one could shut down a conversation quite like my Bubbe.

Maybe it is up to me. My mother has placed in my care the stories of hundreds of women who have fallen in love with foreigners and followed them home. Maybe I need to be their voice. And hers too.

The problem is this. I am not in the right space. I've stopped counting down the days (or months) until my next visit home but I still miss it every day. And I'll never stop being people-sick. I'm happy here and I love my husband, but I still struggle with my decision to follow him to the bottom of the world. I've been reading the stories my mother gave to me, and I know I'm not alone. We're all conflicted. If I'm to write about this experience, I don't want it to turn people off. Yes, a woman should follow her heart, no matter where it takes her. But she should know that if it takes her far far away, it may not be easy. She may even lose herself in the process. And that sounds way too negative.

I want my book to be a positive experience, and I'm not yet ready to write it. I'm not there. Actually, I probably could use a bit of guidance from my grandfather. Gramps was good at guidance. I miss my grandfather. Warts and all.

27

Annie's Diary Entry

August 24,1946

Why are there so many mosquitoes in this country?

Late in the afternoon, when the day is very hot, there are big thunderstorms and tremendous lightning. Thunder and lightning are comparatively rare in Auckland, and so this is quite fascinating. Mum and the twins would love it, but Fletcher's father's dog hides under the bed. Mum would also enjoy something they call fireflies here, or lightning bugs. Thank goodness, we don't live near the tornadoes. I saw a snake the other morning while pottering in the garden. I reckon it was poisonous. Fletcher chided me and said as I have never before seen a snake and there are no snakes in New Zealand, I'm hardly to be relied upon to determine a venomous snake from a non-venomous snake. I don't care what he blooming says — I heard a rattle and I will not return to the garden.

Fletcher's stepmother seems unhappy with my appetite. The wicked dragon gets in a flap over nothing. That I don't eat all the food served to me (on her miss-matched plates!) upsets her terribly. She seems to think New Zealanders went hungry during the war as if in Europe and so I should be grateful for the food I receive. I have explained we didn't starve but she claims I am too thin and need fattening up. As if I were a prized cow.

A Lucie Lunchtime Letter

Ma puce,

The American journalist Henry Mencken once wrote that Puritanism was "the haunting fear that someone, somewhere, may be happy". I agree with him. I loved your grandfather also, even though I always believed him very much a throwback to his Puritan ancestry. Twelve generations are not enough dilution, the apple still has yet to fall far from the tree. And yet your father is a jovial soul. Maybe it takes thirteen.

Not everyone died on that seven-week march up north. And not all captives chose to go home when they were finally able to. Of the ninety who made it to Montreal alive, some sixty were safely returned within two to three years. But about twenty-five chose to stay and married into French or native Mohawk communities. Which goes to show you that even the difficulties involved in international relationships appear far more attractive than living in Puritan New England.

Did you know that several generations later, a grandchild of one of the assimilated captives declared himself to be Marie Antoinette's son? Oui! Eleazer Williams, grandson of the captive Eunice Williams, claimed he was the legitimate heir to Louis XVI. Marie Antoinette had four children but only two who survived infancy. No, not everyone agreed on whether or not they indeed did belong to her husband Louis XVI (after the seven-year penis-problem, rumours of infidelity dogged Marie Antoinette) but nonetheless, poor little Louis-Charles was kept in prison after his mother's death and soon succumbed to tuberculosis. Among other things. He did not die well. The boy was just ten years old. But with no one on hand to identify his body, rumors of an escape circulated for decades. According to one, he was whisked out of France (much like his mother's cats) and sent to live with the Mohawk nation near Montreal. Eleazer rolled with the story for quite a long time and enjoyed the popularity. Reaction was mixed, bien sûr, but the claim itself was not fully discounted until just a few years ago with DNA testing.

We humans love a good mystery, don't we? If it is not the missing Anastasia Romanov, daughter of Tsarina Alexandra, it is the Lost Dauphin of France…

Lucie

28

Annie's Diary Entry

September 28, 1946

Autumn is beautiful here. They call it 'fall' as all the leaves fall from the trees. This I figured out on my own, I didn't have to ask Fletcher's reptilian stepmother. It is getting cold, much colder than I'm accustomed to.

My best shoes are puckeroo, and I don't know where to have them mended, where to find a cobbler. None the matter. I have no pocket money nowadays.

I suspect I am being shunned. Once again, I called into the hairdressers this week and all the girls told me they were too busy to cut my hair. Fletcher's stepmother informs me it is because I am a GI bride and it's believed we've stolen their men.

Fletcher's stepmother has also told me there is a woman here in Vergennes who was Fletcher's girlfriend before the war and that our marriage broke her heart. She says she was a lovely girl and Fletcher was a fool to let her go. She waited for him. I haven't asked Fletcher if this is true but I suspect it is. Vergennes is small, perhaps fifteen hundred people. If we have crossed paths, I'm sure she knows who I am. I don't think it fair that I have not been extended the same courtesy. I should approach Fletcher on the matter but he has lost his job on the farm and now is not a good time as he has the sulks. Unemployment among returned soldiers is considerable. Here in

Vermont, it's very bad. Fletcher says men are looking for work everywhere without success.

Meghan's Method

I'm sure it was Ally who told me the story about The Lost Dauphin of France years ago but it's only now that I cannot follow up on my spur-of-the-moment-intense-and-dying-curiosity that I desperately want to go and check him out. I suck at emotional regulation. But it's like Tim Horton donuts. I had no idea I loved them until they were no longer right in front of me. Or up the street. I knew I was passionate about bagels and Sahadi's hummus and peanut butter chocolate ice cream and expected to go without when I got here, but I had no clue about my love for Tim Horton donuts. Sometimes it's all I can think about. All those times I ignored the shop in Canada now seem like wasted years.

Eleazer Williams died in 1858 in a place called Hogansburg, which is just south of the American-Canadian border and no more than an hour's drive away from my Grand-maman's house. It's the sort of road trip Parker would love — going after the dead — and if I were home right now and asked him to take me, we would be there in a flash. Why did I not take advantage when I had the chance?

There's not much about Deerfield and any of its obscure connections that my sister doesn't know about. She recently informed me that some of the young Deerfield captives taken in by French Canadian families were raised by the Filles Du Roi. You know, they are the girls who left France to breed babies in Québec in exchange for one measly pair of shoes. I say this to remind myself how easy I have it these days because, gosh, life was hard not so long ago. And I wonder if some of those Filles du Roi who opened their homes to the young Deerfield captives are from Grand-maman's family tree. If yes, it sure would be interesting to hear what dear old Gramps would have to say about that.

I so miss not having a history here. In that little corner of the world that is New England and the old New France, it seems everywhere I go, my DNA is in the soil. I miss being excited by small graveyards on the side of the road and wondering if I stop to have a look inside, what will I find. When I spilled my guts out to Ally today, she told me to stop whining and that she would take me there herself next summer if I promised to just shut up. This would be Ally, the one who spends her life researching the past, who feels the spirit of her ancestors wherever she goes, who talks to dead people who don't talk back and who's morphing into the great empath that is my mother. Like I said, it happens. We all become our parents. And for some, sooner than others.

But that would be good if we could all go to Hogansburg in July to have a look because Ally says that while Eleazer Williams may not have turned out to be who he said he was, he still managed to get himself a marker whereas Hepzibah didn't.

July used to be my favorite month of the year but now it depends on my location. I like it in New York. And Montreal too. But if I'm in New Zealand, I hate the whole of July because it's cold, wet, muddy and miserable. And then I hate it even more because it's sunny and beautiful back home. But I do like the month of January now. And February. And March. Because it's summer at the bottom of the world when it's cold at the top. Except it never gets really hot here and I miss the dog days.

'Dog days' is a weird expression. When I was little, Gramps told me it has nothing to do with the thermostat but rather, the ancient Romans and the dog star, Syrius and its position in the sky in the month of July. Diēs caniculārēs.

29

Annie's Diary Entry

November 2, 1946

We have shifted. We are now in a town called Brockville in the Canadian province of Ontario. I was not consulted about this move, but I don't find myself objecting as I care little where we are as I have no attachment to any place here. As Fletcher's late great-great uncle is from an established family in Brockville, he felt certain he would find more suitable work. I am simply glad to be free of his stepmother.

Fletcher works for the local paper, which he says was founded by his ancestors a century ago. He is a reporter now. This, too, is strange to me as I didn't know he was qualified to write. I know very little of this man, I am beginning to see. Except that his drinking is excessive.

Fletcher sleeps badly and groans in his sleep. He is nervy and irritable. He won't talk about his nightmares. He's a different person to the one I married before he went off to fight.

Once again, we are living with members of his family but thankfully, they are much kinder. We've rented out a room which will do us for now. I try to help his great-aunt, Mrs Buell, with the cooking but none of my favourite recipes, which I so painstakingly copied from Mum's books before leaving New Zealand, taste the same here. The ingredients must be different although flour and butter are the same all over the world, one would think. We have electric power and indoor plumbing and what a joy after Vergennes! Still, I am not with child.

A Lucie Lunchtime Letter

Ma puce,

Today in class I suggested the First World War was the result of one international marriage.

For a hundred years, historians have debated the origins of the First World War and have yet to reach consensus. There are many questions and many what ifs. International marriage never comes into the equation.

You should know that the German Kaiser Wilhelm's mother was English. Vicky was the first-born child of Queen Victoria and Prince Albert. Vicky was married to Wilhelm's father at age seventeen and sent off to Germany. Crown Prince Friedrich of Prussia was devoted to Vicky but his people rejected her. Vicky was particularly homesick though I am not sure for how long. After her husband's death, when Vicky was forty-eight years old, she chose to stay in Germany even though her mother and seven of her nine siblings were alive back in England. Yes, Vicky still had teenage daughters to care for but another reason she did not go home was to keep tabs on her son, whose actions before and after he became German ruler were a source of worry to her. I know what I would have done if I were Vicky. I would have returned to England and I would have taken the girls with me. Vicky did not live to see her son go rogue. She died in 1901, just a few months after her eighty-year-old mother.

Naturellement, I have a few 'what ifs' of my own… which I shared with my students.

The German population and the Prussian court rejected young Vicky almost immediately. But what if, instead, they had welcomed her with open arms?

What if the Germans and Prussian court had not turned on Vicky for her 'Englishness'?

What if Kaiser Wilhelm's mother had had a greater support system in her adopted country, would she have been better equipped to care for her son with the bad arm and raised him to be happy and well-adjusted instead of the erratic mentally unstable human he turned into?

What if Vicky had not been rejected and excluded, would she have constantly denigrated her son's German heritage, his 'nasty German habits' and 'terrible Prussian pride'?

What if Vicky had been welcomed in Germany and had not been made out to be an evil foreign queen, would she still have made her son feel like he was living in some medieval backwater?

Seriously, to what extent did Vicky's experiences as a foreign wife impact on her son's character and his need to prove himself to be better than others? If at all.

It is worth thinking about, non?

Bien sûr, as I explained to my class, all three major players in WWI had foreign mothers so perhaps it is a non-issue. George was an English king with a Danish mother (Alexandra of Denmark) and his first cousin Nicholas was a Russian Tsar also with a Danish mother (Minnie, formerly Dagmar of Denmark and sister to Alexandra of Denmark). So maybe having a foreign mother has little impact on who and what we become. Except maybe there is something to be said that in both England and Russia, Alexandra and Minnie were accepted by the people while in Germany where Vicky was future Empress, she was completely ostracized.

So many what ifs…

30

Annie's Diary Entry

December 12, 1946

I have never felt such cold in all my life. Worse than brass monkey weather. I feel disoriented as well as December is the start of summer in New Zealand. As I sit here, I think of all the beautiful pohutukawa trees which must soon be in bloom. And how beautiful they look along the beach. Here the trees are bare and everywhere there is snow. It is lovely when it falls from the sky and it's all quite magical but then the cold comes and it gets crunchy on the surface and not as fluffy as one would think. It's quite heavy also. We had a blizzard a fortnight ago which was quite exciting to me although Fletcher was not so amused. He says it was too early in the season for it and serves only to leave more snow on the ground. It becomes deep and old people suffer heart attacks when shovelling it away. After it's shovelled, it's piled high on either side of the path and the path then becomes slippery with ice. It is dangerous. Especially for the elderly who may fall and break bones. I'm looking forward to a white Chrissy, however.

Meghan's Method

Only my mother could take World War One and spin it into a tale on the promises and pitfalls of international marriage. And our beloved former neighbor Monsieur Obama is also the product of international marriage and, of course, there's Winston Churchill, child of Jennie J. So it can go either way and she says she knows that. And that if Versailles had a better floor plan which allowed for the proper flow of universal energy, the French Revolution could have been completely prevented and Marie Antoinette would have lived to be an old woman with a lot of large cats even though she was more of a dog person. But no, Versailles has missing corners so bad fortune comes to all those who live there. Yes, we do dabble a bit in Feng Shui in my family. On Lucie's last visit, she told me my junk room was sulking. Because that's what unused rooms do. They sulk.

Now this, according to lessons learned in eleventh-grade history, is my nutshell version of how it all went down in 1914. The end of year exam was in short essay form and not only did I ace it, I still remember what I wrote more than twenty years later. Except I didn't include the who's who in the family tree.

Start.

Franz Ferdinand — heir to the Austro-Hungarian throne and sideways descendent of Marie Antoinette — is shot dead by a Serb nationalist in Sarajevo, so Austria-Hungary declares war on Serbia. Tsar Nicholas II mobilizes his troops in support of Serbia because Russia and Serbia are allies. Tsarina Alexandra's cousin Kaiser Wilhelm in Germany declares war on Russia because that just will not do. Germany declares war on France because France and Russia are also allies, and Germany feels boxed in. King George V in England (cousin to Wilhelm and Alexandra on his father's side and Tsar Nicholas II on his mother's side) declares war on Germany because England and France are allies and King George fears that once France is mopped up by Germany, England will be next on the agenda.

Canada, India, Australia and New Zealand are involved as they are part of the British Empire. The US keeps out for a while but finally declares war on Germany in April 1917.

End.

The exam question did not ask for a psycho-social analysis so I left it at that. Thanks to Mizz Nadler, my eleventh grade English teacher, I also remember word for word William Shakespeare's famous soliloquy in Macbeth, Act 5, Scene 5. Tomorrow, and tomorrow, and tomorrow…

But seriously, is Kaiser Wilhelm's agenda all because his mother was a sad sucker foreign wife? Obviously, Lucie is more Team Adler than Team Freud nowadays. Yes, fundamental personality characteristics are set early in life but not all behavior is ruled by instinct. We know social relationships play a huge role in human development and we know Kaiser Wilhelm appears not to have got on well with his mom from day one. And she was far too obsessed with her garden, which explains a lot of things.

Could Kaiser Wilhelm's motivation also stem from the bad arm thing that Lucie mentions only in passing? The heir to an empire should not be born with a disability and little Wilhelm, unable to compensate for his annoying weakness, develops a complex. He too, does not play well with others. Alfred Adler called it Organ Inferiority. Little Wilhelm's attempts to mask his feelings — by putting on airs and showing off — causes people to dislike him. His contemporaries — and perhaps more importantly, his cousins (including the future King George, Tsar Nicholas II and Tsarina Alexandra) — socialize without him and talk about him behind his back. At the same time, he doesn't feel the love he should expect from his mother and begins to resent her. Soon his resentment extends to her country of birth (England) and all the countries England gets on with. And then one day he has a good excuse to go to war with them. So boom.

I think the origin of World War One was a combination of things. The perfect storm. Which would never have happened if the guy two notches ahead in line to the Austro-Hungarian throne before Franz Ferdinand — one Crown Prince Rudolf of Austria — hadn't, some years before in a hunting lodge, murdered his delightful teenage mistress and then turned the gun on himself. That hunting lodge was torn down and a church was put in its place. Presumably with better stronger Chi and no missing corners.

Crown Prince Rudolf, by the way, was also the product of an international marriage. Son of Franz Josef I and his unhappy German spouse, Elizabeth of Bavaria. AKA the sad, sad very sad Sisi. Not to be confused with my mother's departed Coon cat. Before he topped himself, Crown Prince Rudolf had a long list of lovers, but I find no record that Jennie J was one of them. Poor Sisi went on to be murdered. You should look that up. As well as 'missing corners'. Trust me, you do not want to live with missing corners.

31

Annie's Diary Entry

January 16, 1947

I did not enjoy Christmas. I felt very alone. Fletcher seems not to care about my loneliness and goes about his day as if this life is normal for us both. Perhaps to him it is, but to me, it is completely foreign. I think sometimes he thinks me a nuisance and to be quite silly. I think he also wonders why I am unable to give him a child.

It is dreadfully cold outside and the snow is clinging to the trees. One would think inside would be no better than outside but in fact, it's quite cosy and warm and more agreeable than most homes in New Zealand. Mr Buell, Fletcher's great-uncle, receives coal regularly and he and Fletcher go into the cellar to mix it up in some way and this keeps the entire home heated. It's much better than the one fire in Mum and Poppa's house which only kept us warm when standing directly in front of it. I had not seen a house with a basement before coming to North America.

As you go north in North America it becomes colder. In New Zealand, it becomes colder as you go south. I've told Mum of the cold, and she posted me some woollen clothing to keep warm, but it will not suffice. I find the cold here is unmanageable. Mrs Buell says I will get used to it. I am glad now I don't have work as I do not wish to walk anywhere in this weather. I just wish to be inside the house. I am reading many books. Mrs Buell also says that Fletcher isn't the same man he was before the war. She says the Fletcher she knew before was kind and thoughtful and caring, and she doesn't recognise the man who has come home. She says he used to smile all the time. I told her this was the Fletcher I fell in love with and I too don't recognise this man. What horrors did he encounter after he left New Zealand? He will not say.

Mum writes that she is feeling very tired these days and that Paula is with child. How wonderful for Paula and Stephen. When I receive a letter from home, I am so happy. And then I become so sad. Sometimes I wonder if it would be easier to bear if all ties to my former life were cut.

A Lucie Lunchtime Letter

Ma Puce,

When Tsarina Alexandra and her family were taken prisoner by Russia's provisional government (before the Bolsheviks got to them), King George V wished to offer them exile in England. After all, Tsar Nicholas II was his first cousin and they had been close since childhood. But I have read that 'Cousin Georgie' did not provide sanctuary because doing so with Europe's most notorious autocrat would threaten the then-fragile stability of the British monarchy, particularly as the autocrat was a relative. I have also read that the real reason King George V did not save Alexandra and Nicky was because his wife Queen Mary had a bone to pick. You see, before she married the future king, Mary of Teck was a low-ranking royal and the young Alix of Hesse, the future Tsarina Alexandra, never let her forget it. Yes, Alexandra was a snob. And when word came by note at the breakfast table one morning in 1917 that the British government was ready to send a ship to rescue the former Tsar and his family, George passed the note on to his wife Mary who looked at him and simply said, "No."

It was an exchange observed by and later recounted by their firstborn son, the future but fleeting King Edward VIII, who married Wallis. Tsarina Alexandra and her family were executed the next year.

King George never forgave himself for not saving his cousin and his young family. I do wonder what might have happened had they lived.

Lucie

PS. Do you know that Queen Mary was the first English born Queen Consort in four hundred years? Before Queen Mary, the English endured four centuries of evil foreign queens. Bien sûr, they embraced Bertie's long-suffering Danish wife Queen Alexandra but I wonder if it was mostly because they felt sorry for her. His extra-marital affairs were no secret. Especially after his coronation when word got out that all his special lady friends, including your Jennie Jerome, were seated together in a special box right above the royal family. Had Queen Mary's firstborn son carried on as King Edward VIII and made Wallis his consort, she would have been yet another evil foreign queen. Thank Goodness Elizabeth Bowes-Lyon came in to save the day, and such a sweet English Rose she was. Pity the next outsider to marry into the British Royal Family. God forbid she be an opinionated American woman with a bit of background and is anything less than a quiet beautiful girl with a delicate, fair-skinned complexion regarded as typically English.

32

Annie's Diary Entry

February 12, 1947

I believe I am pregnant! I can't wait for this belly of arms and legs! Fletcher is so excited. He is not drinking as much which means we have a bit more pocket money which we will need now that a baby is on the way.

I have met another GI bride and she is from England. How exciting. She's also pregnant though much further along, almost near her due date. Fletcher thinks her a fallen woman because she smokes fags and thus has discouraged me from seeing her. Regardless, I have decided that Kristine is quite wonderful and I will see her again. I can walk to see her as it's not too far. And not too cold.

Mrs Buell and I share cooking duties now, and she's been teaching me some of her special recipes. She is a delight. She makes a delicious mince (which she says is 'ground beef') dinner called goulash. She says it's an old family recipe even though her family is not Hungarian, and goulash is meant to be Hungarian. Today she complimented me on my 'stunning blue eyes' and wanted to know if it was a family trait. I told her I suppose it is as the twins also have the same blue eyes as does Poppa, and I told her that Mum says it's the first thing she noticed about my father and the first thing she looked for when we were all born.

I am feeling like I may settle into this new continent after all. If only it were not so cold. I quite like the yellow school buses they have here just like the ones I have seen in Vermont. It's a particular yellow unlike any other. But I will never accustom to the cold.

Meghan's Method

First, you get the call. At least mine is not in the middle of the night. Lucie's not dumb. She's had a call or two of her own in her lifetime and she knows that from where I'm at, there's not much I can do at two in the morning. She also knows flights from Auckland to New York via Los Angeles leave late in the evening, so if I need to, I've got all day to get to the airport and make the long ten thousand miles plus journey home.

I suppose every one of us gets that call at one point or another. I know now that your immediate reaction is to go numb. Your world stops. You put down the phone and fall to your knees. If you're lucky, you have someone by your side to bring you back up. I'm lucky. I know that you cry and you pray. You go straight to Kubler-Ross stage three — you bargain. Even if you don't do God, you haggle with him. Just in case. Please God, just let me get there in time.

When my dad collapses, he and Lucie are just about to take their seats at the Lincoln Centre. Years ago, my mother told me the real reason why she and Parker chose to live in the States rather than Canada was that she had three siblings and he had none, and you don't take an only child away from its mother. Not if you don't have to. I never forgot that because it struck me as a really selfless thing to do. But on my last trip home, Parker stated that wasn't the reason at all. According to my father, my parents live in New York because Parker needs to be near the New York Metropolitan Opera. This is so that for nine months of the year he can indulge in the season until everything shuts down for summer and then he and his model airplanes head north with my mother to Grand-maman's house. Of course, he doesn't go to the opera every day. He actually probably only manages three or four shows a year, but the thing is, my father says he's able to go if he needs to. I noticed Lucie didn't seem at all troubled by Parker's unusual revelation but I'm not sure I could play second fiddle to Carmen or Madame Butterfly. Mind you, both of my parents were wine-drunk at the time, so they might have been having me on. I left for New Zealand the next morning and wasn't able to explore the topic further, but since that day, I've pondered if there's an element of truth to it. Ask any New Yorker and they'll tell you New York is the centre of the universe. If you are born there, it's in your blood and hard to give up. Even to follow your heart. But I would not dare declare the Met as my deal breaker. I always thought my mother goes home so much because she's homesick, but now I wonder if it is to get even. And I wonder if her marriage, like some I read about in her catalogued notes and personal stories, is based not just on passion and companionship but also a never-ending game of tit for tat. And are all marriages like that or just those where one partner feels to be a follower is to somehow get the short end of the stick?

Anyway, I got home in time. I even snagged an upgrade into Business but that's because I suppose the man next to me thought me an inconvenience and informed the crew of my situation. Not that he knew exactly what it was because I didn't tell him, but when the flight attendant came to see me, I broke down. Try as I might, I can't tuck messy emotions into neat packages just because I'm on a plane and there's a guy with dark sunglasses and a black leather jacket, who I know spends too much time at the gym, sitting next to me. They don't include 'quiet into your blanket' sobbing in your usual insider upgrade tips, but let me tell you, no one (and especially not the Terminator type) wants to sit for thirteen hours next to the poster child for grief. If I may make a suggestion, however, in case you are thinking of giving it a try — be well-dressed. Wardrobe speaks volumes in the airline industry where many front-line employees lament the days when passengers donned their Sunday best to fly. I know what I'm talking about. Not only did I grow up in the airlines but I worked for one too. A career in journalism doesn't always pay the bills and part-time airport customer service is a great place to pick up stories and watch the world. Especially when the uniform can be tailored to fit your form and any black shoe will do.

Now Parker didn't die that day. Or the next day. Or the next day after that. We thought he would, but he didn't. But this is how my family and I found out about the cancer that will kill my father.

There are many things about my father I will never forget. Like the time I told my dad that Blu and I were getting married and I was moving to New Zealand to be with him. Frankly, I don't remember Lucie's reaction even though I know she was there. Lucie, being Lucie, had it figured out. But poor Parker, he just never saw it coming. Probably even more so because Blu had gone home and everyone thought, especially me (but maybe not my mother), that we were over. Parker was sitting down in his usual chair in the living room when I showed him my engagement ring and he went silent for a minute or two. My father then quietly stood up, muttered 'Jesus Christ' and walked out of the house. I don't know how long he was gone but I'll never forget the look on his face. He said he walked over to Grand Army Plaza and then through the park to revisit the markers commemorating the Battle of Brooklyn. It's funny that I don't remember my mother's reaction, but I imagine that, even though she predicted it and that she also had done the same thing to her mother and thus-ergo understood my reasons, I broke her heart too.

Two things stick out to me about my wedding day. The first is how bad I felt for Blu that his kith and kin couldn't be there for him. His mother and some Central Park rugby mates made it but the rest in New Zealand either couldn't afford the trip or the time off, especially on short notice. My entire French-Canadian tribe turned up on the day and every friend I held dear. All that was missing was Bubbe and Gramps, but we had a chuppah and broke glass in her honor and Parker wore Fletcher's old tux. I also held on to the note my grandfather mailed to me from two blocks over when I was accepted into Journalism at Sarah Lawrence. In my little bubble of happiness, I don't think it occurred to me that Blu might feel somewhat alone. In my defence, our entire relationship had played out in my backyard and so I didn't see what was missing. It was only when confronted with my whole life at the reception did I realize his wasn't in the room.

And yet, to this day, I haven't asked him how he felt about this because I don't want to know. Deep down, in that dark place where couples go to keep score of grievances but shouldn't, I am sure part of me was already thinking you get the country, I get the wedding. Fair is fair.

The other thing is the last conversation I had with my dad as a single person. As we left the house for the church, my dad turned to me and put his hands on my shoulders.

"Are you completely sure this is what you want?," he said to me.

"Because if you want to call it off now, that's OK, don't worry about it. Don't worry about the money, don't worry about the people at the church, don't worry about anything, just worry about you. We will still love you and support you no matter what you do."

"It's OK, Dad. I'm sure. This is what I want," I replied. And off we went.

And it was what I wanted. Ten years plus later, I still want it. But my dad's words haven't left me. They never will.

Parker is my hero. My sister feels the same. Lucie says we have residual Electra vibes, but Lucie didn't have a dad growing up so she can't comment on that relationship from a first-hand point of view. Secondly, even if you live in a house where you can observe, with or without bias, you don't really know what goes on elsewhere. I'm well aware Sigmund Freud uber-researched and had three daughters of his own so was onto something, but is it not possible for Ally and I to glorify our not-same-sex parent just because he's a really nice guy? Does it have to mean we didn't get the phallic phase memo? Must people like my mother dig so damn deep for answers and meaning and instead just accept things at face value? Let cigars be cigars…

Here's the thing. My dad doesn't try to change me and make me a better person. He accepts me for who I am and always has. Lucie, who's always searching for teachable moments and finding ways to improve me and yet remains oblivious to it, struggles with the concept of unconditional love. Freud said people are incapable of pure love. Not like dogs. Freud was a dog person. Ally visited the Freud Museum on her honeymoon (can you believe she married a shrink!) and says that there's no evidence he said that thing about cats. In fact, he wrote, 'I, as is well known, do not like cats', in a letter to his friend Arnold. Arnold kept the letter and it was on display the day my sister and the good doctor visited, and she took a photo and put it on Instagram for my mother to see. But Lucie didn't because she believes all social media platforms are sinister and lead to increased rates of anxiety, depression and poor sleep. And low self-esteem and poor body image. Be that as it may, I really enjoyed my sister's holiday pics.

Lucie contends a lot of people struggle with unconditional love and that's why many of us prefer friends over family. Because blood may be thicker than water but blood is bloody hard work. Family is disappointed when you don't measure up or toe the line. Friendships are easier because the level of commitment is different. You can always walk away. Friends are like dating and family is marriage. To unfriend is not the same as to divorce or disown.

I now know I am exactly like my mother. I look back on my life and I see it. The apple may move to the bottom of the world but it still does not fall far from the tree. Having said that though, and knowing how my father adores my mother, maybe that's why he accepts me for who I am. Because I am her all grown-up mini-me.

I have to stop overthinking this. But as I sit here, next to my dad, watching him sleep in his hospital bed, it's all I can do. I think of all the times we had together as a family and all the times we could have had together as a family that I have missed.

I'm not ready for our relationship to end. Lucie says it won't. It will just take another form. My mother has an answer for everything.

Lucie claims not to be at all jealous of my feelings for my father. As my boys get older, she says I'll learn it takes far more strength to be the bad cop parent than it does to be the good cop parent. Which I think means that in some way, she thinks my father was a cop-out. I'm not sure this is fair. If one parent is going to be over-bearing, then the other parent has to go the other way and be under-bearing. For the sake of your children, you must find a balance.

And speaking of children, soon I will head back to New Zealand where Blu keeps farming, where I keep house and where our babies keep growing. I am torn. I will cry the whole way back and not because I'm hoping to score another upgrade. I miss my boys — big and small. The twins are at the stage where it's like having little fans. They don't try and change us and make us better parents. They think we're chill. And Blu and I agree on most every aspect of parenting. Neither over or under bears. We're on the same page of a new book we've been kind of making up together as we go along. That's a metaphor btw.

And when I speak French to my boys the way my mother spoke French to me, Blu partakes. Neither of us understands why anyone would want to limit another's learning just because. I guess my dad isn't perfect after all.

It has just occurred to me in the last month that no one here asks me where I'm from. There is a certain comfort in that. Being always asked where you're from reminds you all the time you're not from where you currently are and that you're different. Like a cactus in the rainforest.

33

Annie's Diary Entry

March 20, 1947

I received a letter from Poppa today. Mum is unwell and he is worried. He says it is a lung disease but not tuberculosis. Regardless, he fears for her life. It's all rather sudden, and I feel I must return home, but Fletcher says we don't have the funds for such a long journey nor should I be travelling while I am pregnant. I have begged him but to no avail. Fletcher doesn't understand. I feel that since his mother died at his birth and with such an unkind stepmother, he can't comprehend the love I have for my own mother — or hers for me. He is also unable to understand how I long for home. He thinks I've been here long enough that this is my home, and I need to get on with things here and put New Zealand behind me. As if I can stop how I feel. As if a time frame exists for homesickness. I do wish I could forget what I have left behind. And what I have lost in coming here, in choosing Fletcher over all that I have ever known and loved. Oh, how I wish I could stop feeling this way. How I wish Fletcher could know how it feels to be so far away from home. I find him uncaring. He's not the man I married. The man I married in New Zealand was a jovial sort and this man whom I'm living with now is not. What happened to him in the war? To be honest, I don't have the strength to care anymore. I must go to Mum. I've not told him that Poppa secretly gave me enough money for a return passage if need be. I can do it. I just don't know if Fletcher is right and I should wait to go until after the baby is born.

Kristine understands my longing and has been a great support. She seems much happier here than I. She says it's because there's so much food here and in England during the war she was hungry and she doesn't care that she can't find crumpets and sausage rolls at the shops. And that life in England during the war was terribly difficult and remains difficult. This must be so because what troubles me seems to bother her very little. I do wonder however, if perhaps there are greater similarities between Canada and England than Canada or America and New Zealand. It is certainly much closer. Her journey on the boat was only six days compared to my thirty. Her husband Gordon Leroy is quite a nice chap. She says that when she arrived in Halifax some men weren't there to meet their wives and some European women were even divorced from their husbands without their knowing.

A Lucie Lunchtime Letter

Ma Puce,

I have always been able to compartmentalize my life. Not like in psychoanalysis where the goal is to separate conflicting incompatible cognitions from each other. I just mean boxes. How else can one study at university and be a full-time mom at the same time? I will not allow my feelings to consume me. But I will say this. I had a feeling. I knew it from the moment Wallis and Ed began cuddling up to your father last summer. They never cared for Parker before and suddenly he was their new best friend. So I knew it.

But I do not want to talk about your father. There is nothing to say. He will get better. I refuse to believe otherwise.

What I do want to talk about is my class tonight. I have not changed the curriculum much since last year but discussions with my students always bring forth new ideas and this is very exciting to me.

Tonight, I am once again concentrating on the First World War war brides who were the first en masse foreign wives. While the dollar princesses came before, their numbers were relatively few (only about three hundred) and so not en masse. Mind you, it is difficult to know how many women gave up home and country for a man after World War One because few countries have proper figures.

Take the women who came to Canada for example. About 425,000 Canadian men went off to war. While the battle took place on the continent, England was a sort of home base. England was where Canadian Expeditionary Force soldiers were trained and sent on leave and if wounded, where they received medical care. Makeshift hospitals were located all over the country, including inside Blenheim Palace and other great country homes belonging to the dollar princesses. In England, as well as the continent, romances formed. At one point, three hundred marriages per week took place between our soldiers and their British and European girlfriends.

Records indicate that during and shortly after the war, Canada 'repatriated' 54,500 dependents of soldiers (women and children) to Canada. But this number also includes wives of Canadian soldiers who moved to England during the war to be closer to their men. It sounds like a strange thing to do, but if you think of how many people living in Canada at that time who were British-born and recent immigrants, it is not so hard to understand. Many, I suspect, welcomed the opportunity to go back for just a little while. To help with homesickness.

Because these women returned to Canada after the war, knowing the number of true First World War war brides (foreign-born women married to Canadian soldiers) is tricky. Or that of how many Canadian men went back to Europe to retrieve their sweethearts when they had the chance. Estimates place the number between twenty and thirty-five thousand. I suppose language and cultural differences between Canadian soldiers and British women were much less an issue than with women from the continent.

I would suppose this was also the case in the Antipodes, which was also home to many first — and second — generation English immigrants. I have read Australia took in twelve thousand war brides during and after the war but can find no record of how many war brides arrived in New Zealand although it was mentioned in the papers at the time.

This is from an article published in *The Weekly News* in May 1919 after the ship *Ionic* docked in Auckland. This *Ionic* carried one hundred and sixty-eight war brides and their children.

"Some of the little brides approached the gangway with the pathetic, bewildered look of those who find themselves in an unknown land, with only strangers to give them greeting, and in their minds a great deal of uncertainty as to what that greeting will be. However, they were not left long in doubt; one girl-bride spoke afterwards with a depth of feeling of her anxiety and wonderment as to how her coming might be viewed by the people of her husband's land, and of her relief and gratitude that her welcome had been so kindly."

Little brides? Girl-bride. Ben coudon! Would the same thing be written about men in their circumstance? Would they too have had a 'pathetic, bewildered look' about them?

And I wonder if one of those cultural difference between old country and new was attitudes towards females. New Zealand and Australia did not witness the contributions women in England and Europe made to the war effort. As a result, women's roles and expectations in and out of the home changed. Did they change in the Antipodes? It is a fair concern as you yourself like to point out its patriarchal misogyny every now and then.

Et oui, les Antipodes. I have only just heard this term in reference to New Zealand and Australia and I think it amusing. It sounds like a name you would give a bug.

I thought the United States would have official statistics on war bride numbers, but I have checked with the people at the National WWI Museum and it appears not to. Although I have heard it to be about five thousand. The United States only joined the 'European War' in 1917 and since most American Expeditionary Force soldiers trained at home prior to going overseas and did not spend a lot of time in England, I believe there were more French War Brides than English. But I do not know for sure. There were many Irish war brides too as the AEF was stationed in Cork. I would be curious to know how well these women were received as Americans were particularly anti-Irish and anti-Catholic at the time. I do know that when the French brides arrived in America, they were not always accepted. Because joie de vivre and flirting (and good fashion-sense, no matter what!) are part of their culture, French girls here had an unwarranted reputation for promiscuity. And the people here were resentful because they were convinced their unsuspecting vulnerable homesick boys had been trapped into marriage. Many war brides were treated as parasites, prostitutes or predators. Perhaps it is true in some cases. Certainly, some girls believed life in America far more attractive than staying put in war-torn cities and villages and probably did take advantage. Mais, tu sais, it takes tremendous courage to go it alone and many were likely shocked at their new and probably primitive circumstances. Yes, I am biased, but the French have always been more sophisticated than Americans. I would assume these poor girls must have felt like they were going back in time. I do not know how many French girls married French Canadian soldiers, but I suspect they might have fared a little better, if only because they all shared a common language. Before you call me a snob, I suspect Canada was equally backward, so do not accuse me of picking on your people.

Oh, and of course, some of those French war brides fell in love with English soldiers so Britain received some war brides too. But again, I do not know how many.

Hiraeth is a word which makes me think of the war brides who left war-torn countries behind. Most of us, no matter where we go, we can go back. We can come home whenever we want and nothing much changes. But for many war brides, their homes were destroyed in the war, the home they knew is gone.

Your father is craving kettle chips once again and we have none left in the house. Did you know that chips were invented in Saratoga Springs?

Lucie

34

Annie's Diary Entry

April 25, 1947

The days are getting warmer. Spring is near. Kristine had a baby girl! On Anzac Day! She is simply delicious. Her name is Elaine! Such a pretty name for such a pretty bubba!

Meghan's Method

I love cats as much as my mother but to be fair, mine strike me as remarkably unconcerned with my well-being. Particularly changes in my internal body chemistry. Although I did notice Wallis and Ed cosy up to my dad a lot last summer, but I thought it was because he was taking longer naps on their sofa than usual.

As far as I know, my mother has not once set foot in Saratoga Springs, so I have no idea why she should know or care that that is the home of potato chips any more than Québec is the home of poutine because she eats neither. Like the outlet malls at Lake George, Lucie never took detours on the way up or down to Montreal. We only stopped for the cats. Parker, however, is big into deviation. Ice cream, donut, cute donkey or interesting mailbox on the side of the road, whatever. Lucie says it's because Parker is a free spirit stifled by on-time departures.

Flying off course and unscheduled landings are generally frowned upon in his line of work. But driving off course, now that's fine. So Parker, Ally and I have, in fact, been to Saratoga Springs. A few times. So we know the origin of potato chips, just like WWI, is a mystery.

According to some, Cornelius Vanderbilt is responsible for the invention of potato chips. But only because the nineteenth-century railroad and shipping magnate was rich and rude at restaurant staff who served him soggy French fries with dinner one night. His plate was returned to the kitchen where a none too thrilled chef spitefully re-cooked the potatoes sliced super-thin and crisped in oil before maliciously dipping them in salt. To everyone's surprise, Consuelo Vanderbilt's great-grandfather loved his revamped spuds and potato chips were born. Consuelo V was a dollar princess, remember? I may not talk about the dollar princesses as much as I used to but I keep up. I recently read online that Jennie J was 'covered in tattoos' when she hooked up with Randolph Churchill. Which may be a bit of a stretch.

Anyway, back to the crinkle cuts. I prefer the kinder gentler version where that same chef (his name was George) was cooking donuts in oil when his sweet Aunt Katie popped in for a visit and when, by accident, he dropped a slice of raw potato into the fryer. George mindfully rescued that slice, had a taste and declared his discovery far too delicious not to share with his beloved customers. Auntie Katie and George were both Mohawk Nation so it's a Mohawk invention.

I digress. If only because I am a hot mess as I now live on stand-by. I can't compartmentalize. My heart skips every time the phone rings. And lately, I find myself seething. Just like my mother said it would, rage has come back to bite me in the bum. Or maybe I'm Kubler-Rossing at livid (anger plus-plus). I no longer know which is which.

I'm ready to leave at any moment. Like most New Yorkers, in the months after 9/11, I kept a bug-out bag and like most New Yorkers, after a while, I forgot where I kept it. Now I have a similar bag, my go-to, clothes and passport at the ready. Parker could worsen at any time — next week or next year. I dare not be caught unaware. I also dare not let myself get pregnant again. Not just because I'm too old to have another baby but because airlines don't let you fly after thirty-five weeks and I need to be able to get on a plane no matter what.

Blu would like another child. He wants a girl. But I can't be having any more babies anytime soon. Especially not since Ally had her twins. Twins seem to run in my small family all of a sudden. The question is why.

I don't know how this works. I don't know how it feels to gradually lose a loved one. I was there when Bubbe and Gramps died, but the way it happened was different from anything I'd ever imagined. Mind you, everyone in the city was grieving for someone in the days and weeks and months after what happened and lots of us had a pathetic, bewildered gangway look about us. You don't have to find yourself in an unknown land to rock that particular style. I still think about that day now and then, but Lucie says it's best to honor loved ones by remembering not how they died but how they lived and that's what I try to do. It was harder for Parker. It was his mom and dad who were killed.

My poor father. All I can do here is wait. I can't help. I can do nothing. A while back, my dad told me that what he hated most about his parents' death was not how it happened but that he didn't prepare for it and get to spend more time with them beforehand. Which is weird because Gramps was in his eighties and so you would think Parker might have been on to it but I guess not. Maybe no matter how it all pans out, we just walk away stunned. Anyway, here I am, able to prepare. I've been put on notice. I've seen the change in Parker. I've been told by doctors that he will die, and yet I can't spend more time with my father before he does. I feel awful all the time.

Frankly, I have no idea where I'm at with the whole Kubler-Rossing thing. I thought depression in survivors happened after death, not before. I'm consumed with guilt. Guilt that I'm not there for and with my dad. And guilt that I'm not there right now for Lucie because she needs me too. And worry because what she calls compartmentalization is what I call denial. She will not talk to anyone about my dad's illness, not even my Grand-maman. My sister's husband, the good doctor, says Lucie needs an intervention but I know that should it happen, my mother would laugh him off. The way she sees it, beautiful David Weisz-Levy's equally hot little brother is only just out of med school and so what does he know. And he's a young man, and young men have this need to piss on trees for no particular reason. Tish Louise used to say it too, and Lucie insists you don't need a psych degree to know that. And I have more guilt because when the time comes, I still won't be there for Lucie because, in the end, I'll leave her too. Lucie's homesick handbook never said anything about the guilt.

My mother promises to call me when the end is near. I struggle with the possibility that when my father dies, I won't be at his side. All those years ago, I made a choice. I chose Blu over the rest. I'm happy here. I have a loving husband and adorable children. And yet at this very moment, I regret it all.

35

Annie's Diary Entry

July 14, 1947

It's just too hot here. Dog days of summer indeed. Fletcher wants us to go back to Vergennes so the baby can be born an American. I don't care either way. It's nothing to me where this child is born. All I know is that I don't wish to go back to Vergennes. I prefer life in Canada. Mr and Mrs Buell are so kind and I have a friend here now. The people of Vergennes were awful to me. I cannot go back to that.

A Lucie Lunchtime Letter

Ma Puce,

Potatoes can be grown in pots and bags. Lorne — he is one of my students — told me about it. It is very low maintenance. You should try it.

Lorne also told me that potatoes were pig fodder in eighteenth-century France and illegal as a human food source because it was thought to be the cause of leprosy. I thought I knew everything there was to know about eighteenth-century France but apparemment non. After years of bad harvests and famine in the 1770s, Louis XVI legalized potato crops but still, the hungry peasants stayed away. Until potato advocate Antoine Parmentier came along. Parmentier survived solely on spuds whilst in Prussian captivity during the Seven Years War and was willing to bet his life on the fact they did not cause the illness. He devised a clever little plan to get the people on board. Marie Antoinette also helped — she wore pretty purple potato blossoms in her hair.

The plan worked. Potatoes became a food source but massive famine continued into the 1780s as a result of weather-related widespread crop failure. In 1783, a volcano erupted in Iceland which caused ramifications worldwide for years to come. In Europe, haze covered the sky for months on end. Summers became exceptionally hot and winters extremely harsh. Heavy rains and flooding were followed by severe drought. Shortly before the French Revolution, a gigantic hailstorm decimated almost all farm crops in and around Paris. Potatoes were also destroyed because while the tuber is below ground, its foliage is not. Starvation ensued. Alors, Marie Antoinette is not to blame for everything. And neither did she suggest anyone eat cake. She may not have understood her people's plight but she was not a monster.

I am finding peace in my potato pots just as Marie Antoinette found peace in her gardens although I am not sure her fingers touched soil on the little farm village she had built near the palace so she could get away from all those prying eyes. But she did milk cows. The cows were scrubbed clean by servants before being presented to her. And the milk was poured not into wooden buckets but monogrammed porcelain vases. And her sheep were dyed pink and wore perfume. But that is beside the point.

Lucie

36

Annie's Diary Entry

October 2, 1947

I have a son!

And I have a daughter!

Twins!

I thought I was rather fat but imagine my surprise when straight-away after the first baby arrived, out came another. And a little girl! We have named the boy Parker after Fletcher's maternal grandfather. My daughter is Julie — just like Mum! They are beautiful. And they are American as Fletcher wished them to be. Parker is dark haired and brown eyed like his father and Julie is fair haired with blue eyes like me. Of course, it is early days so it's hard to imagine how they will look when they are all grown up. Both sleep well and seem content but I'm still very tired as two is heaps of work. Fancy me having twins just like Mum. This too, must be a family trait! I am so happy to be a mother. At the same time, I am so incredibly lonely for my own. I know no one in Queens and can't understand why we're even here, although I suppose it is better than Vergennes. We are staying with one of Fletcher's soldier mates from the war until we find a place of our own. All this shifting about makes no sense to me. How I miss my Mum. I hope she is keeping as well as can be.

Meghan's Method

My mother must be in denial because never have I known her fingers to touch soil either. I know my dad has got a serious thing for kettle chips since he got sick but why her sudden passion for potato plants and flowery blodyn tatws when she doesn't even like potatoes? But then, as Parker says, 'Whatever gets you through it' and I guess he ought to know.

I'm not big on spuds myself, but I couldn't live in a country without French fries. That's a deal breaker I never knew I had. Luckily, Blu's grandmother tells me they go back in New Zealand at least as far as she does. When I was little, Fletcher — who used to take me and Ally out for Nathan's Crinkle Cuts at least once a week — told me that Thomas Jefferson served up fries at the White House in 1802 so it has been a while on my end too.

Gramps also told me that nine-banded Armadillos carry leprosy and depending on who you believe, because the Belgians beg to differ — Montreal and New York bagels are not the only foodstuff at war — fries first showed up in street vendor stalls on the Pont Neuf in 1789. That's the same year Marie Antoinette and her family took up residence in the Tuileries Palace after their 'removal' from Versailles by angry mobs of starved revolutionaries. So for about two years, Marie Antoinette was just a five-minute stroll from the chip shop. And it's not entirely impossible that she liked to pop down for a feed of pommes frites now and then.

Maybe it is a stretch but even though they were under guard, Marie Antoinette, Louis XVI and their children had a certain amount of freedom to walk about and even managed an escape into the countryside. The midnight getaway arranged by Marie Antoinette's lover didn't go to plan because Marie Antoinette refused to split up the family and so the group was not as inconspicuous as one would hope. That nice fancy carriage, a few servants and six well fed horses in times of famine probably didn't help. Nonetheless, they made it one hundred and sixty some odd miles out. Of course, this was before Captain Clough's mythical Maine-to-the-rescue rescue which never did take place because Marie Antoinette would not leave her imprisoned children behind. Especially since Louis XVI had by then been beheaded and she had good reason to worry about their safety. Yup, say what you will about Marie Antoinette but she was devoted to her kids.

And yes, those rumors of infidelity appear to be bang on. But I don't think it was as bad as her haters made it out to be. And I'm not convinced she is an eighteenth-century lesbian icon — or Yesterqueer — all because of her close friendship with the Princess de Lamballe. Marie Antoinette was no Jennie J. She had only one lover. She didn't have a string of men as one might think with all the pornographic cartoons, pamphlets and nasty engravings of her and whomever — male or female — doing the dirty which circulated Paris throughout her reign and which helped to fuel the onset of the French Revolution long before Twitter hit the streets.

Marie Antoinette was madly in love with the Swedish Count Axel Von Fersen for twenty years, but she also loved her husband. And he loved her. Just not in the way that mattered. Louis-Auguste was a mediocre king with a penis-problem and a bit of a bore, but he was also a stand-up guy. He didn't mind his wife's extra-marital relationship because he wished her the peace he knew he couldn't provide. You know, live your best life, that sort of thing. But I'm not sure what he thought of the rumors surrounding the paternity of their children.

What's fascinating is that with all the men with whom she came into contact, Marie Antoinette fell in love with a man who was a foreigner. Did she feel a certain kinship with Count Axel Von Fersen because he was also an outsider and perhaps not familiar or comfortable with French manners, custom and ideologies? Was her initial attraction to him because he too, likely spoke French with a foreign accent and he didn't treat her as if she didn't belong?

I wonder, if I ever took a lover, would I too seek out an outsider? Is it a conscious decision?

And what about her BFF, the immigrant Princesse de Lamballe, born and raised in Italy until shipped off to France to marry a Frenchman? Is that too, coincidence?

And had Marie Antoinette not been from outside the country, would French revolutionaries have been so hard on her? But maybe her fate had nothing to do with her nationality. Maybe French revolutionaries were just really mad about her spendy habits and pink sheep because they were hangry and it didn't matter where she was from. Maybe it mattered only that she was up at the castle eating bread (and cake) when they weren't. I say this because when Marie Antoinette's sweet ten-year-old son Louis-Charles died in captivity eighteen months after his mother, he was covered in bruises and scars. Supposed cause of death is tuberculosis but the poor French-born boy had clearly been abused and his nationality had nothing to do with it.

I should tell you that during his autopsy, the boy's heart was smuggled out and passed around for two hundred plus years until 2004 when it was finally buried — in a proper royal funeral — next to the remains of his parents north of Paris. While DNA from the heart compared with Marie Antoinette's hair prove a link, cynics say the heart could be that of Louis XVII's older brother, Louis-Joseph, who died young six years earlier. So score one for Eleazer Williams. Maybe the Lost Dauphin of France didn't die and did go live with the Mohawk nation after all.

I have always wanted to know what the weather was like the day of Marie Antoinette's execution. Did the sun shine bright or was it more of an overcast sky to suit the sad occasion? I still don't have an answer to that. I guess it wasn't important. After a too-short trial, the all-male jury found her guilty of trumped up charges including incest with her son. Empress Maria Theresa's prized and precious daughter was beheaded in a simple white cotton dress less than twelve hours later. She was a fortnight shy of her thirty-eighth birthday.

Not long after her execution, the exotic royal gardens in Le Palais des Tuileries were converted into potato fields. Count Alex von Fersen returned home. He never married. Nor did he die well. His end — some twenty years later in Sweden — was violent. As with the Princess de Lamballe. This foreign wife was killed by angry mobs at the height of the French Revolution (and before Marie-Antoinette). Marie-Antoinette's only surviving child, Marie-Thérèse left France and lived most of her life in exile. She was married but had no children. Antoine Parmentier remained in Paris and seems to have had a good long life. Parker and I have been to his grave too. My dad used to take us on layovers a lot. Back in the days when kids could travel in the cockpit with their piloting parent. Back in the days before 9/11. You can spend hours and hours in the Père Lachaise cemetery. It's that good. Parmentier is in there with Jim Morrison and Oscar Wilde. When people come to visit, they leave restful flowers. Parmentier gets potatoes. I know this because we took the guided tour. I saw potatoes. It's not something you forget.

Yes, 'fortnight' is a new word. Methinks it's very English. Like Gramps, I also say rubbish instead of garbage now too. But only because it slips off the tongue easier.

37

Annie's Diary Entry

December 1948

The babies are doing so well, and I am so happy to finally be a mother. We are still living with Fletcher's war buddies but now that he has a job at the paper, he hopes we'll be able to find a place of our own soon. Now that I think about it, I do like Queens and it does feel like winter will be less brutal here than in Canada, although I do miss Canada now also. And New Zealand, of course. But the days pass quickly as I am so busy with two bubbas and not one. Fletcher seems happier also as he has found a job in the city. He writes all day and all night when he returns from work but twice this month, he's come home with the most delicious pair of shoes for me! What lovely surprises! And yesterday the four of us went out for breakfast in Bay Ridge. This Narrows Coffee shop seems a rather long way to go for a feed but we made a day of it and spent the afternoon at Prospect Park. And I so enjoyed our visit to the Brooklyn Botanic Garden. I have been so full on of late that I only have time to write to Mum and Poppa and no more. But Mum seems to be getting well again so I believe even though I will be away from home once more, I'll have a happy — and white — Christmas!

A Lucie Lunchtime Letter

Ma puce,

Bien sûr, war brides did not stop with the end of the Second World War. Over six thousand came following the Korean War and about eight thousand when Les États-Unis got involved in Vietnam. I have no idea how many arrived during or after the Iraq War as, apparemment, the US Military has no information on how many women — or men — married American soldiers in this time. I have read the number can be anywhere from a few dozen to one thousand. En tout cas, the number is low.

Why? Unlike in WWII, there was little real contact between military personnel and Iraqi nationals. Certainly, there were no weekend visits into local homes as there were for American soldiers in New Zealand and England. Bien sûr, homestays are not a requisite for romance as several thousand Royal Air Force, Royal New Zealand Air Force and Royal Australian Air Force airmen who trained in Canada went back after the war to fetch their Canadian brides whom they met at dance halls and stores and cafes and even train stations.

But yes, Iraqi-American marriages did take place. I will assume most of the war brides were female though I have read of one male Iraqi married to a female American soldier. Sometimes couples met while he was patrol captain in her neighborhood or maybe he was directing traffic on the streets. Often it was when she — or he — was working for the Army, either in the office or as an interpreter or security guard at the compound gate. Usually she was from a more cosmopolitan Baghdadi family and she was educated and spoke some English. More than likely, she was not veiled — but her sense of identity as a Muslim was strong and cultural divisions going into the marriage were formidable.

I have interviewed five Iraqi war brides to date. One war bride was widowed shortly after her arrival in the United States. Of the four remaining couples, two are together and two have divorced. None have returned to Iraq for a visit.

Unlike European women, whom I have found enjoy the attention received as war brides, my experience with Iraqi war brides is that they prefer not to talk about their new lives in the USA. I believe there are two reasons for this. One, they are somewhat distrusting of Americans. Two, they do not wish to bring harm to their families. In marrying American men, these brave women (and that one man!) have put relatives in Iraq in a dangerous position. As the situation in Iraq continues to be unsettled, it is best not to draw attention to themselves.

Why am I telling you this now when you will be here tomorrow? With your father so sick, I am at a loss. My mind is all over the place. Do you think the Iraqi war brides remain quiet also because they are subjected to prejudice and in some areas, not generally approved of?

Lucie

38

Annie's Diary Entry

14 February 1949

Fletcher came home with roses today! I am pleased to see Valentine's Day is also celebrated in America. Mum says it is a British tradition so it would make sense. Either way, I'm happy with my beautiful bouquet. And chocolates too. Fletcher is so good with presents lately that I have to wonder if he's up to something. It's funny to think I have been married to this man for five years and I still don't know him very well. Sometimes I feel like we are from different planets rather than countries. But then perhaps all wives feel that way about their husbands. It's hard to know sometimes, when we argue, if we do so because we are not well-suited or because our backgrounds make us simply too far apart.

The babies are doing well. How I wish Mum and Poppa could see my littlies. I'm constantly reminded of when Mum had the twins and how they slept hand in hand. Poppa always said the bond between 'womb-mates' was a joy to watch. Mind, they don't look much alike as Julie is so fair compared to her brother. Already they have their own personalities. Parker is happy-go-lucky and placid and Julie is very serious and observant. Fletcher calls her Queen Victoria because she's now quite plump and not easy to smile. I'm tired much of the time and feel quite alone in that I have no one here to talk to or help me as I would if I were in Auckland (why did I ever leave?!), but I am pleased to be in our own home and Fletcher is able to work when so many returned soldiers are not. I don't seem to mind the cold so much right now although to be fair, the winter here is not nearly as severe as in Vermont or Canada, and in any case, I rarely venture out the door nowadays as doing so with two wee bubs is an overwhelming task. It's good we are so close to what the locals call a bodega (Mum says it sounds like I live in Spain, but I told her it's the same as a dairy), and I have a green grocery right on the corner so I never have too far to go. Fletcher insists I serve something called broccoli at tea (or should I say 'dinner'?) every day. I do remember him asking Mum about it in New Zealand. I can't say I like it very much. It's green and tasteless. The vegetables here are quite different to home. Courgettes are called zucchini.

Meghan's Method

My dad didn't know. And my mother only found out when we were cleaning out Gramps and Bubbe's house before the sale. Since Ally and her family needed a bigger place, Parker was finally willing to let it go. We questioned the timing (should he not be taking it easy?) but Parker wanted his affairs in order before he died so Lucie didn't have to deal with it alone. I think Lucie would have preferred to tidy up the house in her own time after he was gone and not in a big rush before because she too had a lot of things on her plate but Parker didn't think that was fair as they were his parents and as such, his responsibility. And besides, she might have a lot more on her mind when she was alone.

If it wasn't for my mother-in-law, I probably wouldn't have been able to go home for so long. As usual, she was great. Blu's mother offered to look after all my boys in New Zealand for as long as needed and so off I went. I will forever be grateful as I was able to be in Brooklyn for

Parker's last few months. We all pitched in with my grandparents' house. Lucie, the Coon cats and I stayed there on the days my dad was in hospital. Ally, who was pregnant with Sabrina and busy with family and work came when she could. Of course, it didn't take us as long as I make it out to be but because my grandparents' deaths were so sudden, no one had ever taken the time to slowly and gradually empty the house of all its contents like when people die super-old and you get to downsize from house to condo/co-op to senior citizen residential complex with movie theaters and lap pools to retirement home to hospital room and hospice. Of course, in the years since they've been gone, Parker could have slowly and gradually emptied the house of its contents, but he just couldn't bring himself to do it. Lucie was fine with that, she predicted gentrification long before the rest of us and over time the house turned into a goldmine. And you can't rush the grieving process, Lucie knows that. So Parker kept the house and put in a whole lot of lighting and extra big windows because it's so important to have your space nourish and support you. When Ally and I moved out of mom and dad's, we took advantage of the free furnished accommodation a few blocks over and congratulated our smug selves as we shoved everything we didn't want into the attic because clutter not only does not nourish and support but is pretty annoying also. Especially when it belongs to someone else. And in that respect, emptying the house was not Parker's responsibility or my mom's. Salem was born there. Heck, I'm sure she was conceived there too. As were Sabrina and the twins. Hers, not mine. Oh, and it's where Blu stayed most of that first summer. Our love nest before things got real. What I am getting at is that Ally and I both lived there long enough and it was our responsibility too.

We had fun when Parker was feeling good. He never lost his happy-go-lucky joie de vivre and off-beat sense of humor and it was just like the old days when it was the four of us. I kind of miss those times. The family I was born into is my human equivalent of comfort food. The whole experience was not bleak because in finally shutting down my father's parents' lives, we almost forgot that soon we would be shutting down my dad's life too, and we would never just be the four of us ever again.

But then my mother found the box with Annie's diary. My dad was almost at the end. When he was not in pain, he was heavily medicated and not quite there. It was the first time in my life I saw my mother not know what to do. But only for a second. Lucie doesn't do cognitive dissonance. Still, I knew what thoughts were going through her head. Should she tell him the woman he had known all his life as his mother was not his mother? Should she tell him his parents had lied to him about his parentage until their dying day? Should she tell him he has a sister? Or should we just let him die in peace?

Of course, it was Lucie's decision. It had to be. She was the only person on this earth who loved my father as completely as his own mother did. And Bubbe adored my father with all of her being. She was a good mother and I will not take that away from her. But why the deception? Why did my grandparents hide — or fear — the truth? We are left with so many questions, the answers to which we will never know.

Parker took it as well as could be expected. It was all too late for him to do anything about it, but he did tell me even though he knew Bubbe loved him, it helped him to make sense of things. But he made me promise I would try to find Annie and look for his sister Julie. If not for his sake, he said, then at least for mine. He could have half-siblings in New Zealand. He said I might have cousins on his side after all. And Kiwi ones to boot. I promised him I will do my best with the few clues I have from Annie's diary.

Does Lucie regret telling him? She says she doesn't. That this was a truth Parker needed to know. But I wonder about that.

Because I have mixed emotions. I feel such immense admiration for my Bubbe who selflessly and lovingly raised another woman's child. Even if I know she must take some blame in the destruction of Fletcher's marriage to Annie. I thank Bubbe for being a wonderful grandmother to both Ally and I. But did I need to know my Bubbe was not really my Bubbe and know that our whole relationship was based on a lie? Did I need to know that I'm not part Jewish? And that, fuck me, I'm actually a little bit Kiwi? Because the only thing those two have in common is the letter *W*.

Oddly, Ally isn't too worried about her new status as total gentile. But she does lament the loss of her Russian heritage.

"Russian women are hardcore," she says. "Russian women know how to walk on ice and snow in stilettos. Russian women run into burning buildings. Russian women can stop galloping horses."

Her intel — bar the heels — is courtesy of Ukrainian poet Nikolai Nekrasov. Gramps quoted him in response to Lucie's occasional comment that French-Canadian women are strong. Like it was a competition. The one time my mother hit back with a "I cannot imagine Tsarina Alexandra ever running into burning buildings let alone stopping a horse in a hurry," he retorted with a "Yes, well, Alix of Hesse was not really Russian, now was she?"

I used to think those two didn't get on because they didn't get on. These days I wonder if there was more to it. I may have trust issues.

The only positives I can think about is that now I know why Ally and I both popped out multiples. That sort of stuff runs in families, right? If it does, now I know which family. And now I know where Ally — and Salem too — got her blonde hair and stunning blue eyes. And why my grandfather had such a soft spot for her. Maybe that's what Parker meant when he said Annie's diary provided pieces to one puzzle at least. Did he suspect something was off all along?

Lucie says no, Parker didn't suspect something was off all along. But when my grandparents were killed and Parker couldn't find any state record of Bubbe's birth in order to register her death, he was miffed. I remember that even though everything else is one big blur. But since the city agreed to waive the usual three-year waiting period for 'missing persons', families of 9/11 victims were able to get all the necessary paperwork done in a matter of days and so, death certificates in hand, he put it out of his head. We all had other things going on. Anyway, Lucie says I'll get over it in time. Closure will come. She says Bubbe and Gramps had their reasons and I don't know enough to pass judgement. I wonder if she would say the same if she were in my boat. Or my dad's. And when did she start believing in closure?

In the meantime, I grieve for my father. Stage four to five. If I think the day he died was the saddest I've ever known, it is closely matched by the day I had to leave my mother and sister behind. I know Ally will be fine, she's just living her dream. Not only does she have two Maine Coon cats but a lookalike dog too. She calls them her triplets. And it turns out the one thing she likes more than her long dead ancestors are her direct immediate descendants. Where I struggle with full-time motherhood, Ally has taken to it like a duck to water. And she's not done yet. Ally will tell you that since she can't count on me to keep her company in her old age and I'm a disgrace to the sisterhood, she must surround herself with more kids. Who knew my decision to live overseas would have a direct impact on the global population? Lucie says don't be ridiculous, it's just Ally's excuse to keep going until she has a boy. Just as Tsarina Alexandra stayed on course. According to my mother, my sister can keep at it because she has a huge support system and basically, I don't. And because I have sons and am the only female in my home and I'm a girly-girl and better suited to raising XXs. Wow. OK. And because I'm isolated on a farm when I truly belong in the city. I suppose that's true. But Ally disagrees. My younger sister, who claims to have personal insight into my parenting skills insists I lack maternal instinct and am the type who eats her young. I guess I should've been kinder to her while growing up. Anyway, I like my home — it has lots of windows to let in the sun and now that it's fully insulated, is warm in winter — but I've never gotten used to living so far away from civilization. How nice it would be to step out your front door and walk to a bodega, deli, corner store. Any store… Like, just for a bag of kettle chips or whatever. Shoes maybe. And, of course, I long for a nearby take-out pizza place but no, just no.

But I'll be fine too. I have Blu and the kids. My man understands Kubler-Rossing all too well — his older and only brother and sibling died two years before we met and he also struggles with loss. It's Lucie I worry about all alone in Brooklyn even though Ally and her gang are not that far away. I'm not sure how my mother is coping because she doesn't talk about that much either. Which is weird considering her predilection for free association. Ally tells me she's wearing tons of blue clothes all of a sudden, which is also weird because I've never seen her wear blue before. And she runs a lot more. I'm not sure if that's rage sublimating or transference. But she pushes both Wallis and Ed in the mornings because those two howl when separated and she doesn't think it's important for cats to explore their solitude because cats, unlike humans, don't experience existential moments and so it makes no difference. I have no idea what this means but, personally, I just think she likes the company. And thanks to a snapchatting Salem, I've never seen her limbs so toned and biceps so mean. I'm jealous. I don't think she's going back to the office any time soon (those sad suckers will just have to wait) but she has kept up her university classes because they're full of young people like her potato-guru Lorne with bright curious minds and those kids make her happy. And she needs some happy.

Now that I'm in New Zealand again, I'm not sure I have the energy to look for Annie even though I know that if she's alive, she may not be for very much longer. Neither Lucie or Ally are pushing me to keep my word. She left us after all. Salem, on the other hand, keeps pointing out that if you think about it, Blu and Ally share many similar physical characteristics and that alone is something I might wish to explore fully and sooner rather than later. In case I feel the need to reproduce again. I hit back safe in the knowledge that not all blonde, blue-eyed people in this world are related and more importantly, there are no missing war brides in Blu's family. Everyone is accounted for. Poor sweet Salem would really like to know her New Zealand great-grandmother because Lucie and Grand-maman took her to a war bride exhibition in Ottawa a few years ago which she really enjoyed and now she thinks it's pretty cool that she has a direct link. That it comes with secrets, lies and betrayal doesn't bother her. She says it only makes it all the more interesting. And chic. Lucie says when Salem is old enough to have a meaningful existential crisis, she'll probably rethink it.

39

Annie's Diary Entry

7 March 1949

Last week I received a letter from a woman in Vermont who said she is Fletcher's lover. She said their relationship has been going on for yonks!

I burnt the letter. I thought I could make it go away. How naïve I am. This woman, the lady who wrote the letter, she came to see me today. She confronted me outside the flat after my tiki tour of the neighbourhood with the children. Can you believe it? It was such a beautiful morning. A spring, push-bike in the park kind of day. Even though I still think of spring as better suited to September and October. But the sun was shining so bright and I really haven't seen much of the area since we got here, it being winter and all and my being cooped inside with babies and I just wanted to feel like me again. At first, I thought I was dreaming, that I was wrong, that I was not being followed. But just as we arrived home, she ran ahead past me and stood on the stoop and looked me straight on. She was hesitant at first, losing her words. She is no more than just a girl. Even though she was two steps higher, I could tell she was much shorter than I. What is my husband doing with this child? She told me she and Fletcher are in love. I just stood there looking at her. I was unable to move. Gob-smacked. Finally, I came to my senses and told her to leave me alone and I pushed past her with the pram. Which took all my strength. Thankfully Mr Goodfriend from the flat upstairs (Fletcher calls him

Nelson even though he told me his real name is Narcisse as he is French from Canada) was on his way out and helped me through the door. I didn't look back. I ignored her. And then just as the door shut, she shouted so loud I'm sure Mr Goodfriend heard it too even though he's old and seems partly deaf. "I'm pregnant." That's what she shouted. I have felt crook ever since.

I couldn't stay in the flat. I returned to the park with the children. I met a lady there. A tall woman who spoke with an English accent, very elegant. And such a fine scarf she wore. I cannot for the life of me remember her name but her boy was Neville. When she said she was a war bride, I lost the plot. I told her everything. Absolutely everything. And she listened to it all. And she held my hand. For a little while today, I felt an angel by my side.

A Lucie Lunchtime Letter

Ma puce,

We had a visitor in my class today. An Iraqi war bride!! Her name is Mona and she lives in Tucson but is visiting Brooklyn as her sister lives here and her brother-in-law had heard about my class. The world feels so big when you leave your corner behind but it still can be small too.

She has not been home in fourteen years. It is not safe to return. She says she misses her family most but is quite happy with the level of freedom her new life here allows her.

Freedom is a funny thing. I wore blue today, for Mona's visit. Parker did not like the color blue and did not like when I wore blue. And I wore blue shoes and carried a matching blue handbag. Now that your father is dead, I can finally wear blue.

Lucie

Meghan's Method

I wouldn't have married Blu if it meant not going home for fourteen years. As it is, I still think once a year isn't enough. I also wouldn't have married him if he didn't let me wear blue. WTF? Blue is a magnificent Feng Shui color.

Gosh, am I wrong too, in the way I've lived my life? Other than Blu and one or two friends, I share my life with the people I left behind — on the phone, through email and Facebook. Is that a bad thing?

40

Annie's Diary Entry

27 March 1949

He says he doesn't love her. And that she is not a child. She is at least twenty. Fletcher claims she seduced him. It was the time we took the twins to visit his father and stepmother and he went off one night to Burlington. He said he was going drinking with his mates. Which he did, he says, but then they all had a bit much to drink and things got out of hand. He says I drove him to it because I am tired all the time now with the babies and forever whinging about home and I remind him of the war, and she was just a bit of a giggle. Of course, I told him, why wouldn't she be a giggle — she's a bloody teenage girl?! He insists it was just harmless fun and it meant nothing and he never meant for this to happen. I don't know who's the bigger idiot, my husband or myself. I feel such a fool. I have two babies and I am stranded and alone on the other side of the world. I gave up everything for this man and this is what I receive in return? What do I do?

A Lucie Lunchtime Letter

Ma puce,

Out of everything your grandfather has written, I would have to say this was his most impressive work. It is a shame he kept it hidden for so long. You know, after Parker died and I went through all the papers in the house, I did think it strange I never found their marriage certificate. Now I am left wondering if Bubbe and Fletcher — whom your father said would never support our union if we lived together in sin — were even married. I never thought it unusual their wedding anniversary was on her birthday as some people do that. I wonder if it was another lie because how could your grandfather marry Bubbe if he was already married? But now I see that if what I am thinking is possible, it serves as a way to both detract from and yet to remind of a certain date. Maybe it was just a clever way to ensure neither of them forgot the devil in the detail. Or whatever. I am still not sure what that means. But did you ever see a wedding photo? I did not. I feel bad for your father, he should have seen this long, long ago.

Lucie

Meghan's Method

My mother is talking about the letter. I don't know when my Gramps meant for it to be found but it was tucked away in a Buell family history book he gave my sister the year he died. Ally knows the history well so rarely needs to refer to it but Salem is only now becoming curious about her North American ancestry and was having a look. And that is when Fletcher's letter became 'untucked'.

I thought Annie had deserted my grandfather and father. I think that's probably what Parker thought too, when we told him. All this time I have been angry at her for leaving my dad behind because how could a mother do that? I wish that my grandfather's letter had been found earlier so we could have told Parker what really happened.

Seriously, how is it fifty years plus and nothing was said? Or known.

Ah, but maybe it was known, says my mother. Maybe Parker was in possession of the letter before it was tucked away. Maybe he put it there when he was done with it. Maybe that's why he didn't seem so surprised when we told him. Because what kind of kid doesn't at some point ask to see his parents' wedding photos and marriage certificate? I don't know, I tell her, wedding photos maybe, but marriage certificate? Have I ever asked to see hers? No. Has she ever asked to see Grand-maman's marriage certificate? No.

I choose to think the reason Parker didn't seem surprised when we told him isn't because my father lied to us too but because he was near dead and pretty damn out of it. Or maybe he did ask to see all that stuff years ago and was told it was lost in the fire. Lucie likes to explore all angles but sometimes it's just unnecessary and exhausting. Sometimes a cigar is just a cigar.

Now that I can stop hating on my newly acquired grandmother, Blu says I need to go look for Annie and whatever family I might have (besides him) on this side of the world. It's not just about me, he says. It's about my father's sister and our children too. If they have Kiwi cousins, they should be able to meet them.

I'll do that. As soon as I get back to New Zealand, I'll start searching. I promised him just as I promised Ally after my dad died and now dear little Salem who is not so little anymore.

It's good being home again. I've so missed Christmas in New York and it has been special with Lucie's family coming down. Grand-maman laughed so hard when I told her no one in New Zealand would touch my tourtière pie until I began to prepare it in samosa form and now it's one of the most popular items on the buffet table. This particular re-invention was Salem's idea. A lightbulb moment over Indian curry dinner on a visit home. It was the night I met Ally's then-husband-to-be and his folks. Although they are a great bunch and I would love to get to know them, it's best to keep away from David Weisz-Levy.

Yes, there was more to us than I have let on and maybe I'll expand on that one day but for now I prefer to box it away. As we know, I am prone to falling into a sliding-doors trap mentality where I analyze how my life with Blu might compare to a life without. I don't need to put a face to it.

So, moving on, oy vey, is it ever cold! I'd forgotten what winter was like. I take it for granted my children live their lives barefoot which is a Kiwi thing. No matter what my boys have on their feet when they go to school in the morning, they come back shoeless. Meanwhile, ever since I got here, Ally is forever wrapping her litter up in coats and scarves and hats and boots and mittens. And then they have to pee. Things may be more expensive in New Zealand but at least I save on kids' shoes. And time.

Being back in Brooklyn is wonderful, but it's sad too. It's easier to forget when I'm in New Zealand that my father is gone because there are no reminders. Has it really been over a year? Here, the reminders are everywhere. Now I know the difference between homesickness and hiraeth.

Homesickness is pretty straightforward. You miss what you have left behind and when you go back, it's still there and you stop being homesick. But hiraeth is more complicated. Hiraeth is a combination of homesickness and longing for what no longer exists. This kind of homesickness doesn't leave you even when you return home because a part of what made it home is gone. Like loved ones who are no longer living. So you really can't go home again. Now that my father is gone, home will never be the same.

You don't have to be homesick or away from home to feel hiraeth. You can be in your own house, simply missing the past and what's gone. At least that's my take on it. The Welsh may beg to differ. Just as they might with someone who dares to call Wales a principality. Wales may not rank as a sovereign state but it is a country. Or constituent country. It's complicated. So too, nowadays, are my feelings for Fletcher. But I still remember the things my grandfather taught me.

And I think Lucie needs to revisit how she uses the word *Hiraeth.* Now that Parker is gone and she suffers it too, she actually agrees. It's not the same. It goes deeper. Or maybe that's just grief.

Anyway, Ally the Empath says my father is not gone just yet. Not while he's parked up in the basement. After all this time, Lucie has yet to clear out his model airplane stuff. Not because she can't bear to be parted from them but because she wants them to go where they will be appreciated. And what if one of the grandkids might want it all? Until she knows what to do with it, she's hoarding like a prepper. And we all know that would be fine with Parker since, well, he didn't get rid of the contents of his parents' house and the house itself for years. And like he used to say, 'Whatever gets you through it…'

But there is the issue of what to do with Parker. Or his ashes. Turns out my parents never agreed on a final resting place. Because my paternal grandparents died without remains and there was no point in going for a grave, I think my mother thought it was sorted. And why not? He got location in life, she gets it in death. Lucie wants to be where her grandmother Hermeline lies, where her long-dead father lies and where one day, when my Grand-maman Cyprienne finally lets go, where her mother will lie too. But that's not what Parker wants. He made it clear when he got sick. Parker wants to be in an old burial ground in the Connecticut River Valley he and Ally really like. Of course, Ally loves the idea and so do I, except distance does make it a pain to go and visit. Right now, Lucie is torn. And until she figures it out, she says he's staying in the basement. She also says this — location location location in death — is one of the many perils of international marriage.

I wonder about that. I, who was so into graveyards growing up, am not quite sure now where I want to be in the end. Does it really matter? I don't know that I care. But I do know that Blu does. No way in hell is he going to lie for all eternity in the United States of America. That much I know.

But then Ally says you don't have to be in an international marriage for it to be an issue. She says it's a 'peril' in all relationships. It seems now that it's come up and she quite likes the idea of the old burial ground in the Connecticut River Valley too, she and her good doctor disagree on where to hang out in death. Hopefully they'll have a long time to work it out. Oh, and what happens when your first partner dies and you remarry. What then? Why did Jennie J pick husband number one over two and three? And Consuelo V too, chose to lie forever next to the arrogant nobleman she finally divorced after twenty plus miserable years of marriage rather than her dearly loved second hubby, a one French Lieutenant colonel Jacques Balsan who died before her and is buried elsewhere. Why is that? No wonder ash-scattering is so popular now.

Anyway, neither one of us can get Fletcher's letter out of our heads and boy, I sure am glad I got here so soon after it was found. Major FOMO had I been in New Zealand. Who else but me could be trusted to make a count for evil adverbs? But more than that, it has allowed Ally and I to deal with it together. Although I think we will probably be unpacking its contents on our own for a very long time. When you think of it, that fire was a pretty good excuse for a lot of things and yet why did Annie's diary not burn too? Did my grandfather keep it in the attic or prefer to keep it close by? And if so, how come?

Even though I now know my Bubbe is the reason Fletcher and Annie's marriage fell apart, I feel only sadness for her. She was just a girl and my grandfather should have known better. I think she wanted to come clean but didn't know how. Shortly before she died, she told me she had something she wanted to tell me but that I needed to experience life more in order to better process what she had to say and I no longer saw everything in black and white as "all young people do". Funny, I assumed she was going to tell me she had brought some stupid silly shame on her old-fashioned family which was why we never had anything to do with them. I guess I was right. At the time, I figured whatever it was, it was going to be good because Bubbe hated lies. Sure, she had secrets, we all have secrets, but what you saw was what you got. The deceit must have torn away at her. We don't know what happened to my Bubbe and Gramps in those final minutes before their world came crashing in on them, but I hope that in some way, she found her peace. And I hope my grandfather was able to get it into her head that she was dearly loved. Not just by us but by him.

41

Fletcher's Apology

My son,

I owe you so many apologies. I have lied to you the whole of your life. I have betrayed you and for this I am deeply sorry. I do not expect your forgiveness because it is too late for forgiveness and I do not deserve it. I only wish to let you know the truth.

You were born in Queens after the war. Your sister Julie Sara was born twenty minutes later. That was the prettiest autumn I can ever remember. The leaves were beautiful. Prospect Park was a tapestry of color. Fall has always been my favorite season. But not in 1948. I should have been a happy man. I was finally home after too many years away. I had survived the hell that was World War II. I had a baby boy and girl and a beautiful wife who loved me with all her heart. I should have been on top of the world and all I could think about was I wanted to be dead.

The woman you have known as your mother all your life is not your mother. I met Anna in Vermont the year you were born. Your real mother is Anne Smith. My Kiwi bride.

I met Annie in 1942 in Auckland where I was stationed during the war. A lot of us Yanks were there before going into battle. My camp — Camp Hale — was set up on the Auckland Domain, so we were pretty central. On weekends, the locals would take us in. They were mighty kind to us, they were, those New Zealanders. They wanted to help us not be homesick. It worked, too, even though I never did get used to liking lamb or mutton like they said I would.

It was in the Smith home that your mother caught my eye. She was the loveliest sweetest thing I had ever seen. And she had these stunning blue eyes that just about blew me away. I guess you could call it love at first sight. For me anyway. She took a little more convincing in that department. She insisted there was no way she was going to get involved with a soldier, let alone with one who lived on the other side of the world. First, I had to convince her mother (not easy!) but eventually I won her heart and once I got army approval (also not easy!), we were married. We had a few months together before my unit shipped out.

Your mother was very young and very close to her family. She had two younger siblings. They were twins, in fact, a girl and a boy, aged about twelve or thirteen. She adored them all and I see now I never should have taken her away from her home. I should have gone to her after the war and not have her come to me. But the idea did not even cross my mind at the time. This was not how things were done in those days.

Annie sailed on the *Monterey* which arrived in San Francisco in early March 1946. There were almost two hundred other New Zealand war brides with her and they picked up at least five hundred wives in Australia on the way, so she had lots of company on the ship. It took three weeks and when she arrived in California, she was put on a train to Boston which is where I went to pick her up. I brought her to Vergennes in Vermont the next day.

Our life together was difficult from the start. She was not the same happy, carefree girl I married. I was not the man she knew in Auckland. The war changed me. I saw terrible things and I could not forget. I did not sleep at night and during the days, I cried sometimes for no reason. Finding a job was near impossible and because of the housing shortage, we were forced to move in with my father and stepmother. It was not ideal. Annie was homesick and hated a lot of things in Vergennes. My stepmother resented having both of us in the house and she took that resentment out on Annie.

I could see it happening, but I did nothing to stop it. Ergo, I started drinking. Sometimes I did not come home at night.

I tried to make it better for her and took her to Canada where my great-uncle had family because I thought Canada with its King George VI was more like England in the same way that New Zealand was. She was happy in Ontario and seemed to settle in. She got on well with my aunt and made friends. I worked as a newspaperman at the *Brockville Recorder and Times*. I got the job because my great-great uncle was editor at one time and back then, family name still meant something. It was obvious I could write but I was not in the right frame to be chasing down stories and I continued drinking. I knew it was only a matter of time before I got myself fired and so when Annie got pregnant, I demanded we go back to the States. I told her it was because I wanted my children to be born American but that was a lie. I simply could not face being a failure anymore. She begged me not to go to Vermont so I brought her to New York.

I have always said my first wife abandoned me. On more than one occasion, I have stated that Annie is dead. I have learned that if you repeat a lie enough, eventually you come to believe in it yourself. But it is just that — one big lie. As far as I know, your mother — and your sister — are alive. I have lied about everything and I have lied to everyone, including Anna, the woman you have known all your life as your mother. Please do not blame Anna in any of this. She knew nothing of your sister. She has given you her heart since the moment I brought her into your life.

Anna was a shop girl just out of high school in her father's store in Little Jerusalem in Burlington in Vermont. Hers was a family of Lithuanian Jews which was far removed from anything I had ever known. Anna was so full of life and jovial and except for the similar name, was nothing like Annie. In Anna one night, I found my escape.

Annie and I were visiting my father and stepmother in Vergennes and I begged off after dinner one night so I could go out drinking with some old friends. We ended up at some wing-ding in Burlington where Anna and some girlfriends were clearly letting off steam. I was drawn to her. She seemed so young and innocent and particularly rebellious against whatever constraints her parents had set for her. Things got out of hand and well, I got her pregnant.

Annie found out about Anna after you and your sister were born. First Anna sent her a letter, and when she did not hear back, she came to see us. She was terrified. In those days, intercourse outside marriage was taboo. And young girls certainly did not get knocked up by older married men. She was desperate her family would find out so I paid for her to have an abortion.

I thought this would be the end of it. I thought I could put my indiscretion behind me and go on with my life. But Annie would not have it. The trust was gone. She wanted to leave me but had nowhere else to go but home. I could not allow that to happen.

Finally, we reached an agreement. She would take your sister with money her father had sent her, and I would keep you until such a time as I had earned enough wages to pay our passage to Auckland where, she promised me, she would give our marriage another chance. We estimated that if I saved fast enough, we would be separated a year at most. I was doing well at the paper and I thought I could do it. I really thought I could earn the money to get us both to New Zealand. But then I began to panic. Auckland was so far away, and I realized I could not do it. I could not leave my home. The longer she was gone, the easier it was to convince myself she had deserted us and we were better off without her. And Julie Sara.

When my stepmother said she could no longer care for you and she wanted to return to Vergennes, I did not know who else to ask but Anna. I found her letter and wrote her an offer of employment. It was an arrangement which suited us both as her father had learned of her terminated pregnancy (she told a friend with a big mouth) and wanted her out of the house. She had shamed her family and there was no going back. I felt I was to blame for it and so I let her move in.

What could I do? Annie was gone and the longer she was away, the more she retreated into my past. And it was a past I wanted to forget because to think of Annie was also to think of the war and the horrors of battle and the buddies I had lost. I chose to forget about her honey blonde hair and those sweet blue eyes and what a wonderful mother she was to the both of you. I chose to forget it all because I had let her down. All I could see was what was in front of me and I knew I had let Anna down too. I could not let it happen again. I had done so many wrongs, I had to make something right. Anything. So I chose Anna.

I told Anna that Annie had left me and did not want you and so in our sad little world, I like to think we created a family. We moved to Brooklyn where no one knew us and no one cared if we were married or not. After a while, people just assumed we were. We tried for more children but none came. Passing you along as Anna's was never a problem. School officials and doctors and even you just assumed her incorrect name on your birth certificate was a typographical error. With your dark hair and brown eyes, you even looked like her. Anna begged me to tell you the truth when you were young but I forbid her. I know from my own first-hand experience that substitute parent situations are not always agreeable and as I never felt the power of a mother's love, I did not want you to miss out also. But Anna did love you, with all her heart and as her own, from the moment she first saw you. And I thought it better for you to know Anna as your mother than to believe Annie had abandoned you. I lied to Annie as well. I wrote her and told her you had died of pneumonia, and I had changed my mind about coming. She had no way to reply as I did not leave a return address. It was easy to disappear back then.

I do not know what became of Annie or your sister Julie Sara. In recent years, I suppose I could have looked them up on the computer but I have remained a coward. How can Annie and Julie Sara possibly forgive me for what I have done? How can you? To this day, Anna begs me still to tell you about your mother and I refuse. Anna has always been by my side and for this I am grateful, but the untruths hang over our relationship. My lies have destroyed me. I suspect they have destroyed — or have the power to destroy — others as well.

My son, I am so very sorry I have kept you from your mother and your sister and lied to you from day one. I have no excuse other than I did it to save my ass. Not a moment goes by where I do not regret what I have done and it is only fear of losing you (and now your beautiful family as well) which has kept me from telling you the truth you deserve. But you are entitled to know your full story. Know first that while I am a wordsmith by trade, I will never find the words to express to you how truly sorry I am for my deceit.

I know you will want to find your mother, and I will do anything I can to help. Annie's full name was Anne Jane Smith and when we married, she lived on Cecil Road in Auckland. Her birthday is August 9th. We married at Saint Mark's Anglican Church on May 25, 1943. She was the most beautiful wonderful woman I have ever known and I have never stopped loving her.

Sincerely and with love, Dad

Meghan's Method

Yeah, so not his best prose but hey, it's quite the spiel, yarn, tale, whatever.

Gramps always used to say truth is stranger than fiction. I just didn't know he was talking — or writing — about his own truth. And yes, I know Mark Twain said it before him. But probably only because Samuel Langhorne Clemens was born first. *One Question* was my grandfather's biggest book. The movie was huge. Who would've thought it was semi-autobiographical?

What I find weird is that my grandfather was a prize-winning novelist. I mean, he wrote all the time. Opening lines and perfect sentences and paragraphs were always forming in his head, and he carried pen and paper with him wherever he went so he could put it all down in front of him before he forgot. Not that he went out that much. Most of the time he just stayed at his desk, plugging away, word after word. And yet, with all the stories he had to share with the world, he never bothered to tell the people closest to him the one which really needed telling.

Gramps said he used a nom de plume because he valued anonymity. Parker figured it was also because he man-crushed Mark Twain who made it a de rigueur thing to do. I never thought it strange that my grandfather didn't do interviews or that you would be hard pressed to find an author-bio or photo of him anywhere online. For a long time, I was sure no one outside our immediate family except his agent, editor and maybe the IRS knew what he did for a living. Just like JD Salinger, his other man-crush, he was the ultimate anti-celebrity. I thought it was because he wanted to be left alone. Now I know it was more than that. He needed to be left alone. Long before the Hague Convention was a thing, he was in hiding. Because if Gramps used his real name and showed his face, Anne Jane Smith would know where to find him. And Julie Sara might come looking for him. His was too big a can of worms.

But none of it makes sense to me. Bubbe told me Annie was the love of his life. Why then deny her her son? And if Annie came to find Gramps, this meant he might see his daughter again. Money wasn't a problem — certainly not after his first few best-sellers — so 'passage' was hardly an issue. Not for him anyway.

And is it possible Tish Louise somehow figured out my grandfather's deception? Or at least part of it. Was she the tall elegant English lady with a son called Neville who Annie spilled her guts out to that day all those years ago? Why not? For all I know, they could have lived on the same block. I choose to believe that if my friend was aware of the whole story, not for a minute would she have let that sleeping dog lie. Because Tish Louise would have known it was ultimately very much my business. And my family's business too. Especially in light of the fact the distraught woman in the park had two children with her, not one. But then, maybe that's what threw Tish Louise off track and made her doubt her suspicion. Because Tish Louise lived an honest life and I think my grandfather's duplicity was far beyond the scope of her imagination.

But what about Bubbe? Exactly when was the moment my grandmother first saw my father? Was it after Gramps invited her to come work for him or the morning she confronted Annie on the stoop? Did Bubbe examine the contents of the pram? I know I would have. Did my grandmother realize my father had a sibling? And if she did, did she not question what happened to the second baby?

I'm mad at Gramps. Fucking furious actually. Bubbe not so much. Bubbe was trapped. Strangely, Lucie's more sympathetic than I these days. She blames the war. Because war changes people, plain and simple. The Fletcher Annie Smith fell in love with before he went into battle was not the same Fletcher who came back to her when it was all over. He was damaged. He was a drunk. And he was in no position to care for a homesick wife. And when she left him, he was broken. Even if it was all his fault in the first place.

Of course, my mother is thrilled at this most recent example of the perils of international marriage. The problem for the rest of us — well maybe just Ally and me — is this isn't a case study. It's personal. Parker is gone and we are left with the fall out. I am no longer the person I thought I was. Neither is my sister. Who are we if we are not Bubbe's granddaughters?

Gramps once told me that JD Salinger was traumatized as a young man when he discovered that he was not fully Jewish but only half-Jewish. Because his mother was born a Catholic. Did it never occur to Gramps that losing part of our heritage might cause us to react in the same way?

I feel my grandfather's betrayal on so many levels. He Nevilled it.

Big time.

PART THREE

SOMEWHERE ON THE OTHER SIDE

OF
THE

WAR BRIDE TEN YEAR
(MAYBE FIFTEEN)
TIMELINE

Epilogue

Meghan's Method

There is a cemetery two hours north of Auckland in a small settlement called Matakohe. This is where my grandmother, Anne Jane Smith Buell not Buell is buried. Next to her are her parents — my great-grandparents.

With a name like Buell, I thought finding my Kiwi grandmother would be a breeze. There are only four in the entire nation but after an hour on the phone one night, I realized Annie — or any descendants of Annie — wasn't one of them. Which means she had either left the country or gone back to using her maiden name. Or maybe had a new married name. All three scenarios of which were problematic and totally overwhelming. Tish Louise was right — Smith is way too boring and way way too common a moniker. So I gave up the search for a while. A few years, in fact. I told myself I was busy with my three kids, busy with my husband and busy with my work. But then on a whim not long ago, I put out a Facebook message seeking a long-lost 'World War Two War Bride Grandma' and this is what her name is and this is what her daughter's name is and can you help me find her. By the end of the week, it had gone viral. Four days ago, I got a call from Julie Sara Smith in Auckland.

Soon I will come face to face with my Kiwi aunt, my great aunt and my great uncle and my Kiwi cousins. Soon I will know more about the grandmother my sister Ally and I never knew. Soon I will tell Julie Sara

Buell not Buell Smith her truth. And I will tell her about the wonderful brother she never got to know.

What I know now is that Anne Jane Smith died the year my sister was in New Zealand and says she went looking for her. She remarried and had five more children. Parker has many siblings after all. He would have liked that. But now poor Ally is completely gutted. Ally says if she only knew Annie was her biological grandmother and not some random ex, she would have looked a hell of a lot harder. I tell her not to be so hard on herself (that's on my Gramps) because there are over eight thousand Smiths in the phonebook and the only things that went viral back then were infections.

"Still," she says, "what if I had found her? How would things be different?"

Funny thing is, I may have already met Julie Sara Buell not Buell Smith. She's the owner of the New York Deli where I pick up bagels when I'm in the city. She says she's never been to Brooklyn but I don't believe her. One bite of her beauties tells me otherwise.

I love my grandfather, I always will. But I doubt I will forgive him for the super-size lies he told and the what ifs in their wake. Frankly, I am not immune to acrimonious victimhood and wouldn't mind a behavior template to fall back on for a bit of guidance. Lucie advises forgiveness is a process (OMG!) and empirical research shows that hanging on to toxic anger, resentment and bitterness is harmful to my physical and mental health in multiple ways and on multiple levels. And that a bit of baking soda in the bath might do me some good. She always forgets my water is sourced from the roof and not the plentiful Catskill or Delaware aqueduct and my tub soaking days are a thing of the past. Lucie also says my aunt Julie Sara Buell not Buell Smith likely has issues of her own — if not before, she will soon — so perhaps we should group counsel our way through it. She also suggests I just get me some more cruisy Coon cats to help alleviate potential emotional instability even though Blu keeps telling her that, with my current cat menagerie plus three indoorsy dogs, I should be able to regulate just fine. But we're all facing emotional instability right now because my Grand-maman says it's time. For years my French-Canadian grandmother has been campaigning to have her beloved Doré's body (remains?) returned to her and now that he's finally home and where she wants him, she's ready to die. So Lucie is going home to be with her mother in her final days. I try not to be too down about that knowing my grandmother has both her men waiting for her now, lying next to each other in one plot. You kind of have to wonder what her local Catholic priest has to say about that.

Lucie says when Grand-maman is settled into her ménage à trois, she will return to Brooklyn. She's sad but also matter of fact about Grand-maman's impending death. I am too but take comfort in the knowledge that Grand-maman has promised to wait until I can get to her first and have a proper goodbye before she goes. I have no doubt she will keep her word. I guess Kubler-Rossing is different when it's for the very old. A little less anger and depression and more acceptance. My mother says she doesn't plan to stay in Montreal longer than necessary because 'Les États-Unis' has (have?) been good to her (hah!) and she loves her life in New York. Even if my dad isn't in it anymore. You get used to anything, I suppose.

Even New Zealand. So many things about this country upset me when I first got here. Now I just let it go because it's true — after a while you make a life (and friends) and you come to terms with blah footwear and garden-zombies. Especially if married to one and you still think he's a nice guy with fabulous forearms. No, there's no special cure for the dull aches in your heart and soul that don't seem to go away but you get on with it because you know you still have it pretty good. But it's funny how I used to complain about my lack of connection here. How I had no history. I'm told that's not uncommon. By Lucie, of course. She says lots of her sad sucker clients long to feel a sense of continuity and deep community with their adoptive land but maybe, I felt it stronger because dead people (dead dollar princesses, dead ancestors, etc.) are my thing and that's fine, we all have our thing. But now that it's been a while, now that I've had a chance to step back from my father's passing (she still hates that word) and reflect on my newfound family (the one I will meet soon) and the fact I do have a link, I realize that all along, I've been putting in roots. Baby roots, maybe, but roots just the same.

New Zealand's Māori indigenous people have a word which really speaks to me. 'Tūrangawaewae' is usually translated into English as a place to stand or where one has the right to stand. Because 'Tūranga' is standing place and 'waewae' is feet. But 'Tūrangawaewae' is more than that. Much more. Because often words on paper don't convey the true meaning or intent of spoken communication.

"Māori have a strong oral history," informs my friend Aroha who is teaching me about her culture.

"Māori ancestors believed in a world where supernatural creatures lurk in the water and where mountains and trees and rivers and streams are alive and have names and command our respect. On the marae, our communal meeting ground, elders pass on ancient myths and legends and share the stories which form the basis of our beliefs."

According to Aroha, Māori, or 'Te Reo' is a language of the heart and soul. Aroha, by the way, means love.

And 'Standing Place' means more than just standing place.

"My Tūrangawaewae is not where I'm from," says Aroha. "My 'standing place' is where I connect to all the other dimensions."

I think I know what she means. I may not share the same beliefs as my friend, but I get the need to connect with the land on which I stand. And I choose to believe it's possible to have more than one standing place, more than one Tūrangawaewae. And gosh, how my Gramps would love that word. Maybe he did and just never let on.

That war bride timeline can be pretty daunting at the bottom end but I really think it does take that long. But finally, I feel like I might be in the right place. I've learned I can be people-sick and miss New York every day, but I can be happy here too. And yet, I would still go home in a New York minute if I had the chance. No, it doesn't make sense. I guess nothing ever does.

I am clearly conflicted and I probably always will be but I no longer let it bother me.

I no longer struggle with my decision to follow my beautiful Blu to the bottom of the world. He's my beloved, my treasure, the joy of my heart. How lucky am I he chose me to sit next to on the steps outside the central library that day?

Finally, I feel I have found my feet. Or waewae. In more ways than one.

Maybe it's time for me to open that new suitcase no doubt now covered in fly shit lying under the bed in the sulking spare room, the one with all my mother's beautifully catalogued notes and personal stories. Maybe it's time I put my grandfather's word-nerd genes and iambic pentameter know-how to more challenging use. Peut-être I am ready to write my mother's book now.

Our book.

My book?

Nah, it's our book. With all our stories. Throughout all of this, my mom has been my greatest support. That's something I need to let her know.

And today, I have a graveyard to visit. I have to say hello to Anne Jane Smith Buell not Buell and maybe have a nice long talk. That's the thing about graveyards — they are full of possibilities.

The End

Acknowledgements

I know I've been a pain. Thank you to David W (my beloved and treasure and joy of my heart!) and wonderful family and friends for putting up with me. Also, a big thank you to the many wonderful foreign wives and World War II who shared their immigrant journeys with me so I could finally write my book!

About the Author

Danielle Murray grew up in Montreal where she fully intended to stay until she fell in love with a wonderful Kiwi man and followed him home. This is not her story. TWO QUESTIONS is a work of fiction based on information gathered in conversations with World War II war brides and modern-day foreign wives as the author waited for decent bagels to arrive in New Zealand. It took far too long and so she got to interview a whole lot of women. This is their story.

Manufactured by Amazon.ca
Bolton, ON